THE FAIRY
STEPMOTHER INC.

Maggie Hoyt

MAGGIE HOYT

Quill

Published by Inkshares, Inc., Oakland, California
www.inkshares.com

Cover design by CoverKitchen
Interior design by Kevin G. Summers

eBook ISBN: 9781947848634
Paperback ISBN: 9781947848627
LCCN: 2018955127

First edition

Printed in the United States of America

To my three good fairies:
Mom, Pat, and Nita

PART 1

PROLOGUE

THEY TOLD ME there are never any good stepmothers. All of my friends said, "Haven't you heard the stories? You'll end up hating her eventually. That's how it always goes."

I dislike stories. Stories tell you how to be, and then it never occurs to anyone that you could ever behave any differently. People can only seem to imagine one future.

For example, in stories, girls either clean or sew. In finishing school, which classes do you suppose were most popular? Stain Removal and Embroidery. Of course, Weaving and Improvised Dusting Tools gave them a run for their money. I was the only student in Household Economics. Since I already knew my sums, Master Basnage had to come up with three whole weeks of new material.

In stories, girls become princesses. None of my classmates became princesses, but they did clean and sew their way to lesser titles. I spent four years at Furnival's Halle for Sounde Business Procedures and would have graduated top of the class had any of the professors ever recognized my presence.

You see, in my experience, stories only tell you what you can't do. I dislike stories. So when my friends all said, "Evie, there simply are no good stepmothers," I said, "That's your opinion."

"Besides," I said, "the kid is a saint. How hard could this be?"

My friends didn't spend much time trying to convince me I was wrong. They simply moved on to their next topic, which seemed to be which young woman had the best chance of marrying a prince.

Girls today are always waiting for a prince, but I'm never sure why. It's the fairies who do all the work in the stories. They wave their magic wands, and the dewy-eyed ninnies can't help but fall in love.

I can't really say if there are any good stepmothers. But one thing I know for certain: there are absolutely, definitely, no fairies.

CHAPTER ONE

I MET HENRY AT A PARTY. I like the idea of parties. I like looking nice. I like watching men imagine the length of my legs under a smock, a petticoat, a kirtle, and a gown. I like the idea of drinking wine and talking. In actuality, Lord, people are dull.

Despite its pretensions, Strachey-on-Stout wasn't half as stratified as its residents wished. It was, and had been, a fully functioning small town that at some point in its history became the ideal spot for the titled and/or wealthy who weren't important enough to receive adequate attention in the Capital. Thus, Lord Whitcomb, who was inordinately wealthy with no political sense, could throw an annual ball that drew everyone from the elite to the untitled widow of one of the kingdom's leading entrepreneurs—that's me, of course.

Henry found me against one of the manor's oak-paneled walls, drinking wine and not talking. He was clearly nervous, terribly interested in the carvings on the panel above me and unable to make eye contact with me at all. He needed help, but I wasn't in the mood to offer.

"Lord Whitcomb is certainly enamored of the pineapple motif," he finally managed to sputter. It was true. Lord Whitcomb had succumbed to the current trend of turning every knob or slightly curved piece of paneling into a pineapple.

"It's a terrible investment," I said.

"Really?"

"Look at it. He's taken a whittling knife to every piece of wood in his manor. At least when the fad was cherubs, one simply affixed them in places. When this craze runs its course, he'll have to replace anything remotely round."

"I'd never thought of it that way!"

"What's fashionable makes a poor foundation for a luxury purchase. It won't stay in style long enough to create any sort of return."

"That makes such obvious sense when you think about it. I wonder why more of the wealthy don't abide by it."

I just laughed, a sharp, one-note "ha."

"Has anyone ever told you that you have a wonderful voice?"

He liked to explore. He liked to walk through the woods, collecting oddly shaped leaves and flowers he didn't recognize. He'd dry them and press them and put them in a large blank book. He liked to watch clouds. I liked to watch him watching clouds. I made him go to the theater, and I think he preferred to watch me. He was friendly to absolutely everyone. I swear he'd even made friends with the geese by the lake.

The first time I met his daughter, she was on the front porch, her right hand gently turning a spinning wheel while her left fed wool onto a spindle. Birds chirped in the trees. My heart sank.

"Ellie!" he exclaimed as she ran to him and threw her arms around his neck. "Ella, I'd like you to meet Evelyn."

"Hi," I mustered. She was gorgeous. Her hair was so blonde it was almost white, and it would have run halfway down her back if it hadn't been in a braid demurely piled on her head. Her blue eyes were as bright as the flowers in the garden, and her skin positively radiated light.

"It's so nice to meet you! Father's told me so much about you. I was helping Lucy with supper, Papa. I think it's almost ready." Cooking. Right up there with cleaning and sewing.

"She's an angel," I whispered. Maybe literally, I thought. Henry beamed.

"Oh, I have to tell you about the tree, Papa! I left a little dish of milk for the fairies, and they came!" she said as she led him into their modest little thatched cottage.

She didn't look like him at all. He was awkward, with scruffy golden-brown hair and cheekbones that weren't quite even. His face was long and hers was round, his smile a little crooked while hers was wide and perfect. She looked like her mother, his dead wife, who was probably, in fact, actually an angel. I'd consider myself a catch, but that's a level of competition I can't begin to touch.

I found it difficult to leave the entryway, as my feet were seriously considering bolting in the opposite direction. Then I felt a soft hand on my elbow.

"He's been so happy since he met you. Thank you."

I can be much more cynical than everyone else, but it's impossible to mistrust Ella. (Mostly because, as I later learned, she's a terrible liar. Guile doesn't pay off for her.) She knew just what to say, and she believed every word, and I fell for her completely.

That was not how Henry's first meeting with my daughter went.

"I thought she would be home. I told her to be home," I said halfway through the meal.

"Don't worry about it. She's young!"

"She's rebellious. That child has it out for me."

By the time my maid came home with her, we'd finished supper.

"Fanchon!" I cried.

"I'm fine, Mother!" she said as she attempted to push past me.

"Don't you walk past me," I said. "I told you to be home for supper. Where have you been?"

"Where have I been?" she asked, wide-eyed. "Regina and I were planning outfits for a fancy-dress ball." The maid nodded. "I don't get what—"

"You are grounded for a week."

"What?"

"Fanchon, you can't do this! You told me you would be home tonight, and then you weren't! For all I knew, something had happened to you!"

"Mom, why is this suddenly a big deal? I'm always with my friends!"

"I reminded you last night. We were having supper tonight so you could meet Henry."

"Oh! Was that this week? I thought it was next week!"

"See, she forgot! No harm done!" Henry said as he stepped up by my side.

"I'm so sorry! It's nice to meet you. I'm Fanchon." She shook Henry's hand.

"We're going to be late for the show," I said, clenching my jaw as tightly as I could. Anyone could tell Fanchon was lying, but clearly Henry didn't have much practice with obnoxious teenagers.

"Then I'm not grounded?"

"It was an honest mistake," Henry said.

I rolled my eyes. "Three days," I said. "Next time, tell me where you are."

"I hate you!" she shouted as she stomped back to her bedroom. What else was new?

"Let's go," I said.

"She's spirited," Henry said when we'd left the house.

"She's—" I started but was interrupted by a cry from the house.

"Mom!" Fanchon leaned out of the front window. "Mom, you're too old to have more babies, right? So I don't need to be worried?"

One of the downsides to the death of Husband #1 is that Fanchon seems to be entirely my fault.

Husband #1 was the only thing I got out of business school that my parents appreciated. We met when he beat me out for a consulting job. I was jobless, unmarried, and quickly realizing that both prospective husbands and prospective employers saw only what I couldn't do. He was self-made and needed a wife who could work a crowd and wouldn't squander the fortune that was coming. We were attractive. We oozed charm. I'd persuade potential clients to have supper with us, and my husband delivered the pitch. We could seal deals during famines, the pox, and barbarian invasions. I thought we were partners. I thought I was valued.

There are different kinds of needing, I realized a little too late. In fact, Husband #1 cared about two things in life: himself and his daughter. He had graduated first in his class, so he soon earned the obscene amounts of money needed to satisfy this adoration, and Fanchon quickly became spoiled.

In the beginning, we both gave Fan anything she wanted. We were new parents, and she was an adorable little lump of baby fat. I was the first to say no—probably because I have a limited tolerance for children, or maybe because I was home all day with her. I just felt she ought to put away her toys, eat her vegetables, and speak like a decent human being.

But Husband #1 read her stories and told her she was a princess and the fairies would find her a prince, and he let her skip the part where she cleaned and sewed her way to the top. If I tried to discipline her, he shouted at me. Pretty soon, little Fan learned that Daddy always overruled Mommy. If Mom said no, Dad said yes. If she didn't want to put away her dolls, Dad paid someone to do it for her. If she wanted to stay up another hour, Dad held her on his lap. She had about as much respect for me as he did.

I'm sure there was something I should have done differently. I don't know what it was. Mothering never came naturally to me.

I didn't cry when he died, when his heart just suddenly stopped. I hadn't loved him in a very long time. Besides, I didn't have time. Fanchon was fourteen. She screamed. I tried to calm her down; she hit me. I put my arms around her, I stroked her hair. She tried to bite me. She shut herself in her room, and when she finally came out, she stormed out of the house.

I planned the funeral, sorted his belongings, and called for the solicitor. He arrived the day after the funeral.

"Ma'am, my condolences for your loss."

I sighed. "Thank you, Mr. Sherman. Please have a seat. Would you like tea?"

He nodded, so I brought over the tray and began to pour.

"I have looked over the contents of your late husband's will . . . ," he began hesitantly.

"And?"

"It is quite clear. He left everything to your daughter."

Everything seemed to freeze as the solicitor's words sank in. I set the teapot down very slowly. I felt panic welling up, so I closed my eyes and took a sip of tea—black, bitter, and scalding hot. I wanted to scream. I even wanted to cry, I was so angry. I was his wife, and I'd been faithful. I'd been trapped for fifteen years because if I'd ever left him, I'd have been destitute. Our whole marriage, he'd known he controlled me, and he wanted it to be clear that he still did. I took a deep breath and tried to exhale my anger, letting my mind race with solutions.

"Fanchon is only fourteen. She can't run her father's business," I said.

"No. Your husband appointed a board of directors to run the company until Fanchon comes of age."

"And then?"

"She gets her seat on the board."

I sank my nails into the cushions of the sofa. "Surely she must get an allowance."

"Yes . . . your husband appointed me overseer of Fanchon's monthly allowance." Mr. Sherman removed the lid from the sugar bowl and carefully spooned two lumps of sugar into his tea.

I took him in with a glance—the laces on his cuffs were tied in symmetrical bows, and he nervously ran his hands over the meticulously drawn boxes on his sheaf of forms. This was my one true edge over Husband #1: I knew how to read the people he considered trifles.

"Of course," I said, shaking my head in disgust. "He would assume you had nothing better to do."

"I am a busy man . . ."

"I'm sure you must be! He was like this with everyone. Always assumed serving him was the most important thing you had to do that day."

"I met your husband on a few occasions, ma'am," Sherman said, looking nervously at me through his spectacles.

"I'm sure he was impressive."

"Oh, quite." He picked up his teacup with a shaky hand, sloshing a few drops over the side. He took a sip. "So much so, the rest of us didn't really seem to merit."

"None of us did."

Mr. Sherman paused. I waited patiently.

"Ma'am . . ."

"Call me Evelyn, please."

"Evelyn, it is in my best interest to see this will executed fully, meaning I wish to see your daughter inherit her father's fortune. If Fanchon's guardian were unable to care for her, I would be interested in doing something about that. After all, Fanchon shouldn't be expected to care for her guardian—quite the opposite. Anyway, it seems to me within my rights to transfer Fanchon's allowance to her physical guardian. Until she turns eighteen, of course."

"If it would put your mind at ease, Mr. Sherman . . ."

"It would, I think." He shuffled through his papers and found something appropriate for me to sign.

"One more question, Mr. Sherman. What happens to her inheritance if Fan gets married?"

"Oh!" Mr. Sherman looked puzzled, as though he couldn't fathom why a person would ask such a question. "Her husband would take control of her finances. Probably the board seat as well. It's hard to imagine a woman running a company like that, isn't it?"

I smiled wryly and negotiated my allowance. If I'd had this dowry, Husband #1 would have stolen it from me before the honeymoon was over, and in this world, even I couldn't have stopped him. I wasn't going to let that happen to Fan, so I had to prepare her to go it alone.

Fan and I ate supper in our usual silence the next evening.

"Fan, if you want to talk about anything . . ."

"I don't."

I paused, at a complete loss as to how to speak with her. "I've spoken with the solicitor. Your father left everything to you. When you're eighteen, you'll inherit everything, even a seat on the board of directors."

"So I'll be rich?"

"And you'll help run your father's company. You'll have to learn how to make wise business decisions."

"Whatever. I get the money when I'm eighteen?" She stabbed an asparagus stalk with her fork.

"Yes."

"And until then you'll try to steal it from me?"

"Of course not!" I exclaimed.

Fanchon shrugged. I took a deep breath. She was grieving.

"What do you see yourself doing in the future, Fan?"

"I'm going to marry a prince, just like in the stories." She let her knife drop on the plate as she took a bite of quail, and the clanging seemed to echo through our dining room.

"Which stories are those?"

"You know, where the girl's dad dies and everyone's mean to her but a nice fairy comes and helps her marry a prince."

"Well, I'm not a fairy, but I'll do my best . . . ," I said with uncharacteristic cheerfulness.

"Sometimes I think you're not my real mom."

"I'm really sure I am," I said slowly.

"Someone could have switched the babies when you were asleep."

"Fan . . . you're my daughter."

She shrugged again and didn't say another word the entire meal. That's when I realized she'd cut me off. Fanchon wouldn't spare an allowance for her dear mother. It was a terrifying thought, having to go back into the world all alone. As much as I hate to admit it, I needed help.

CHAPTER TWO

"YOUR VOICE is like velvet," Henry said.

I laughed. More of a giggle, I reluctantly admit.

"Marry me," he said, kneeling by the side of the bed.

"Of course," I breathed, and he kissed me, and I held on like we were one person.

I felt the relief the next day. I had a safety net, and it was a happy one.

I looked over Henry's finances and sent a few queries to Mr. Sherman. Within a few days, we gathered the girls around my dining room table to break the news.

"Well, girls, your mother and I—I mean, well, Fanchon's mother and I—Evelyn and I . . . ," Henry fumbled. He kept clasping and unclasping his hands over his knee. Ella smiled patiently, but Fanchon gave an exaggerated eye roll. I decided to speed things up.

"We want to tell you that we're getting married."

"Yes! That's it! That's the news!"

Curiously, neither girl reacted. I'll admit, I was expecting Fanchon to hit the roof, and I figured Ella would either smile weakly and cry later or squeal about weddings. If I were a gambler, I'd have lost a bundle. Unnerved by the silence, I went on with the speech I'd planned.

"Of course, neither of us would dream of replacing the parents you've lost. I know you miss your mother, Ella, and I'm certainly not her."

"And I know you were close to your father, Fanchon, and probably don't want a new one," Henry joined in.

"But it's a hard world to go through alone," I said. "And we think we could all take care of each other."

"Are you girls all right with this?" he asked. Henry always assumed the best of everyone, but I think even he was surprised by the lack of reaction. He started drumming his fingers on the table.

"Of course," Ella said, her blue eyes starting to glisten. "I want you to be happy, Papa."

"Whatever," said Fanchon.

"Well, in that case . . . ," Henry said cheerfully.

I wasn't convinced. I eyed Fan, wondering why she was saving the firestorm.

"We're not planning much of a ceremony," I said, "so we won't need to busy ourselves with wedding plans. But first and foremost, Fan, you and I have to get ready to move."

Fan stiffened. Ah, here it comes, I thought. Now she'd finally put all the pieces together.

"And Ella and I are happy to help pack crates! Aren't we, sweetheart?" He gave her an enthusiastic smile; she nodded faintly.

"What?" Fanchon bellowed, turning Ella's hesitant smile into a quavering pout. "We're moving? Why aren't they moving? Our house is so much nicer! They ought to move in with us!"

"Well," I said calmly, "theirs has an extra room, so you and Ella can each have your own room. In ours, you'd have to share."

"She can sleep on the floor!"

Tears welled up in Ella's eyes.

"I think not, Fan. The best option is to sell our house and move into Henry's."

"But you can't sell the house!" Fan crowed, rising triumphantly from her seat. "It's mine! It was Dad's, so it's mine! I knew you would try to steal my money!"

"Fanchon, sit down. I am doing nothing of the sort. The entire sale will go into your inheritance, which you will receive when you are eighteen."

She plopped back into her chair with a huff.

"No one is being unfair to you," I continued. "I understand this is a change you don't want to make, but that doesn't give you the right to be rude. I think you owe Ella and Henry an apology."

"Sorry," she practically spat.

"I forgive you, Fan," Ella said. Fan rolled her eyes again.

"Well!" Henry said. "I guess that's all the news. Just let us know when you start filling boxes, Evelyn!"

As we started to rise, Fanchon bounded to her feet and stomped away, shoving her chair to the side.

"Just wait until I'm eighteen," she shouted back. "You'll all be sorry when my fairy godmother finds me a prince!"

I am, ultimately, an optimist. For example, despite my previous failures, I still hadn't given up on parenting. I thought I would have a better chance with Ella. Her father adored me, after all. He didn't mind that I was an inch taller, or that I kept my graying hair short. And most importantly, he didn't seem to care that I was better at running his business. Acceptance is the family style, I thought.

Ella spent most of her time on the front porch engaged in various crafts projects while a family of sparrows serenaded her from a hedge near the side of the house. The sparrows had adopted Ella, it seemed. I never quite figured out where they made their nest, but eventually I got used to their singing. Apparently, they came with the house. I think they appreciated the gifts Ella left for the fairies.

"What are you making, Ella?"

"It's a quilt. I'm using the fabric from Fanchon's and my worn-out dresses so nothing goes to waste. Fairies hate wastefulness."

"It's beautiful! You're quite talented. You know, you could probably sell your wares in town."

Her eyes widened in horror. "Oh no, Stepmother, I can't do that! I just like making things for our home."

"Why not? I'd be happy to help you set up a small business. You'd only need a bit of marketing. We'll want to sell to the nobility, so we could blitz a circular—No! We have events. You have one woman throw a party, and then everyone comes and looks at the different quilts and patterns—if you wanted to do custom, they could even pick out which options they wanted for their personal design. You could charge—"

"Oh, I don't want to charge! The girls in the stories never sell things. They give them away, to anyone in need. It would be cruel to sell things!"

She gave me an angelic smile and went back to making small hand movements whose purpose I couldn't possibly discern. How had she gotten a whole blanket doing that?

The next time Lord Whitcomb held a party, the girls were both sixteen, old enough to come along. I had more than a few misgivings, but Fanchon had pleaded, and Henry thought it would be a nice family activity. Ella hadn't had a strong opinion. She'll be nervous, I thought. She'll need me to introduce her to people.

"Had to get rid of all the pineapples, I see," Henry said as we entered.

"I can't tell what he's replaced them with," I said.

"Wolf motifs," Fanchon said. "They're all the rage. Just so you know, Mom, we're the laughingstock of the county because we're not up to date."

"Thanks for the warning."

While Fanchon searched the crowd for a reason to ditch us, Ella took the scene in. We'd entered into the main hall, which was abuzz with chatter and laughter. Near the back of the room were several long tables piled with desserts, where guests chose their sweets and then milled about the hall, positioning themselves to be seen by as many as possible. The ballroom was in the adjoining hall. I could just barely hear the musicians over the din of society.

I tried to see it from Ella's point of view. Nearly all of Strachey was here, and she hardly knew anyone. We were barely through the door, and we were already assaulted with strident voices and strong perfumes. She's probably scared, I thought.

"There's no need to be nervous, Ella," I said. "Come on, girls, I'll introduce you to people."

"Sir Kingsley!" I heard Fan say. "How delightful to see you again!"

She'd gotten away from me, I realized as I turned. Fan had left our little cluster and was slipping her hand through the arm of a tall, darkly handsome young man whose eyes went straight to the ample bosom threatening to burst out of her gown.

"Her bodice was not that tight when we left," I said. "Who is he? He's too old for her."

"Did you break the stallion you were telling me about?" Fanchon asked.

"Telling her about? They've talked before? Fanchon!"

I know she heard me—we weren't that far away—but she just batted her eyes as he said something masculine.

"I feel a little bit bad for the poor horse! Promise me you won't hurt it!" she minced.

"Fanchon!" I tried again, but she just turned him away from me. Fan may not have paid attention to sewing or cleaning, but she had mastered the art of meaningless conversation, and that was a dangerous tool.

I must have looked ready to vent steam because Henry spoke up nervously. "I'll go find out who he is." He scurried off, leaving me and Ella standing barely a few feet inside the doorway, continuously jostled by a stream of entrants.

I took a deep breath and turned brightly to Ella. "Well. There's no reason we can't enjoy ourselves! Shall I introduce you to my friends?"

"Oh, no, Stepmother, that's really all right," she said, her eyes darting around as she looked nervously at the crowds of people.

"Ella, you can't just stand here!"

She shrugged and looked over toward where Fanchon had gone. I was filled with pity.

"Darling, there's no reason to be nervous. You're beautiful and sweet, and everyone will love you. Just be yourself! You don't have to be like Fan to have people like you."

She nodded, but made no real signs of action.

I put my hands on her shoulders. "Ella, I'm going to teach you my three steps to introductions. They're not hard. One: shake hands firmly—not too strong, not too limp. Two: give a compliment. Three: ask a question. If they're nice, they'll ask you a question, and, then you have a conversation. If they're rude, they'll just talk about themselves and you won't have to say another word. All right? Let's give it a try."

I looked around the ballroom, hoping to find someone gentle. When my eyes lit on Maribelle, hovering over the sweets with an air of indecisiveness, I put my arm firmly around Ella and steered her toward the pastries.

"Maribelle!" I called with forceful cheeriness.

"Oh, hi, Evelyn! Don't they all look so good? I can't decide which to try!" She giggled, causing her overlarge gable hood to shake. I wasn't surprised; Maribelle never made a decision for herself. She was a young housewife with seven children who were raised by nannies but all wore homemade clothing. Maribelle never gave anyone a gift she hadn't made herself, and while she generally made me cringe, her preserves were fantastic. I figured in about fifteen years Ella would be her.

"Maribelle, I want you to meet my daughter Ella. Ella, this is Lady Frandsen."

"Oh, you can call me Maribelle, Ella! It's so nice to meet you. I've heard a lot about you!"

Ella shook hands and smiled faintly.

I waited. "Maribelle, your gown is lovely," I said finally. Ella just nodded.

"Oh, thank you! I made it myself!"

I gave Ella a chance to jump in on step three. No luck.

"Ella loves sewing!" I said. "She makes quilts and does the crossing stitch, and she does the little embroidery things with the hoops."

"No, Stepmother, um, cross-stitch and embroidery are pretty much the same thing," said a helpful little voice at my side, a little too loudly. She turned back to Maribelle. "Sometimes I use a hoop, but not with lacework, of course."

"Of course!" Maribelle laughed. "Do you make clothes?" She picked up a delicate pink sandwich cookie, took a bite, and set it on her plate.

"No, I've never tried. I'm not sure I'd be any good."

"But you do all the stitching on the quilts so well! I'm sure you could do it," I said.

"They're different kinds of stitching, Stepmother. And the processes would be different."

"Well, we'll just have to have lessons! We'll start with undergarments and work our way up!" Maribelle waved her free hand in excitement. "You should come too, Evelyn. Stepmother-stepdaughter bonding!"

"I don't know if you would like it, Stepmother. You might get frustrated."

And here I'd thought she was nervous.

"Oooh, yes," Maribelle said, an iced ginger biscuit hovering inches from her mouth. "Evelyn doesn't like it when she's bad at things. We'll probably have to start you with a pillowcase."

I just stared at them.

"Oh, excuse me! I think my husband's waving at me. Oh no, that's not him. Should I try one of these jam cookies? Ooh, that might be him, though. I'd better go see. Bye!" Maribelle floated away.

"She was very nice," Ella said. "I think that went well for my first introduction."

I rolled my eyes, picked up one of those sandwich cookies, and stuffed it in my mouth. I looked around. Servants were circulating with glasses of wine. I made a beeline for the nearest one.

"Who should I introduce myself to next?"

I don't know, I thought. How about someone who washes her own windows? I've never been sure what you mix to keep them shiny and streak-free. (Is lemon juice involved?) You can exploit that. I snatched a glass of red wine off the tray of a passing servant and took a large, unladylike drink. Those cookies were dry.

"Why don't you introduce yourself to one of those young noblemen?" In my defense, I regretted it as soon as I said it. There's no need to be petty, Evelyn, I told myself.

To my surprise, Ella gave a long look over at a pair of young men jawing in a corner, chests puffed out experimentally.

"No," she said finally. "I don't think that's how it's supposed to go. They're supposed to come introduce themselves to you. Because they think you're beautiful, so they just have to talk to you."

I winced. "Or other characteristics," I said. "Intelligent, funny, kind. . . All great reasons for people to be interested in you. And there's nothing that says you can't introduce yourself to a man!"

Ella just shrugged. We'd parked ourselves right in the middle of the hall; people flowed past us, but none paid us any attention. I leaned in a little so I could hear her over the chatter.

"Where do you see yourself in ten years, Ella?"

She blushed a little. "I want to marry a prince. Everyone does, I know. But it would be just like the stories."

"Which stories?"

"You know, where the girl's mother dies and she's all alone, but then her fairy godmother comes and gives her a magic dress and magic shoes and a magic carriage and then she marries the prince."

"That godmother's a busy woman. Do you have a fairy—do you have a godmother?"

"I don't know." Ella frowned. "But she'll be there when I need her. I'm not really worried. I just have to wait for her. That's how the stories always go."

"Well. I suppose if young men are going to sweep you off your feet, you don't want your parents hanging around."

Ella laughed. "They might be scared of you, Stepmother. You should probably find Papa. He's all by himself somewhere."

I stood with my mouth open for a moment as my mind finally caught up. She isn't nervous; she just doesn't want your help. "I don't want to leave you by yourself . . ."

"I'll be fine."

So I left and found Henry, and we stood centrally, with both daughters in sight. The thing about waiting, I wanted to say, was that you couldn't control who would show up.

I tried parenting with Fanchon too. Heavens knew the world didn't want a woman to control her own fate. But you didn't have to let it take advantage of you, if you had knowledge and willpower. She had the willpower. She just needed the knowledge.

Despite my own experiences, I'd tried to send her to finishing school. For the discipline, at least. Her father had refused, so we'd compromised on tutors, although I couldn't afford them after he died. None of them were ever sure whether she was inept or just lazy, but I thought she'd have a chance with business. After all, between her father and me, she ought to have been an economic genius.

I called her over to the dining room table. "Fanchon, it's time for you to learn about the world. You'll be eighteen in a couple of years, and I should teach you what I know."

"I know what sex is, Mom."

"I'm talking about economics, Fan. Let's start with the supply-and-demand principle."

"Henry! Where's Henry? Someone tell Henry she's demented!"

"Fanchon! When you're eighteen you will inherit your father's business, and if you don't know what you're doing, you'll drive it into the ground! You have to be responsible—"

"Fine!" She plopped into a chair.

"How do you think a company like your father's sets prices?" I asked. Maybe if I kept her focus on her inheritance, she'd pay attention.

"I imagine Father set them as high as he wanted. That's how he was amazingly rich."

"Not quite. You see, the higher the price, the less people want to buy."

"Well, then that's their problem, isn't it?"

"But if no one buys your product, you don't make any money. That means it's your problem too," I said gently.

Fan stared at me blankly. Fanchon had her father's deep black hair and ghostly pale complexion. She would be pretty if she weren't constantly sneering. Where Ella radiated love, Fan exuded hatred. They were almost opposites, except they both achieved that same vacant stare.

"Let's think about this," I tried. "Imagine you have a stock of one hundred." I wrote the number on a piece of parchment.

"One hundred what?"

"Um . . . quilts," I said, my mind turning to my failure to pass down my business acumen to my other daughter.

"Like Ella makes? Then I will make no money because no one will buy those things."

"Well, we haven't done the consumer research. Let's pretend people will buy them."

"But they won't."

"Fine. Pretend you have one hundred bales of wool."

"This is stupid."

"You can sell ten percent of your stock for five sovereigns each, or sixty percent of your stock for one sovereign each. Which price scheme makes you the most profit?" I wrote the details on the parchment and turned it toward her, offering her the pen.

"How am I supposed to know something like that? Aren't you supposed to be teaching me?"

"You can do this, Fan. Start with the percent. It's out of one hundred, so I've made it pretty simple."

"So I'm stupid then because I can't answer your little question. Thanks, Mom."

"No, I'm sorry, Fan, of course that isn't what I meant. I just thought you knew how to do this. I told your tutor to teach you your sums and a few more advanced topics, like percent."

"That was years ago. Why would I remember that? I'm never going to use it. Real women aren't like you, Mom. When my prince shows up, he's not going to care if I can do percent!"

"Evie, no board of directors is going to let Fanchon do that much damage," Henry said.

"They'll use her. They'll lie to her, manipulate her, and buy her vote while they gradually edge her out!"

"So we'll find her a husband."

I'd avoided this topic. Of course I could find Fan a husband, even if he wasn't a prince, but I didn't want her to need one. There were too many men like her father and not enough like Henry.

"He'll do the same thing! He'll assume control, take over the company, and leave her. Fanchon is my daughter, and I love her, but if we're perfectly honest, she is not pleasant!" I paced up and down the bedroom, barely keeping my voice at a sort of screeching whisper. Henry put his hands on my shoulders and sat me at the vanity.

"First of all, we don't know that's what would happen. Think of all the unpleasant married women we know!"

"Her father didn't think. He didn't think about actually protecting her," I said.

Henry held my hands. "And isn't that why we're here? Fanchon's got to make her own mistakes. And when she does, she can come back to us. We'll be here for her."

"She's bound to learn some common sense before we're dead, right?" I sniffled.

"Has to." He kissed me on the forehead.

"Thank you. Really, thank you, for taking both of us . . ."

"You worry too much, love! Everyone will be fine. Fan's just needled you today. You need something to take your mind off it. Do you want to look over my list of potential acquisitions?"

I nodded.

"That'll make you feel better. And I need you to help me make up my mind . . ."

CHAPTER THREE

HE DIED in our second year of marriage, when bandits attacked his caravan. I don't remember who brought us the news. Ella screamed and sobbed. I put my arms around her, and I stroked her hair. She didn't fight me, but she was distant and a little bit cold, like she was pretending I was someone else.

There always seemed to be a reason for me not to cry. Ella was distraught. Fanchon was cruel to Ella. Nosy neighbors came by, wondering how I was putting on such a brave face. The funeral. The closest I came to losing it was at Mr. Sherman's arrival.

"No. We are not doing this today. I do not care about the will, or the money. Just go away! Go away!"

"I know you are grieving, madam, but surely you will want to know where your family stands."

"I don't really care right now."

"For your daughters, madam? It will only take a few moments."

We sat down at the kitchen table.

"Once again, a fairly simple will."

"Oh good." Everything would be Ella's, of course.

"He left everything to you."

It took me a moment. "Wait, what? That's not right. He would have left something for his daughter." Henry was sweet, but not stupid.

"He trusted that you would treat her fairly."

That was a lot of trust. I sat there with my mouth hanging open. "I believe his words to me were 'I'd have to ask Evelyn the best way to distribute it anyway, so it might as well be hers.'"

"That sounds like him. Thank you, Mr. Sherman. This was much less painful than I thought."

He squirmed a little in his seat. "Well, I have bad news too, madam."

"Of course."

"Your husband didn't really have any business for you to inherit. His clients and trade routes reverted to his business partners. He could only leave you the money he'd saved."

"He was always good about saving."

Mr. Sherman hesitated. "He was, yes. He stored it at a goldsmith's not too far from here . . ."

"Yes, my first husband did the same thing. They've got vaults and everything."

"Unfortunately," Mr. Sherman began, "the town was pillaged by marauders a few days ago. They couldn't, of course, take everything, but since your husband was unable to defend his own interests, I'm afraid he has two thousand sovereigns remaining."

Defend his own interests. Of course. As soon as the marauders left, undoubtedly every nobleman within earshot descended upon the vault to "determine" which coins belonged to whom, probably with the help of three-hundred-pound bodyguards. Everyone except Henry.

"So in essence, Mr. Sherman, you're telling me that I have complete financial control over what amounts to a few months of survival."

"Um, yes. Yes, I suppose. Um. I'll have the money sent here to you?"

"Well, I think you'd better. We used up most of the mattress savings just paying for the funeral."

He stood to leave, and I ushered him out impolitely.

"Until next time, madam."

"I'm not getting married again."

"Ah, no, um. Won't Fanchon be eighteen soon? I imagine we'll have some paperwork to fill out then."

We began cutting back. One by one, I let the servants go. Ella cooked all our meals, and even though I'd started purchasing blander fare, she somehow made it palatable. Fanchon did the dusting and the floors poorly for three weeks, so Ella went through and cleaned all the spots Fan had missed until Fan quit working altogether.

Meanwhile, I went looking for a job. It was what had to be done. My father was only a chemist, but I never had to sit on the streets and beg, mostly because no one knew how to wring copper flats from stones better than my parents. If he lost a few customers and times looked lean, Mother tightened belts and Father worked harder. He peddled sleeping draughts outside the nobles' mansions in the middle of the night. He'd predict the next plague and sell preventative cures. "Money is out there," he always said. "You just have to work hard enough to find it."

So I tried. I could consult, I told potential clients. I had exemplary marks from Furnival's and would have been a consultant if I'd been a man. I had advised both husbands (not a lie—just because Husband #1 didn't listen didn't mean I hadn't given advice), and I had years of experience managing my husbands' households. No one was really impressed. A few kindly told me they'd consider my offer. Most looked at me like I'd sprouted horns. Women didn't do this sort of thing. It wasn't in the stories. Even Henry's business partners had no provisions for widows and orphans.

Laundry was my chore, but I was out constantly, networking, job hunting. There were even a few nights when I begged at taverns for leftover food because I knew we only had enough at home for the girls. I'd sit down to do the washing late at night at the end of the week, and it would already be done. The beds were already made, the fireplace already swept—even the kitchen garden had already been tended. The first time I noticed, I felt a little surge of hatred for Ella. She was all the house needed. What had I ever been good for,

anyway? The second time, I just fell into bed, supremely grateful I
didn't need to scrub clothes.

The storm hit after the first month. Our thatching wasn't quite
up to the task.

"Find containers!" I shouted. Ella ran to the kitchen. Fanchon
tried to stand between the holes. I dropped an armful of linen cloths
in Fanchon's arms.

"You can't dry the storm, Mother!"

"It'll damage the wood. Any water that doesn't land in a bowl,
wipe it up. I knew we should have switched to tiles."

By morning, the ceiling sagged and dripped. Ella lay asleep on
the floor, drops falling on her waist. Fan had found the one dry spot,
and since she hadn't mopped up like I'd asked her to, she was using
the dry towels as blankets. I took one and put it over Ella.

I reassessed the placement of our containers, adjusting the vases
and pans until the house resounded with plinks. The drops sounded
almost like coins clinking into a metal vault. That was wishful thinking. All the coins around here were being washed away with the
flood.

We couldn't begin to afford to fix the roof. That storm was a
fluke, I said. We shouldn't have more for a few months. The roof
didn't need to be done right away. Unfortunately, I'd also run out of
options. The only non-cleaning, non-sewing jobs for women in their
late middle age were in childcare.

It galled me to think I really couldn't provide for the three of us,
but I had to admit I needed a new plan. I covered the dining table
with the parchments of both wills. Henry's was useless—he had truly
left me everything and nothing—but I hoped there was a loophole
in the first one, something that could prevent Fanchon from hanging
Ella and me out to dry. Because the more time I spent at home, the
more obvious it became that she would.

"Ella! You touched my dresses, didn't you! I told you not to
touch my things!"

"I was getting your washing, Fanchon," Ella said and carried an
armful of clothes into the washing room at the back of the house.

"Stupid little serving-girl!"

"Fanchon! Leave your sister alone!"

"Stepsister, Mom. I would have thought you'd be on the side of your real daughter."

"You're being rude, Fan."

"It's because she's jealous that I have nice things and she just has rags," Fan taunted.

"If you actually did your chores, you wouldn't wear velvet either," I said.

"She doesn't have nice things because the idiot sold all her gowns."

I rubbed the bridge of my nose. "Ella!" I called.

She entered with a basket of neatly folded clothes.

"Did you sell your gowns?"

She froze, eyes wide like she was going to get in trouble. I could almost see her mind trying to formulate a lie. She wordlessly opened and shut her mouth several times, and then started a very faint humming noise. "Umm," she'd say, clenching her fists and swallowing hard, but she couldn't get another word out before she'd started humming again. We'd have waited all night, if it hadn't been for Fanchon.

"She hid all the money from you. She's stealing. She should be punished for being wicked."

"I didn't steal!" Ella cried, her eyes brimming with tears. She dropped the laundry basket and ran to her room. She returned with a coin purse, which she placed on the table.

"I wanted to fix the roof, but I didn't have enough, so I was saving it until I could get more."

"But now you don't have any clothes," I said. I heard Fanchon snort.

"The girls in the stories never do."

"How much did you get?" I asked. The purse didn't look very full.

"Thirty-eight sovereigns."

It took all my willpower not to wince. She'd been cheated something awful. Ella kept her clothes in good condition.

"Ella, why don't I put this with the rest of the savings. When we have enough, we'll use it to fix the roof."

Ella nodded and scurried away with the laundry basket.

"She's so stupid," Fanchon said.

"Fanchon! You are being unacceptably rude, and I don't want to hear it! Find a way to help!"

"You like her better because you hated Dad. Well, you'll end up sorry. This is just like in the stories."

"Which stories?"

"I'm like the princess who has to live in filth because an evil fairy takes everything away from her. But soon I'm going to get my money, and then I'll marry a prince, and you and Ella can starve for all I care!"

I was too exhausted to scold Fan. If she really thought about it, any prince would be embarrassed to have his mother-in-law sitting in a ditch begging for coins, but Fanchon wasn't going to marry a prince. She was going to end up with someone like her father, and I'd have to move back to the city, where I could beg from my husband's former business partners.

The person who ought to end up with someone like her father was Ella. The girls might disagree, but that was better than a prince in my book. He'd take care of her, he'd listen to her, he'd appreciate her. He'd feel guilty enough to help Ella care for Fan and me.

I started to feel a twinge of guilt myself as I pictured how well this would work. Really, Evelyn? You'll marry your stepdaughter off to avoid becoming a washerwoman? But he has to be kind, I thought. He has to be good, or it won't work. I could solve everything, if I could just find Ella a husband. The only problem was, every time I tried to be helpful, neither girl cooperated. I sighed. I didn't even know who was eligible. I needed my connections.

CHAPTER FOUR

THE NEXT DAY I went looking for my "friends." They'd disappeared ever since I started flirting with poverty. I found them, finally, near the King's Woods, having a luncheon under a pavilion.

"She said that whoever wants to marry her son is going to have to pass some sort of test. Like weaving a carpet with gold thread or something. I said—" Delia jumped as I approached. "Evelyn!"

"Evelyn Radcliffe. What a surprise," Cora said, hiding her shock much better than Delia had.

"Evelyn! It's so good to see you!" Maribelle gushed.

"It's been a while, hasn't it? I had a few spare minutes today and thought I'd say hello."

"We're so glad you did! Here, we don't have an extra chair, but I've got a footstool." Maribelle paused her knitting and handed me a little footrest that put me barely six inches off the ground, with my knees pulled up to my chest.

While Maribelle was welcoming me, Delia had put all her focus into consuming a poached fig so she didn't have to look at me, and Cora gave me a pinched smile that didn't extend all the way to her eyes. They were probably wishing they'd officially uninvited me.

"It's really so awful what's happened to you," Cora said. Delia nodded her agreement, mouth stuffed with fig.

"I felt so bad when I heard!" Maribelle said, and she possibly actually meant it. "Here, Delia, pour Evelyn a cup of tea."

Once I'd accepted a cup of tea, Delia brought up two noble-women who'd shown up at a ball in the same dress, and the gossip hour continued as if I wasn't there—although that's not exactly accurate. I had a feeling that when I wasn't there, they were gossiping about me.

"How are you feeling about it all?" Maribelle finally asked me.

"I just don't know how you do it. I don't know what I'd do without William." Delia started sniffling.

"Evelyn and Henry just seemed like a match made in heaven!" Maribelle said, knitting needles clacking.

"We heard you had to let go of your servants," Cora said. "Looking after your own house, caring for your own children—you must cry yourself to sleep every night."

"No," I said crossly. Cora gave me a smug smile. I pursed my lips. I needed information out of them, so I had to throw them a bone.

"I just make Ella do all the housework anyway. It's all she's really good at."

"Congratulations, Evelyn! We knew you'd turn wicked eventually," Cora said.

"Just like in the stories," Delia trilled.

"Well, wicked or no, I've somehow got to get the two of them married or I'll be stuck with them forever."

"That might be difficult, given your . . . current station," Cora said.

"Not for Fanchon," Delia said. "Not with her inheritance."

"I don't even know who's eligible these days."

"Ooh . . . there's the Kindler boy," Maribelle said.

"Isn't there a Kingsley?" Delia asked.

"I thought he was married," Maribelle said.

"No, there's another one," Cora said. "But he's dreadfully pocked."

"I suppose Cora's son is too young," Delia said.

Cora grinned at me and winked condescendingly. I gave her a withering sidelong glare.

"There's a Windham, a Quincey, and a Meekley," Cora said. The others nodded in agreement.

"Good luck finding anyone for Ella," Delia said.

"Men never want to marry orphans, do they?" Maribelle said. "Unless they're a prince. In the stories, princes marry orphans all the time."

"The girls both seem to think they're living in one of these tales," I said. And I need to make one happen, I thought. "I'm afraid I'm not familiar with them."

The knitting needles stopped. "Not familiar with them!" Maribelle cried.

"I don't like stories."

"But you have to have heard them!"

"I wasn't paying attention."

"There are all kinds of stories about pretty young girls with an evil stepmother and a wicked stepsister," Maribelle said.

"And the father always dies and the girl is treated like a servant," Cora said.

"And then she meets a prince!" Delia said. There, I thought. Reason #23 for why I can't stand these stories: contrived and impossible chance meetings.

"How on earth does a common girl meet a prince?"

"He usually throws a party," Delia said.

"Except the girl is always forbidden from going, so her fairy godmother gives her a beautiful ball gown, and a carriage, and glass slippers," Maribelle said with a sigh.

That was familiar, but even Ella hadn't made it sound so ridiculous. "Glass slippers?" I snorted.

"She loses one of them when she leaves," Cora said.

"The prince is so in love, he goes all over the kingdom and tries it on every girl, but it only fits the princess," Delia said. Reason #5: irrational methods of identification.

"Hm," I said out loud. That is a stupid story, I said in my head.

"It's so sweet," Maribelle said.

"What happens to the stepsister?"

"I think she usually cuts off her toes. To make the slipper fit," Delia said.

That sounded like Fan.

"I think I heard one version where the stepmother and stepsister had their eyes pecked out by birds," Cora said. I tried hard not to roll my eyes.

"No, it doesn't have to be so gruesome," Maribelle said. "I mean, the princess is always so nice! I think she just forgives them and they all live in the palace happily ever after."

"Well, the girls are convinced they're going to marry princes. I may be evil, but I still don't have the heart to tell them we don't have any."

"Yes, we do! Prince Aiden!" Delia said.

"And he's what, fifteen?" I said.

"Well, someone's been out of the loop," Cora said.

"He's twenty-one!" Maribelle giggled.

"I hear he's a perfect gentleman," Delia said.

"And he's incredibly good-looking," Maribelle whispered.

"Why do you think we're out here?" Cora said.

I looked around, uncomprehending.

"He comes here to hunt," Maribelle said. "All our husbands go out with him. He doesn't have a retinue, but if we sit right here, we can catch a glimpse of him."

"He's in Strachey all the time now," Delia said.

"Rumor has it, the king's mind is all mush, and the queen does most of the ruling. Everyone suspects Aiden's trying to shore up support for his own rule," added Cora.

"We support him!" Maribelle said dreamily. "My husband organizes all his hunting trips. That's how we know where to come."

I was struggling to think of a response that wasn't dripping with disdain when we heard a small commotion in the trees.

"Here he comes!" Delia exclaimed.

Sure enough, a little way in, the prince and company came into view. He seemed so young, especially next to the other gentlemen. Sure, he had a royal bearing and a kingly smile, but he was still thin and gangly, with a mop of brown hair.

We all watched for a little while. The other men preened and boasted. The prince laughed good-naturedly at their jokes but never really joined in. He wasn't impolite, just bored, I thought, with posturing noblemen attempting to impress him. After a few minutes, the prince went off by himself, and my friends turned their attention back to the luncheon with wistful sighs. Even I stared after him. He seemed so . . . sweet. I started to think.

"So he's here to make connections?" I said.

"Also I think he really likes our trees," Maribelle said. I raised an eyebrow.

"He's probably got to make sure we're all coming to his party!" Delia said. "It's in a few weeks. I think he's looking for a wife! Didn't you get invitations?"

I opened my mouth to say something nasty, but I thought better of it. "No," I simply said. Of course I didn't get invitations! I hadn't been to a function since Henry died. My ever-popular friends had ignored me for a month. I had holes in the roof the size of my head.

"I hear it's very exclusive. You have to be extremely well connected to get in," Cora said.

I set down my teacup. It was time to leave before I throttled one of them.

"Well, I should check on my daughters. Find something wicked to do to Ella."

They said goodbye and pretended it was nice to see me. I hurried out of earshot before I could hear what they said about me.

I wasn't ready to go home yet, so I walked for a while. I found myself at the lake. I bit my lip as I sat in the grass, slipped my shoes off, and dug my toes into the dirt.

Fanchon turns eighteen in two months, I thought. She'll inherit her father's fortune, and Ella and I . . . we'll be homeless. No reason to sugarcoat it. Even if Fanchon didn't kick us out, the house would be uninhabitable before long. We'd really, truly have nothing, and I knew what would happen to Ella on the streets. I'd have absolutely no way to protect her. And of course, Fanchon would join us in a few years after her father's business sharks took everything away from her. I chucked a stone into the lake.

What could I do with them? They wanted marriage, so shouldn't I give it to them? It had to be better than destitution. They'd be happy, I guess.

Happy like whom? Happy like Cora, who spends entire luncheons castigating her husband for flirting with barmaids and drinking too much? Happy like Delia, who might go a whole year putting up a pretense of wealth because her husband hadn't yet recouped his losses at the gambling table? Happy like Maribelle, who calls herself stupid whenever anyone disagrees with her and only really gets her husband's attention when she bursts into tears? She'd looked just like Ella, adding row after row to that massive blanket. No wonder everyone wanted to marry a prince.

Maybe I thought the stories were stupid because they never happened. Was it really too much to ask to be loved, respected, and financially solvent? Which one were you willing to give up? Which one was I willing to let the girls give up?

And even if you did manage to hit all three—love, respect, and a steady income—there was no guarantee he'd stay alive. I looked out at the geese waddling in the grass. Then I looked at the lake, I looked up at the clouds, and I felt a giant sob catch in my throat, so I buried my face in my arms.

I took a ragged breath. The prince. Why waste time with minor nobility? The more I thought about him, the more I felt certain he'd fall hopelessly in love with Ella. All she had to do was show up. Of course, even that would take some initiative on her part. I remembered Lord Whitcomb's party. Life wasn't going to happen if she waited for it to come to her. Even if I pushed her, she'd just sit around and wait for that stupid fairy godmother. I bit my lip. What did the godmother use? A magic dress, magic shoes, and a magic carriage.

I stood up and exhaled. I'd tried everything, and I'd tried to do it all myself. I'd even thought I could get them married on my own, but I was being foolish. Ella needed my help, but it was her story. I pursed my lips. Men were such a risk, but the prince . . . he'd never let his mother-in-law go homeless. And more importantly, he reminded me of her father. Fanchon might have my eyes pecked out, but Ella—Ella would forgive us all.

"Evelyn," I said, "this story is no longer about you."

CHAPTER FIVE

THE FIRST STEP was a trip to the city. I'd show Cora well connected.

The capital city of our fine nation was named Trull, but everyone just called it the Capital. It was everything one would expect of such a large city. Any major street was congested with carriages, which didn't go nearly fast enough because of the pedestrians drifting down the center of the road. You couldn't go a block without being accosted by either a beggar or a hawker, where you would either lose a copper or gain a flyer to the newest opera or freak show. Sanitation and waste removal were what you'd call emerging fields, so the scent was often pungent, particularly in the poorer districts where the wealthy dumped their refuse.

Like any good city, the Capital was characterized by dichotomy. In the Fens, on the one hand, clean water was such a luxury that consumption was rampant. In the Pendolyn District, on the other hand, two-story houses glittered with fresh paint, vividly green manicured lawns, and a much lower risk of fire. I grew up somewhere in between, surrounded by stories of the little chimney sweep who'd suffocated in a chimney and the nobleman's daughter who ate dainty chocolate cakes for dinner. Small wonder I'd never had much time for fairies.

Husband #1 and I had just worked our way into Pendolyn when Fan was born. But we were new money and small fish, and before long he decided he'd be a bigger deal in Strachey. All our friends expressed envy—how lucky we were to move to the countryside. I have never met a resident of the Capital who didn't say they hated it. I knew I would miss the city. I'd miss the not knowing, the never-ending supply of new around the corners. Strachey was too knowable.

Of course, Husband #1 had maintained his connections after the move. He'd visited the Capital frequently, and I have a vise-like memory for names. After a few hours of research, I knew who had invitations; I searched my memory and went down the list, circling all the men who'd adored my husband and crossing out all the ones whose wives he'd seduced. Then I chose my mark.

"Lord Busbee!" I exclaimed. I'd crashed his weekend fete and had to circulate for an hour before I'd finally found him.

"Ma'am, I don't think I—"

"Oh, you probably wouldn't recognize me, but you knew my husband, I think—Bertram Envers. May he rest in peace."

"Oh! My goodness! Yes, of course I knew your husband! A paragon, madam, a true loss."

"You're very kind, sir. My husband always spoke so highly of you. He so valued your thoughtful advice—said you were one of the few geniuses of this generation of businessmen. Anyway, when I saw you standing here, I just had to come tell you how much you meant to Bertram."

He puffed like a robin swelling his chest. "Well, thank you very much, madam. Have you moved back to the city?"

"Oh no. We're still living in the country, my daughter and I. I'm just visiting. Don't you have a daughter as well, my lord? I think I remember . . ."

"Why, yes! You have an impressive memory!"

"Oh, well . . . how is she?"

"She's quite the charming young lady, if I do say so myself!" He chuckled. "She and her mother are quite mad about the ball, although I suspect you and your daughter understand that quite well!"

"I'm sure I don't know what you mean," I said, doing my best to sound sincere instead of sarcastic, or possibly sinister.

"Haven't you received an invitation?" He gasped, socially horrified.

"No! We are completely out of the loop. Invitations for what?"

"Why, the prince is giving a ball!"

"Really? Oh! How disappointing! My daughter would have so enjoyed it. There must have been some mistake. I mean, I certainly don't need one, but surely the daughter of Bertram Envers . . ."

"Indubitably a mistake! How horrifying! Fortunately, I happen to be one of the few individuals with blank invitations at my discretion."

"What a coincidence," I murmured.

"Give me but a moment." He left and returned with two elaborately decorated pieces of paper and a quill pen. "Now, what is your daughter's name?"

"Fanchon. She'll be eighteen in a few months. It's hard to believe."

"They grow up so quickly."

I watched as he inscribed *F. Envers* with a flourish.

"Now, we must send you with her, madam—"

"Of course, I had to remarry. It's Radcliffe now. E. Radcliffe."

"There you are!" Fanchon said when I returned. "Where were you again?"

"The Capital. Did you know Prince Aiden is giving a ball?"

"What?" Fan shouted. Ella's eyes lit up.

"You have to have invitations, of course," I said.

They held their breath. I held up the invitations. Fanchon screamed. I caught a glimpse of Ella's hopeful face and slowly turned away.

"Oh, I'm sorry, Ella. I only have two. I suppose you'll have to stay home."

She didn't say anything, so I continued with my last dart.

"Besides, you sold all of your gowns. You can't go to a ball in rags."

I couldn't bear to look at her, but I could imagine her crestfallen eyes anyway. This is how the story's supposed to go, I tried to reassure myself. She'll be happy as soon as she gets her prince. She'll forgive you. I still didn't think I could turn around, so I pretended to be busy with the papers on the table.

"Ribbit," I heard. A frog leapt out from a cabinet shelf at me. I yelped.

"Don't kill it! Don't kill it!" Ella cried. She rushed over and scooped up the trespasser.

"What in the—"

"We're being invaded," Fan said.

"I think it's because things are kind of damp," Ella said. She stood on a chair and reached up to a shallow tin pail balanced precariously in the rafters. As Ella dropped the frog in the pail, another one peeked its head up over the rim. I could only assume he shared that habitat with several brothers.

"I'm gone two days, and the two of you start saving frogs?"

"I said we should pluck off their arms and legs and eat them."

"No! We can't kill them! They just want a home. I'm keeping them close to one of the holes so insects will just fly in and they can eat them."

I sighed. She was teary-eyed, and I'd already reached my wickedness quota for the day.

"Fine. But when we get the roof fixed, they go."

Ella nodded. "Thank you, Stepmother."

"Ella!" Fan cried. "Let's go pick out what we're going to wear to the ball! Oh, wait! You're not going. You've got nothing to wear."

Ella ran from the room, fighting back tears.

"We can't afford something new, Fan. It cost me enough to get the invitations."

"I guess I can make do. Really, I get to go? And Ella doesn't? It's just about me?"

I smiled weakly.

"I love you, Mom. You are the best."

She ran up the stairs. I sat down, took a shaky breath, and wondered what a good mother would have done differently.

Getting a ball gown for Ella was a problem. We'd made quite a dent in the money Henry left us—my allowance from Fanchon's estate made up more and more of our monthly income. She and Fanchon wore the same size, but Fan would know immediately if she spotted Ella in one of her gowns. I was a good head taller than Ella, and the idea that I might hem anything was laughable. This left me, really, with only one option.

I found Maribelle near the woods, eyes fixated on the spot where the prince and his hangers-on would appear while her hands continued to knit her blanket. She wasn't completely alone; her children screamed in their matching outfits and eluded their nannies.

"Evelyn! What a surprise!"

"Hello, Maribelle. Waiting for the prince?"

She nodded. "Have you ever heard him speak? He's so genuine. He's humble. You wouldn't think he's royalty. I mean, you would, because he carries himself like a prince, but he doesn't act it—superior, you know?"

"He doesn't show it, at least. We don't know what he's like in private."

"You're so cynical, Evelyn. I think he's wonderful. What are you doing out here? We don't usually see you wandering about."

I sighed. "Maribelle, I need a favor. An enormous favor. I'm embarrassed to have to ask."

"Oh, Evelyn, don't be! We're all here for each other!"

That was debatable. I doubted Maribelle ever meant much malice, but that wouldn't stop every word I said from being repeated to Cora and Delia. Oh well.

"No, it's too much. Forget I said anything," I added, the magic words to ensure her cooperation.

"Evelyn!" Maribelle put her hand on mine. I tried not to flinch. "I know things have been hard recently. If you're in trouble, I'd hate to think I didn't do something!" She started to tear up.

I sighed. I was actually asking a huge favor—and it was truly a mark of how desperate I was that I was even going through with it. "I managed to get invitations to the ball through a connection of my first husband. Fan's over the moon about it, but she hasn't been able to buy anything new in months. I just don't want her to be embarrassed to meet the prince!"

Maribelle was about to gasp and gush her sympathies when we heard voices in the trees. Her attention snapped eagerly toward the commotion. I considered the time. He certainly kept to a schedule.

They'd caught something, apparently. Maribelle frowned and attempted to tell her nannies to cover the children's eyes. While servants took the carcass away, the noblemen congratulated one another and chatted. Then once again, the prince excused himself and wandered out of sight.

"Where's he going?" I asked.

"Oh, he always does this. He always goes off that way by himself. Wants some time alone, I guess. I don't know what's down that way, though."

I pictured the countryside. The river, I thought. Henry loved to take me there.

As Prince Aiden's comrades traveled back out of sight, Maribelle let out a sigh. I gave her a moment.

"So . . . I'm sure I can't afford the proper fabric. . . If I gave you some of my dresses, could you use them to make something for Fanchon? Even if you just take them up." If it fit Fanchon, it would fit Ella. All the fairy godmother would have to do is leave it somewhere.

"What? Oh, of course, Evelyn! I'm happy to help!"

"Thank you so much, Maribelle. As soon as I have the money I'll pay you for your time."

"Oh, you don't have to do that."

"I certainly do." Otherwise, I'd owe her a favor, and I really didn't want to find out what she'd call in.

"You're so sweet, Evelyn," she said as I stood up. "You take care!"

I thought I'd feel more embarrassed as I walked away. Past Evelyn could hardly have stomached groveling to Maribelle. But now? Present Evelyn could almost taste a royal wedding.

CHAPTER SIX

"FANCHON! We're going to be late!"

"No one goes to these things on time, Mom." She came flouncing down the stairs in a whirl of red-orange silks that hugged her figure a little more than I would have liked, but only because I still wanted her to be four.

"You look beautiful, Fan," I said. "Your—"

"I know, right?" She turned away from me and walked into the sitting room. She took her matching purse from the console and inspected its contents.

"Your father would be proud of you."

"Hm?" She turned and looked at me. "So that's what we're wearing, Mom?"

She was fighting a grin. I closed my eyes and took a deep breath. I'd sort of expected this. Maribelle had cannibalized my best gowns for Ella's dress, and I'd traded a few others for the shoes, which left me with two options: a severe and tightly laced funeral dress and an old gift from my mother. I'd always told her I was saving it for something special, and it turned out I hadn't lied. I'd saved it for the last gasp of my dignity.

It was pink like spun sugar. The skirt left room for me to hide both Fanchon and Ella. At my height, I couldn't possibly look cheerful enough to pull this off. Fortunately, it didn't matter. I was going to be ill on the way there. I just had to survive the carriage ride with Fan.

"Fan . . ."

"No, Mom, it's fine. I mean, you know there are going to be rich widowers there, right? You might finally find a husband who will die and leave you a fortune."

"Get in the carriage," I said quietly.

"What? I just—"

"Fanchon, someday you might have to learn when to shut up. Please get in the carriage."

She marched past me, throwing her shoulder into me.

"That's a new dress," I realized.

"No, it isn't. I've had it forever."

"You're lying, Fan. I can tell it's new."

"How? You don't know everything I own!"

"Fan! I told you we couldn't afford anything new! Ella, we're leaving!" I shouted and slammed the door.

"You can't afford it, but I can!"

"How?"

"Everyone knows I'm going to be loaded when I'm eighteen. I just used my credit line."

"You have a credit line?" I think I felt my heart stop. "Fan, how—how much have you charged?"

As it turned out, I wasn't really lying when I told Fan I didn't feel well. Nothing makes me ill like a great mass of useless debt. She didn't care, so I dropped her off and immediately turned the carriage around.

I stopped the carriage some yards away from the house and snuck into the stables on foot so Ella wouldn't hear the horses. I'd left the dress and shoes in a sack tucked in the hay, and I now pulled them out. Maribelle had wrapped the dress delicately in a soft white cloth. I stacked the somewhat transparent-looking shoes on top and tucked my ambiguous invitation under the heels.

From the carriage house, I bustled into the garden. We used to have a small knot garden—interlocking manicured hedges surrounding a quaint little marble fountain—but since Ella only had time to tend the vegetable garden and the rosebush, the hedges had become one overgrown mass surrounding a very large birdbath.

It was practically a jungle expedition, and I was intensely ill-attired. I tried to be silent, but I was almost two feet wider than usual. I pushed through the crowded garden like I was wading through molasses, dragging my giant skirt through the snagging bushes. Each rip felt like it echoed, but I reassured myself—Ella had sulked meekly in her room all day. I didn't think she had a chance of hearing me.

Just to the side of the knot garden was a cherry tree, planted by Ella's mother. If a fairy was going to leave Ella a gift, she'd leave it by the tree. I knelt down, although my skirts didn't, and wobbled in my rising layers of pink fabric. Just as I placed my little bundle at the base of the tree, I heard the back doorknob turn. I froze. Ella must have moved to the fireplace after we left. If she saw me, she'd know it wasn't her fairy godmother, and she'd probably refuse to go; and even if she did go, she'd have to lie to Fanchon, and that would never work. I looked around desperately, but truthfully, the garden only had one hiding spot. I dived low under an overgrown hedge.

I tried to crawl through, propelling myself forward on my elbows, but my dress was caught. Twisting, I reached one arm back to swat at yards of pink gauze. I tugged the fabric loose from the branches and pulled my feet under the hedge line.

"Godmother?" I heard as I tried to scoot toward the fountain. Little thorny branches slapped me in the face, but I reached in and tugged on the skirt one last time. I broke free and huddled at the base of the fountain, peeking under the hedge.

"Godmother? Where did you go?" Ella said. She'd come out with a candle and cautiously approached the hedges.

It's a good thing I'm not trying to rob the house, I thought, not that we've got anything to steal. Only Ella would assume a mysterious noise in the back was her fairy godmother.

Look at the tree, I willed her, but her feet just kept coming closer. I crawled to the other side of the fountain. Please don't look over the hedge, I thought. Suddenly I heard a gasp. I hustled back around and peered out from under the hedge. Joy lit up her face, but as I watched her I groaned in inward disappointment. I finally understood why the slippers were supposed to be glass. Glass would have sparkled.

"Oh, Godmother! Thank you!" She scooped the bundle into her arms and ran into the house.

Time for phase two. It has to be quicker to go over the hedge, I thought. I lifted one leg over and straddled the hedge, then swung my other leg over. Except it didn't come, because this damnable dress had become one with the brambles.

Hopping on my free foot, I silently cursed my mother. I pulled and yanked and tried to spring forward until it all came suddenly free. I toppled over, like a giant pink tree.

Get the carriage, I thought, before she's finished getting ready. I picked myself up out of the dirt and ran toward the carriage, motioning frantically for it to pull up to the house. Ella stepped out of the front door just as I leaned against the corner of the house, wheezing tragically. She'd have taken my breath away, if I'd had any left.

Maribelle had worked magic. She had blended the grayish-blue velvet with white satin so that the dress gave off light. I'd clearly fallen short. Glass would have looked so much better. Ella hadn't had time for an elaborate hairstyle, so she'd simply piled it on her head, and a few strands had fallen out of place. I'd never seen her look so much like Henry.

She turned toward me. I spun around the corner with a wide circle, narrowly avoiding the bush abutting the house.

"Godmother, I know you're there. I saw your fairy dress."

She took a few steps closer to the corner. I was going to have to speak. What did a fairy godmother sound like, anyway? High and thin, perky? Maybe a nasal tone? I took a deep breath.

Suddenly, one of the sparrows landed on the bush. My eyes widened. Stay put, I thought.

"Fly away, child! Fly away!" I squeaked, in my best impression of a tiny talking bird. I hesitated. I wanted to chirp, but if I did it poorly, and then the actual bird chirped . . .

Fortunately, Ella squealed in delight. "Oh, hello, little sparrow! Did my godmother send you?"

"Mm-hmm! We always look after you!"

"I knew it! Will you thank her for me? I wanted to go to the ball so badly, but Stepmother only had two invitations because she hates me and—"

"She doesn't hate you! Don't be too hard on her. She's doing her best!"

"She is?"

"Now get in the carriage!" My sparrow voice made my nose buzz, which then made my ears pop. I yawned. "It'll take you to the ball."

But not back, I suddenly realized. Not if it took Fanchon back first. I scrambled. Fanchon would stay there. . . When did it end? Two in the morning? So if I counted the carriage travel time back and forth, plus a little bit of a cushion to give the horses a breather. . .

"But remember this! You must leave the ball by the stroke of midnight!"

"Wait, why?"

"Because the magic will end!" I'd lost the voice. "The magic will end," I tried again. "Your dress, the shoes—all magic!" Nope. I sounded like Maribelle's two-year-old.

"My dress will vanish?"

"Mm-hmm!"

"I'll remember, little sparrow! Thank you ever so much!" She climbed into the carriage.

I waited until she drove off and went inside the house. I poured myself a drink and picked little round green leaves out of my hair.

Well done, Evelyn, I thought. One daughter will get herself a prince, the other daughter will undoubtedly pick up a duke, and you've got the house to yourself. I sat in the stillness and listened to the bellowing frogs. Mm. I didn't tell Ella to leave a slipper behind, I realized. Well, she'd have to think of some things herself. I couldn't do everything for her, now could I?

I heard the front door open and close twice that evening. The first shut with quiet courtesy, and I suddenly remembered the dress was supposed to vanish. Once Ella was safely in her room, I told the driver to pick up Fan (I owed him a tidy sum). Then I waited outside her door until her room was so silent I thought she had to be asleep. I snuck in and took the neatly folded dress and subpar shoes—there were two of them. Well, hopefully the prince could just recognize her. The second time the door closed, it slammed so hard it brought me out of a deep sleep. I smiled anyway.

CHAPTER SEVEN

"WELL, FAN? How was it?" I asked when she finally trudged down to breakfast the next morning.

"Terrible. That was the worst party ever."

"Didn't you get to dance with the prince?"

"No."

"Why not?"

"Because there were like a million people there, Mom! The line was out the door!"

"Oh." I was hoping to hear that Ella had swept the prince off his feet and he wouldn't dance with anyone else. I started to feel a terrible sinking sensation.

"And you could dance with the other nobles, but only if you wanted to give up your place in line, and besides, the dance floor was so clogged with people, you only had a few inches to move. It was like . . ."

"Like being packed in a tin," Ella offered. "And everyone had to move the same direction or you would just bounce off each other."

"Exactly! How do you know that?"

Ella's face froze as all her concentration went toward formulating a lie. Her mouth hung open a little, and her eyes drifted up toward the ceiling.

I decided to help. "Ella certainly has quite the imagination."

"Yes, I just imagined it," she said hoarsely.

"You're so weird."

"Did you see anyone interesting?" I asked Fan.

"No one interesting wanted to talk to me, Mom. All the attractive men had twenty girls hanging on them. They didn't want to talk to me."

"I mostly stood on the edge of the room and got pushed around by all the people," Ella said.

Fan stared at Ella.

"In my imagination."

"How are you talking like you were there?" Fan shouted.

"I just know what it would have been like?" It wasn't a question, but Ella said it like it was. I needed to help her—she was practically immobile—but I also had to keep up the charade.

"As a matter of fact, Ella, I came home early. I didn't see you."

Her eyes widened exponentially. You were in your room, I thought loudly, hoping maybe I could transfer the thought into her head.

"I was . . . not . . . here."

This was a disaster.

"What? Were you there? You didn't have an invitation!" Fan shrieked. "How did you go to the ball?"

"I didn't see you in the living room," I hinted, hoping she would pick a different room.

"Umm . . ." Ella hummed like a bumblebee.

"And you weren't in the kitchen."

She looked down at her plate.

I'm going to have to list every room in the house, I thought. "I didn't see you in the washroom."

"Where were you?" Fan screamed.

"I—I—I was in my room?"

Whew. I let out the breath I was holding.

"Oh, I didn't look there," I said. "I suppose if you were in your room I wouldn't have seen you. Do you think the prince picked a wife, Fan?"

"I doubt it. He had to dance practically every dance. I think he wanted to run away."

"I didn't even get to see the prince," Ella said softly.

"Because you weren't there!" Fan shouted.

I hit my head slowly on the cupboard.

Well, a prince had been a long shot, hadn't it? I revisited the list of minor nobles the ladies had given me and began paying calls.

"Lady Quincey. It's been too long!" I minced, taking a seat in the Quincey family home. Oliver Quincey was the first name on my list, so naturally, I was meeting his mother.

"Hi-i-i," she sang, stretching the word into several syllables. "How are you?"

You'd think by this point I'd have figured out a good answer to that question. Each time, however, I just wanted to let loose. How do you think I am? I wanted to say. My husband is dead. We're just about in the poorhouse, which you already know, because everyone knows! Everyone knows our business, and you're all just looking the other way!

I never actually said any of that, of course.

"It's certainly been a struggle since Henry passed," I said, sighing. "But we're muddling our way through. I suppose there's no other choice, really. One just has to keep going. Still, I've got my girls, and it's such a pleasure watching them grow into such beautiful young ladies. Have you met my daughters?"

"No-oo-oo!" she exclaimed. "And I've always wanted to!"

I found that doubtful. Glendora Quincey was trying to butter me up. "I'll have to introduce you," I said. "How is your family?"

"Oh, quite lovely. Bruce has decided to start a political career, so we're thinking of moving to the Ca-a-a-pital," she said, her singsong voice making her sound more and more like a bleating sheep. "We'd give Oliver the house, of course, but we'd like to see him get married first."

Aha. Glennie knew why I was there, and her bid apparently came with the family estate.

"I completely understand. You want to see him settled. That's exactly how I feel about my daughters. Both Fanchon and Ella are of age now, and the process seems overwhelming."

"I ima-a-a-gine Fanchon has quite a sizable dowry."

Subtle, Glennie. Very subtle.

"Yes, her father did provide well for her there. But then Ella has just the sweetest, kindest personality." I paused for a split second before I said some of the worst words to ever come out of my mouth. You've got to seal the deal, Evelyn. You're desperate. "I'm sure she'd make any young man happy."

"Aww," Glennie purred, stretching her smile and opening her eyes wide, trying to seem interested in Ella. "You really ought to meet Oliver," Glennie continued. "Have you met my son before?"

"I haven't, no. I've heard wonderful things about him, of course."

"You're too kind. Let me see if he's home."

He would be, of course. Glendora had planned her pitch. She sent a servant to find him, and sure enough, within a few seconds he sauntered into the room.

"Oo-oo-oh, Oliver!" Glennie said. "Madam Radcliffe and I were just talking about her daughters. Do you know Fanchon and . . . um . . ."

"Ella," I supplied.

"That's right, Ella. Have you met them?"

"Do you mean Fanchon Envers? Why, I'd be quite the social recluse if I didn't know Miss Envers. You have a charming daughter, Madam Radcliffe."

I murmured my thanks. Fanchon saved her charm for outside the house, I supposed.

"You're probably not aware, of course, but Envers Enterprises is simply the model for all business plans. Any student of investment or manufacturing has studied it, but for womenfolk, well, that's probably too challenging, isn't it? I'm sure Fanchon is planning to hand the company to her future husband. A board of directors really ought to be all men."

Unsurprisingly, I didn't stick around to chat with Oliver. Never mind the fact that the Quinceys were clearly uninterested in Ella.

Oliver Quincey could keep his greedy, chauvinistic hands off my daughters.

After the Quinceys' display, I wasn't exactly keen on continuing these calls, but I had to find Ella a husband before Fan got her inheritance and left us in the dust. Unfortunately, Glennie Quincey had been talking.

When I arrived at the Windham estate, Annalisa Windham welcomed me with an array of cookies and pies and little cakes. Then she introduced her son by having him drift into the room strumming a lute. He said he didn't know I'd be there. Right.

Like the Quinceys, the Windhams were interested in Fanchon's money, not Ella. It was only when I stopped the servant carrying the uneaten desserts to the compost heap that I learned the young Lord Windham had inherited his mother's nasty habit of spending an entire monthly allowance in a week. At least I went home with leftovers.

I might well have given up at this point, but the remaining mothers of eligible bachelors weren't even waiting for me to make a call. The Meekleys ambushed me on the road into town; as soon as I was in view, Lady Meekley did a spectacular, flailing imitation of a turned ankle. She'd probably hoped her son's protestations of care and affection would sound more natural, and I'm sure that distraction was the reason she walked up to me, leaning on his arm, limping on the wrong ankle.

After all the hoopla for the ball, whenever I left the house I was stuck with my severe high-necked jet-black funeral gown. It was starting to feel appropriate.

Joanna Kindler had worked out my usual market time and put in her bid there. I don't think she'd expected that I'd have Ella with me.

"We can afford the cabbage, I think. Should we get a head, Stepmother?"

"I'm so tired of cabbage," I grumbled.

"But you always say if we get cabbage we can also afford cheese."

"I know, I know. What have we got in the garden?"

"The parsnips are coming in nicely. And I think we have radishes ready to eat."

I sighed. "Okay, let's get the usual. A head of cabbage, a cheese wheel, and make sure you get enough rye to replenish your store. You're doing a wonderful job with the bread."

She nodded with a little smile.

Ella had run off and I was debating over whether I could afford sage—if I could just get Ella one spice—when I heard a voice that wanted to be noticed.

"Now then, son, help your old mother with the purchases."

"Of course, Mother. It is my pleasure."

It's almost like they rehearsed it, I thought as I turned around to face the Kindlers.

"Why, Evelyn Radcliffe, as I live and breathe!"

Joanna greeted me like an old friend, which I wasn't, of course, but I could hardly be offended, as this was how she treated everyone. She was one of those women who insisted on a hug plus a peck on each cheek when a handshake would do. She liked to clap you on the shoulders, like she was going to hold you in front of her until she'd inspected you thoroughly. If you were young enough, she'd pinch your cheeks.

"It seems to be market day for everyone!" she boomed in her low, gravelly voice. "Reginald is such a good helper." She patted him on the shoulder, and he smiled impatiently under the weight of a collection of hat boxes and shopping bags. I was fairly certain he'd never been shopping with his mother before.

"You know Reginald, of course. Reginald, this is Evelyn Radcliffe. And how are your daughters, love?"

"They're quite well. Growing up so quickly."

"Isn't that just the way of it!" Joanna's throaty laugh seemed to echo in the marketplace. "It seems like yesterday they were taking their first steps; now, they're walking toward matrimony!"

As pickup lines go, Joanna's wasn't bad. She must have worked on it. I smiled and murmured my agreement.

"Now—how funny is this—if you can believe it, Reginald and I were just discussing your daughter, Fanchon. What a delightful young woman! Reggie and his father have such respect for her father and the company he managed to build. Fanchon will no doubt inherit, I'm sure . . ."

I was no stranger to this meandering way of discussing Fan's inheritance, so I waited patiently for Joanna to mine her information. Before we could find out what Fan's future husband ought to do with her money, Ella returned.

"All right, Stepmother—Oh, sorry."

"That's all right, Ella. Joanna, Reginald, this is my stepdaughter, Ella. Ella, Lady Kindler and her son."

"It's a pleasure to meet you," Ella said, curtsying as best she could with a heavy bag of rye in her arms.

Joanna stared wide-eyed for a moment, as if Ella had grown horns.

"How nice to meet you, love," she said finally.

"I'm sure you met Ella's father, Henry," I said. "He was a partner in a shipping firm, and he raised a wonderful daughter. Absolutely no credit to me, but Ella's the most talented seamstress. Her quilts are as good as anything you could get in the Capital."

"Mmm," Joanna murmured politely. Reginald, however, sighed impatiently and tapped his foot.

"You know, these are a bit heavy, Mother."

"And we certainly ought to be going," I said. "If you can carry the rye, Ella, I can take the rest."

Ella nodded and handed me the sack with the cabbage and the cheese.

"You go on," I said. "I'll catch up with you."

"Well, it's been so lovely chatting with you, Evelyn," Joanna said when Ella was out of sight.

"You too, Joanna. And so nice to meet you, Reginald."

"You take care. I'm sure we'll be in touch," she said, winking. "We mothers are in this together," she whispered as she leaned in conspiratorially.

I'd only turned the corner, separated from the Kindlers by a row of new stalls, when I heard Joanna's always too-loud voice.

"Do you know the other daughter?"

"Penniless," Reginald replied. "Not worth it."

"She is pretty, though."

"She's the type a man has on the side. You see it all the time. Marry the rich daughter, and spend her money on the pretty one. That one's going to be somebody's mistress someday. Mark my words."

I'm sure the woman selling little sachets of potpourri wondered what she'd done to infuriate me. He would plan to cheat on my daughter? Really, he'd use Ella like that? He couldn't find any other reason for her to exist? I was so full of rage, I forgot to put on a happy face when I caught up with Ella.

"Is everything all right, Stepmother?"

"Hm? Oh, I was hoping for some fish, but the seller refused to come down from his exorbitant price," I lied.

I can't find you any kind of future, I should have said. I'm looking everywhere, and no one wants you. I'm beginning to see why those girls in the stories always need fairies.

"That's too bad," Ella said.

"Yes. Let's go home."

The last nobleman's son on my list was Ethan Kingsley, of the pockmarks. I trudged up the hill to the Kingsley manor, visiting more out of a sense of thoroughness than out of any actual hope. The Kingsleys were one of the oldest families in Strachey, and their home was one of those vast mansions that had a name, like Stoke Membley, or Badger's Old Hall. I wasn't expecting much in the way of empathy.

"Evelyn Radcliffe!" Lady Kingsley chirped matter-of-factly as I entered her sitting room.

"Lady Kingsley," I began in my usual tone of deference.

"Oh, please. Call me Francesca. Have a seat."

Francesca Kingsley was older than I, but despite the wrinkles on her face and neck and her thin, arthritic hands, she had a grace and elegance her younger neighbors lacked. She had foregone the middle-aged habit of shaping one's hair into a bowl around the head, and instead wore her long gray hair piled on her head. Becoming Francesca Kingsley would not be such a bad thing, except that she'd had ten kids, which was about nine more than I could have handled—well, honestly, evidence was suggesting I couldn't even handle one. Ethan was her youngest, the last to leave the house.

"I do hope you'll join me for lunch," she said. "I won't be offended if you don't, as long as you're not offended that I'm going to eat in front of you."

Francesca, I decided, had reached that age where she could say whatever she wanted. I graciously accepted her offer, because I was hungry, and I was immensely gratified to learn that her appetites did not run toward dainty watercress sandwiches.

I didn't begin my spiel right away because to be honest, I wasn't at all sure I had a read on Francesca. However, I had to steer the conversation toward marriage somehow, and I assumed flattery was a pretty universal tactic.

"How are—" I started but was quickly interrupted.

"You know, I've always had a lot of respect for you, Evelyn."

Uh-oh. As conversation starters go, that one felt ominous.

"I didn't know you knew much of me," I said.

She raised an eyebrow. "This is Strachey, isn't it?"

I conceded the point.

"No, I am impressed with your resilience. And it seems to me that you know exactly who you are and have never tried to be anyone else. I like that." She took a sip of tea while I sat there, flabbergasted. "You know, I met your first husband when he was working with mine."

I prepared myself to listen once again to a grand eulogy for Husband #1, but that seemed to be all Francesca wanted to say on the matter. I overcame my nervous bewilderment long enough to actually make eye contact. Her raised eyebrow and tight lips suggested she had a very different opinion of my first husband than most of the nobility. I smiled to myself.

"Anyway, my point is, I respect you too much to sit here and ask you how you are, which would be a slap in the face, or force you through the rigmarole of nudging the conversation in the right direction. I mean, really, the minute you left Glennie Quincey's home, her smug mug was in every manor this side of the Stout practically inviting us to the wedding. Don't see the point in playing dense."

I let out a little snort-giggle, trying not to give in to hysterics over the image of Glennie Quincey preening. I didn't know why—well, no, I knew exactly why I'd never really met Francesca. I moved in a very, very different social class.

"And you should have seen the look on her face when she learned you went to Annalisa!" Francesca giggled and sighed. "At any rate, I'm going to be honest with you, Evelyn. I—"

She stopped abruptly as we heard the front door shut. "Is that him? I swear I didn't orchestrate this. Ethan?"

Ethan Kingsley popped his head into the room. "Hi, Mum. Oh! Sorry, I didn't realize you had company."

"That's all right, dear. Come in. This is Evelyn Radcliffe. Evelyn, my son Ethan."

"You're Fanchon's mother, right? I remember she used to hang around with my older brother, before he got married. Nice to meet you."

He shook my hand and kissed his mother on the cheek. Cora had exaggerated the pockmarks—he'd had a few skin blemishes as a teenager, but they hadn't left too many marks, and he had a nice smile that made up for it. His hair was dark and a bit shaggy, long enough to keep falling into his eyes. He looked as though he would have broad shoulders if he didn't hunch them—probably a side effect of having so many older siblings.

"What have you been up to?" Francesca asked.

"I've been working on my project for school. I'm at Furnival's Halle for Sounde Business Procedures," he said to me. "We've got a big summer case study. I've got to advise a yarn company that's seen all their sales drop off after expanding into a big warehouse-sized storefront. I know they need to narrow their business plan—they started selling fabric, and that was a big mistake. But I don't know what to do with the warehouse. Their market just isn't that big!"

This time, the little part of me warning not to engage was even less effective.

"Is renting the warehouse an option?" I asked.

"I thought about that, but I'm worried they'll get overshadowed."

"Not if they rent to something like a salon. Or one of those over-priced oils and perfumes vendors. After all, who buys yarn? Women who need to knit make their own. But bored noblewomen who want a hobby, they're your target consumer. Find another place they'll sink their disposable income."

Ethan's eyes lit up. "Oh! Of course! And if I think about it like that, there are so many changes they should make to their marketing strategy. Thank you, Madam Radcliffe! I'll go write that up. Bye, Mum." He bowed his head to me. "Tell Fanchon I said hi." Ethan stepped out of the room.

"What a considerate young man," I said after he'd left. And how well he'd get along with Ella, I thought. "Have you met my stepdaughter?"

Francesca sighed. "That's what I've got to be honest with you about, Evelyn. I know you've got to get both girls married, and I sympathize. And I don't care one whit about whether someone's an orphan or a stepchild or anything, as long as they've got good breeding. But I can't let Ethan marry Ella."

The bluntness of her answer stung. "But . . . you've got to meet her, Francesca. They'd make a wonderful match."

"I know, and that's why I'm glad he's never met her. I've seen Ella, and he'd be head over heels so fast, I wouldn't be able to talk any sense into him. You've got to do what's best for your girls, but I've got to do what's best for Ethan. He's the youngest of ten, and what with dowries for the girls and inheritances for the older boys, Ethan will get next to nothing. That's why he's putting himself through business school. It's a hateful thing to say, and I'm sorry I have to, but Ethan needs a match that brings just a little bit more than a good wife. I wouldn't be doing my job if I said otherwise."

My reaction at first was pure fury, that she was so callous—toward other women! That she was so controlling, she wouldn't let her son decide himself what would make him happy. But aren't you doing the same thing? I asked myself. Wouldn't you do the same thing, in her position? At least they'd consider Fanchon, I thought, and Ethan was conscientious enough that he would hopefully not let Ella and me starve. If only I had any ability to make Fan marry him, because it was going to take coercion.

"On the other hand," Francesca said, "if I remember Fanchon rightly, it might take a . . . change in character for Ethan to be her type."

I smiled wryly. That was a gentle way of putting it. "Well, I shouldn't take up more of your time," I said, rising to leave.

"I apologize for being blunt, but I thought it ruder to string you along."

"I do appreciate honesty," I said. She put out her hand, and I shook it.

"Can I interest you in taking some of the extra food to the girls? My cook still prepares meals as though all the children were home."

I regret to admit that I wanted to tell her to stuff her charity, but the larger part of me knew that would be stupid and pointless. She's actually trying to do something for us, I thought. And this is probably the only thing she can do that wouldn't utterly humiliate us.

"Well, we'd hate to be wasteful. If it would help, we'll take it off your hands."

I brushed away a tear or two as I walked home with my cloth-wrapped chicken pies. Oh, come off it, Evelyn, I thought. So you've failed to marry Ella to a nobleman. That isn't the end of the world. People have it much worse than you. You're a chemist's daughter—you know Ella could be perfectly happy with a tradesman.

Of course, I had absolutely no idea which young men of the village were eligible, and the only things I'd get by asking were suspicious stares and vague answers. This was the part I'd been dreading. Time to involve the girls.

"Is anyone home?"

"Hi, Mom," Fanchon said, lying on the sofa reading a book.

Ella entered from the back, her gardening gloves and apron spotted with dirt. "Hello, Stepmother."

"Ella, I brought home some leftover pies from my luncheon. We can do something with these, right?"

Ella nodded emphatically.

"What kind are they?" Fan shouted. "Please don't be kidney, please don't be kidney . . ."

"They're chicken."

"Yes!"

Ella took the package from me and went into the kitchen.

"Who were you visiting today, Mom?"

"Francesca Kingsley."

"Are you actually expecting a noblewoman to hire you? Are you asking for a loan?"

I shrugged. "It's always good to keep up your contacts. Women like Lady Kingsley have more influence than you think." I paused for a length of time that I thought would make my next statement seem innocuous. "I met Ethan while I was there."

"Who? Oh, the youngest, right. He's a weenie."

"What? He seemed very thoughtful and polite."

"Exactly. He's spineless. His brothers would always josh him, and he'd never, ever fight back."

"Walking away from a conflict is not a bad thing. That says to me that he knows how to pick his battles."

"But that doesn't impress anyone. You were impressed with him because you're a mom. He impresses moms. But he's never going to be anybody. He's not going to move up anywhere. Dad would never have been successful if he'd avoided conflict. You know I'm right."

"I just know that it's also nice to be around people who are considerate."

"Yeah? Let me know how that goes for you. Look, Mom, I've already thought about it, and I'm never going to marry Ethan Kingsley because he will never take me where I want to be. I want a rising star."

"A change in character" was putting it mildly. I left Fan to her lurid romance novel and went to find Ella.

I found her on her neatly made bed, holding a worn rag doll and staring out the window. I knocked on her door softly. "Could we talk?" I asked.

She nodded, so I sat down on the end of the bed.

I very nearly asked her how she was, but that was as stupid a question for her as it was for me. Might as well borrow a page from Francesca's book and come right out with it.

"You know, you're getting old enough now, it's maybe time to think about marriage."

She hugged her knees to her. If she could have shrunk any farther away from me, she would have. I felt too large for her delicate bedroom, and for a moment I thought I saw myself as she did—a looming giantess. What had I done? She had liked me when we first met. How had I lost her? How had I lost her so quickly?

"It would be a good way to get you a better situation than we have here."

She simply stared miserably at me, so words kept tumbling out of my mouth, as if I could ease the situation by talking it to death.

"Since you don't really have an inheritance, it might be hard to find a nobleman who would want to make such a match. But I'm sure there are plenty of nice young men in town, I just don't know any of them. Do you know many of the boys who work in town?"

She nodded and shrugged.

"Are you friends with any of them? One you have your eye on?"

She shook her head.

"No one? Really? I'd really like to help you make a good match, darling. A happy one."

She shrugged again. "Whatever you think is best, Stepmother."

What I think doesn't matter, I wanted to say. You're the one who needs to be happy. You have the whole rest of your life ahead of you, and that's a lot of years where you'll want to be loved and fed. Trust me. It's a long time to be miserable—my mind stopped its rant. Well, I've come this far, I thought.

The girls needed to be happy. But I didn't.

CHAPTER EIGHT

HE WAS WHITE HAIRED and stooped, chewed with his mouth open and slurped when he swallowed. He'd made his money the old-fashioned way: inheritance. He was a widower with a son and a daughter, both older than my girls. I wore the funeral dress.

"Tell me about your estate," I said, pushing food around on my plate. It wasn't very appetizing after I'd seen it chewed.

He didn't answer right away, but glowered at me. I blinked.

"Your lordship," he said finally.

"Your lordship," I repeated through clenched teeth, my cheeks burning.

"Women should always address their betters with proper titles."

I gripped my fork so tightly the metal dug into my palm. The arrogant, scum-sucking relic of the minor nobility. I forced myself to smile.

"The grounds here are very beautiful. My lord."

"Yes, they were planted by my father's father's father," he said, picking his teeth. "He was awarded the land for saving the king's life. Are you past childbearing years?"

"Yes," I said incredulously.

"Good. There cannot be any challenges to my son's succession, but I would naturally expect my full marital rights."

I put my fork down very, very slowly. Everything had slowed to a crawl. I could see him talking, but I couldn't hear him because I was trapped inside myself, boiling blood and bile rising to my head. Finally, his voice broke through the rushing in my ears.

"You have two daughters, yes?"

I nodded.

"They will take positions in the scullery. They cannot be daughters of this house, but I will allow they must be adequately cared for. Does this offend you?"

It must have shown in my face. I'd rather live on the streets, I thought, but I'm not the one I'm trying to protect. I smiled faintly, gave my head a little shake, and finished the dinner.

It rained again. We all moved a little sluggishly this time, as if we couldn't be bothered to care. None of us would be living here in a month or two anyway. We certainly couldn't fix the roof now, not after the amount I'd wasted on the ball. Fan's allowance didn't stretch far enough for the three of us, so I took odd jobs when they were available. If I was lucky, I could get some work as a scribe. If I wasn't, I was stuck with sweeping, making deliveries, or emptying out rubbish bins. When I couldn't earn a few coins, I usually didn't eat. Time to start getting used to that, I figured. What good were the stories anyway? They weren't meant for real people.

It seemed to be marriage or nothing. Even among the merchants and tradespeople, I couldn't find a suitor for Ella, not without a dowry. I made follow-up calls to the eligible nobles, and I even dared to take Fan with me. She cooed and flattered and enjoyed the attention, but she was oblivious to their haughty smugness, the hunger in their eyes that so terrified me. They're wolves! I wanted to shout at her. They're not safe. I could not let her make the same mistake I had. The more time passed without some miracle, the more I was certain the bride would have to be me.

The mail arrived three days after the storm. The messenger stared past me at our soggy, drooping house. I cleared my throat. He handed me a sack of coins—my monthly allowance. My last allowance, I realized. Fan's birthday was this month.

This was it, then. I considered begging Fan's charity to see if she'd give me an allowance. Even then, Ella and I would hardly have a home, and we'd still have to beg for work. The world of the streets would abuse Ella while the world of the elite took advantage of Fan. The best I could do was pledge myself to a self-important noble and stick Ella in his kitchen. She'd neither understand nor forgive me, but it was all I had. I was getting married this month.

I hadn't been in the house very long when I heard another knock at the door.

"'Scuse me, ma'am. Are you Madam Radcliffe?" the man said. His clothes were stained and his beard unkempt as though he had clearly been traveling for some time.

"Yes."

"Got a letter for you, here." He pulled a crumpled piece of parchment from his pocket. "From your husband. He gave it to me 'cause I was heading this direction, see, only I got caught up with some doings in Farthingdale, so I took a roundabout way, if you catch my drift. Anyhow, I reckon he got here before me, but it still seemed decent to bring you the letter."

My hand started to tremble as I took the parchment.

"Thank you so much, sir," I said with measured voice. "I . . . I don't really have payment for you."

He looked at my house and nodded. "'S'all right, ma'am. Your husband already paid."

Of course he had.

As the man walked away, I stared at the letter in my hand. My fingers ached to open it, but I needed privacy; I needed to be so far away from the dampness and the angst. I shut the door behind me and hurried down the path. I started toward the lake, but then I felt a huge sob rise up, and I bent over like I'd been punched. I couldn't handle losing it completely right now. I just wanted to read the letter. I turned around and went a different direction. I didn't really notice which.

I found myself in town. It was market day, so I stood in a little square by myself, listening to the hum of bargaining in the distance. I sat on the ground, leaned up against a well, and opened the letter.

Dearest Evelyn,

I imagine you'll see me before you see this letter. The fellow I'm giving this to seems a little suspect, but he looked like he could use a meal and a bath, so I've parted with a few sovereigns, and I will probably tell you all this again anyway.

I've missed you more than ever this time. In fact, I've hated this trip, and that's quite the admission, coming from me. When I get home, let's come up with a way to restructure. I just can't bear being away from you and the girls anymore.

I can already hear you telling me I'm being foolish, but you're not being very convincing because the more I listen, the more I long to hear your voice in person. You have the most wonderful voice. You know how a rose petal feels? Soft, but not perfectly smooth? That is how your voice sounds. Listening to you is like being covered in a blanket of rose petals.

Goodness, I'm not much of a poet. I can't wait to see you. Tell the girls I love them. I've got presents for them. It's probably a bad way to parent, but I'm hoping I'll win over Fanchon someday.

Love, Henry

Every tear I'd held in since the moment we heard the news came flooding out. My chest heaved as I tried to stop them, but all I could think of was how I'd never see him again. I couldn't even force my mind to worry about Fan and Ella instead. I'd been using them to shove grief into a back corner of my mind, but now I knew what would happen to them. You can't really worry when you know.

I lost track of how long I'd been curled up, I was so absorbed; so when I heard a voice call out, I was slow to respond.

"Pardon me, madam, I say."

"Sorry?" I looked up. A decrepit, ancient woman shambled toward the well. She was draped with dirty rags and leaned heavily on her staff. My heart leapt suddenly. What if she's a fairy? I thought before my common sense could get a word in.

"Have you got a bucket? Or a cup or whatnot?" she asked.

"A cup?"

She gestured toward the well. "Something for water."

"Oh!" I stood up and held out my empty hands. I hadn't brought my bag, although really, I didn't usually carry a cup.

"I don't have one. I'm so sorry. I . . . wasn't really here for water. There's got to be a bucket around here somewhere." I started looking around. "My stepdaughter probably carries a cup with her, for this very purpose," I muttered. Because Ella probably prepares for fairies, I thought.

"Eh. Don't trouble yourself," the woman said. "My cottage is just around the bend, I'm just being lazy."

"Oh."

"Besides, you look like you've got your own troubles."

I sat down on the lip of the well and fought back another flood.

"Go on. Nothing like telling a crone all your problems."

"My husband is dead and I miss him."

"Hm."

"My daughters are teenagers and they hate me."

"Ah!"

"I'd get them married, but the men around here rankle. I'd teach them to survive in the world, but they don't have the sense God gave geese. I've got no choice but to put myself under a misogynistic crustacean because as soon as my daughter turns eighteen—in a few weeks—she'll leave her stepsister and me penniless and then go blow her fortune paying back her overextended credit."

"Well that's a . . . that's a how-d'ye-do, ain't it?" Drool ran down the old woman's chin as she spoke.

Her voice was grating, as if I'd dragged my nails down a sheet of iron, and she gurgled a little mid-word, which was probably where the drool came from. Not exactly a blanket of rose petals. Wait. My heart started racing as an idea began to compound like interest. I watched as a drop of spittle fell from the woman's chin. What if . . . ? I pictured the house, anticipated Fan's reaction . . . Yes. I just needed . . . the prince's hunting day—tomorrow.

"Um, ma'am?"

"Huh?"

"Do you think you could help me with something?"

As soon as I returned home, I sent Ella to the market. We couldn't afford to buy much, but it was a long walk, so she'd still be gone a while. Fanchon had left hours ago, so the house was mine.

I went into the backyard, where our rosebush had bloomed beautifully under Ella's care. I cut some flowers, here and there so that it wouldn't be noticeable. Then I ripped the buds apart, collecting the petals in a cloth pouch.

I looked at the bag. Rose petals were lovely, but I needed something more impressive. Something . . . valuable. I hurried upstairs and opened my jewelry box. There was nothing valuable there. I'd sold it all, of course. I examined my fakes. If I did this right, no one would be looking at the jewels. I pried bits of brightly colored glass and a few semiprecious stones from their settings and dropped them in the sack.

The next part would be tricky. I stood in the living room, surveying the room. If I were sitting in the armchair, Ella would probably stand . . . there. And then which hole would be most directly above her?

I dragged a chair over and climbed up. I nestled the bag in the thatching at the lip of the hole and secured it loosely with twine. The frogs burped next to my head. There were more of them now; they climbed atop one another to see over the rim of the flimsy tin bucket. I hoped they were too crowded to breed. The beam under their habitat was beginning to sag.

I'd stolen some of Ella's thread, fine and inconspicuously gray. I twisted two strands together and ran it from the bag, along the inside rafters, and let it dangle over the chair. I stood in Ella's spot under the hole. With all the straw hanging down from the roof, the thread was only noticeable if you knew where to look, and neither of my daughters was keenly observant. I tugged the thread experimentally. A fake emerald and a few rose petals fell through the hole. This was, I thought, largely insane. I grinned. Bless you, Henry.

CHAPTER NINE

"ELLA!" I shouted the next afternoon. "The cistern is backed up again. Go down to the well in town, please." I handed her a bucket and a ladle. She left obediently. I waited.

When I saw her coming up the road, I sat in the chair and fingered the string nervously. Fanchon stormed into the room.

"Is she back yet? I need to wash my hair."

Ella opened the door. Don't talk yet, I prayed.

"There you are!" Fanchon shouted. "Give me the bucket!"

Ella crossed underneath the hole and Fan snatched the bucket from her hands.

"How was the walk, Ella?" I said quickly.

"Just fine, Stepmother," she said. I tugged the string. A sapphire fell out with some rose petals. Ella jumped a little as the jewel landed at her feet. She looked dumbfounded at the ground. I pretended to look shocked.

"Where did you get that?" I demanded, drawing her attention away from the hole in the ceiling and the costume jewelry on the floor.

"I don't know! They're not mine!" I tugged the string again. A few pearls hit the floor and rolled as she babbled. She shrieked.

"Ella. What happened?"

"She must have been a fairy! There was a fairy at the well!" A diamond thudded on my floor. Ella clapped her hands over her mouth.

"Is she still there?" Fanchon shouted.

Ella shrugged.

"I'm going to the well! Give me that." She snatched the ladle from Ella's hands and began to march out of the house.

"The water, Fan," I said. Fan made as if she would dump it on the porch. "Don't waste it!" I shouted. "Pour it in the basin!"

Fan just shoved the bucket toward Ella. As soon as Ella had emptied it, Fan snatched the bucket back and ran out the door.

I took a second bag out of my pocket. "Gather everything up," I said, handing the pouch to Ella.

"Will we be able to fix the roof?" Ella asked. Rose petals and a topaz fluttered down.

"I think we just may," I said.

Because you're going to be a princess, I thought. It all made sense now. The one person who wouldn't care that an orphan had no dowry? A prince. And the girls had read so many of those stories, they were utterly predictable. When the petals don't fall for Fan, she'll be furious, and I'll be wicked and kick Ella out, and it won't take more than a subtle suggestion to send her running right into the prince's path.

A few minutes later, Fanchon stomped back into the house.

"I hate you! There wasn't a fairy there! Just a stupid old woman hounding people for water. What's her problem? She lives like a house away!"

To this day, I remember the moment as if time had slowed, as if I were a captive audience member, watching a drama—or probably a comedy—unfold.

Fan was angry. As she entered, she slammed the door open and let it swing shut. She hurled the bucket into the wall. She waved her arms around. She bellowed. She stomped her foot hard and then kicked the bucket back into the wall. I had expected all that. But even I was stunned when a frog leapt from its overcrowded habitat and landed at Fan's feet. Both girls screamed.

"What did you say to her?" Ella shrieked.

I suddenly remembered I was a participant in the scene and tugged the thread belatedly, my eyes still fixated on the frog.

"I told her to bugger off and get her own cup!" Fanchon stomped her foot again. This time I stole a glance at the ceiling. The bucket had shifted so it tilted at a slight angle, held in place by the rafters but giving the frogs a near-perfect diving board. A few more frogs followed their brother.

"And she said, 'May you have the luck you deserve'?" Ella said with increasing panic. More rose petals fell.

Fanchon nodded.

"Fan! That was the fairy! She said the same thing to me! Now you've got bad luck!"

The girls' high-pitched shrieks flooded the house. Fan's tantrum continued to shake the rafters, prompting frogs to tumble out. Ella hurriedly scooped jewels and rose petals into the pouch and tried to rescue frogs from Fanchon's feet. The girls were so focused on each other, neither one ever thought to look up. I just sat there, slack-jawed. It was like magic. I wished I'd thought of the frogs myself.

"It's all your fault! I hate you! Nothing good ever happens to me!" Fanchon screamed at Ella and kicked one of the beams. Frogs rained down as the rafters shook dangerously. That bucket was going to fall. Time to intervene.

"Fanchon!" I said. "Stop talking."

Fan froze. I turned slowly to Ella.

"Go."

Ella took off toward the door. I followed her and snatched the pouch of gems from her hand. I still needed those. She looked up at me with tears rolling down her cheeks. Her lip quavered.

I cut the emotion from my voice. "So you convinced a fairy to curse your stepsister. I wouldn't have expected that of you, Ella."

She opened her mouth to protest, so I quickly talked over her. I didn't have rose petals rigged over the doorway.

"I think it would be best if you no longer lived here. Fanchon is very angry. Run down to the river. You can follow it out of town. Perhaps Fanchon won't look for you there."

She ran away, sobbing. I sighed. Just wait until the end of the story, I thought.

I turned back into the house. I would give Ella a brief head start, then I had to follow. Where were my shoes?

Back in the sitting room, Fan sat huddled on the floor. I knelt next to her and put my hand on her arm. I don't think she looked this helpless when she was born. Maybe, just this once, she could need me.

"We're going to fix this, Fan. I'm going right now to see what I can do. But I think you're going to have to change your own luck, sweetheart."

Fan nodded meekly, mouth clamped shut.

"Now. I'm going down to the well to find that fairy. You catch these frogs and find a nice place to keep them. Put some mud and water in a pail or something."

I could tell Fan wanted to complain, but she didn't dare speak. Bless the frogs too. I kissed her on the forehead and hurried out of the house.

I took a slightly different route than Ella did. I heard her sobbing down on the riverbank as I approached the hillside above her. I needed to position myself directly over her. I stopped as my shoes squelched in an oozing patch of muddy earth. Biting back a sigh of disgust, I looked for a drier way to the edge of the hillside. No luck. Reluctantly, I gathered up my skirts and squatted behind some rocks.

It's just a little mud, Evelyn, I thought. Besides, I knew that farther off, the prince and his admirers were hunting, and Maribelle and her children were waiting for their glimpse. Any minute now, the prince would come through the trees.

We waited. Well, I waited. Ella mostly just cried. Tepid sludge permeated my shoes and tickled my feet. I cursed silently and tried to shift my weight off of my burning thighs. I can't sit in this. Could I kneel? If I hoisted my skirts, maybe it would just ruin the stockings. I tried to lower my knees into the mud, but my legs just hit the surface with a wet slap. My legs slid backward, I leaned forward, and a rock rose up to meet my chest, knocking the wind out of me.

I sat up, struggling to find the purchase to kneel. Where was the prince? The one day we're waiting for him, he breaks his habit. What had I done to a fairy to deserve my luck? I fought against the panic. Now you've done it, Evelyn. You're not going to get Ella back, I thought. You've thrown her to the wolves, when you should have sucked it up and found another husband. How wicked can you get? Then suddenly, I heard rustling leaves.

Ella gasped. I peeked over the rocks.

"Are you all right, miss?"

I wanted to cheer. Instead, I reached my hand in the pouch, pulled out a handful of petals, and readied my toss.

Ella nodded.

"You don't seem very all right," the prince said. He knelt down in front of her. "Can I help you with anything? Can I help you get home?"

"I can't go home," Ella said. I released a handful of rose petals. They drifted softly around Ella. The gem plopped into the dirt next to her. Cue the prince's astonishment.

I immediately tried to duck. That only sent my knees sliding once more across the slick surface of the mud. This time I grabbed at the rock before I could hit it, all while trying to keep my head down. Fortunately, I needn't have worried. The prince didn't look up. He just looked into Ella's eyes. I cautiously peered over the side.

"I helped a fairy and she told me I would have the luck I deserved, but then my stepsister was mean to the fairy and now frogs drop out of the sky when she talks, and she got really angry, so Stepmother kicked me out of the house." That deserved a shower of petals.

"Kicked you out?"

"She doesn't like me. Because I remind her of my father."

It's not true, I thought as I threw another handful. But that doesn't matter, Evelyn, because this isn't about you.

Things were silent for a little while. Come on, El. You can do this.

"I'm Ella." I saw her slowly extend her hand toward the prince. I tossed down a pearl.

"Um, hi, Ella. I'm Aiden." He shook her hand.

"I like your . . . hat."

I winced a little. Well, magic couldn't pick and choose. I let fly a few petals.

"Oh. Thanks."

There was another pause.

"Do you come to the river often?" Ella asked.

"Yes, I come here every weekend! It's a very nice river. It's so peaceful."

"My father used to take me here when I was little. And the lake. Have you been to the lake here?"

"No! Is it nice too?"

Ella nodded. "There are geese."

I sighed and looked in the pouch. I didn't have enough petals for drivel. I willed them to hurry it up. My lower legs were going to get a rash. Instead, the two kids sort of stared into each other's eyes. I say *sort of* because they did a lot of shyly looking away.

"You're the most beautiful girl I've ever seen. Sorry. I don't mean to embarrass you."

There. That was escalation.

"It's all right."

I dropped the fake diamond. Symbolically, as foreshadowing. They paused for another while. I should have brought something to eat.

"Is it too forward of me to ask you to marry me?" the prince asked. "Yeah, it is. Sorry. I don't know what's wrong with me. I mean, we just met. My parents just have marriage going through my head. And I like you better than all the other girls I've met. I'm probably in love with you. Sorry. I'm messing this all up."

"No, I don't think you are," she said.

"It's just, in the stories, when the girl marries the prince—I think you're exactly who they mean."

"I think you're very sweet."

"So, maybe—maybe we could get to know each other better? Since you can't go home, you could come with me. We would take you in."

"Really?"

"Of course!" The prince blushed as he stood up and offered her his hand.

"Thank you so much." Ella took his proffered hand and stood. I couldn't help noticing that she didn't let go.

They started to walk off, hand in hand. Now came the moment of truth. They were out of my reach. I couldn't throw rose petals after her forever.

"I was at the ball," Ella said.

"Really? But I'd remember if I'd danced with you!"

"I was too shy. I just hid in the crowd. Wait—it's stopped!"

"What?"

"The rose petals. They've stopped."

Ella and the prince looked around. He seemed to think for a moment.

"Didn't the fairy promise you the luck you deserved?"

"Yes. Why?"

"Well, you're going to live in the palace. That is pretty good luck."

"Of course! I don't need them."

"Not at all."

I breathed a sigh of relief. Not for their logic—you can justify anything in fairy tales—but for his character. He wanted her, not a constant shower of stones that looked precious from a distance.

"I'll leave the jewels here for someone who does."

I waited until they were well out of earshot before I stood up. The mud made a slurping noise as it suctioned off my stained stockings. I trudged down to the bank, shoes squirting with each step, to pick up the gems. If I could get some back in their settings, I'd wear them to the wedding. Honestly, if I had anything fall out of the sky every time I spoke, I think I'd stop talking. Wouldn't anyone? Stupid stories. Designed to make you shut up and clean.

I pulled the drawstring on the pouch. I only had a few tears in my eyes as I made my way home.

CHAPTER TEN

FAN WAS STILL huddled on the floor when I returned. I was half-worried she'd have figured out the secret of the frogs, or that she'd just decided she didn't care, but as soon as I stepped in the door, I realized just how distressed she was. She'd obeyed me. The frogs were now burping in one of our nice iron kettles. I'll have to wash it really, really thoroughly, I thought.

"I found the fairy," I said, sitting down in front of her. Her nose was red and her big brown eyes brimming with tears, as if she'd been crying the whole time I was gone. "She said that when you're nice to others, you deserve good luck yourself. Since you were rude to her, the curse will be lifted when you show you have nice things to say."

Fan glared at me, her lips hardening into an angry pout. Then she exhaled sharply and closed her eyes for a second, choosing her words—or rather, her gestures—carefully.

She extended one arm out wide, then balled that hand into a fist and punched her other hand.

"What? No, of course I wasn't going to punch the fairy!"

She shook her head and pointed to herself.

"I'm pretty sure you won't deserve good luck if you punch the fairy."

Fan rolled her eyes.

"Well, I don't know what you're trying to say, dear. Do you want to write it down?"

Apparently, she didn't. She raised one finger in the air and rotated her wrist, tracing circles in the air. Then she stuck out her tongue.

"Excuse me, is that supposed to be rude? Because that is not helping your situation, young lady."

She shook her head vehemently and waved her arms in front of her face.

"All right, sorry!" I said.

She crossed her arms in front of her face, and then thrust them down to her sides.

I sighed. "Right, start over."

This time, she stretched out her arms and gestured—aha!—to the area around her. Then, she put her hand to her mouth and pretended to laugh.

"The whole house is laughable," I guessed, which was true.

She pointed to herself.

"You're—oh," I said, finally understanding. "Everyone's going to laugh at you."

She nodded, waved her arms all around her again, and stuck out her tongue. Then she pointed pleadingly at the frogs.

"Everyone else around here is mean, and they don't have any frogs."

Her face began to crumble as she nodded again.

"All I can say, Fan, is that they haven't had the fortune of running into a fairy. You have, and if you want things to change, you're going to have to make it happen. It may not be fair, but it's just the way things are."

She scrunched up her mouth in a fairly decent imitation of a duck.

"You can do this, Fan. I'll help you. We'll just have to practice thinking nice things until it becomes natural. We'll—I don't know, we'll think of a compliment for every person we see."

She shook her head insistently, but her eyes said fear more than stubbornness.

"You don't want to see people," I said. "I don't think we're going to be able to avoid them. We got rid of Ella, remember? You're going to have to help me shop and do the chores."

She threw her head back in despair.

"All right. I'm going to go see what's wrong with the cistern." Nothing was wrong, so it would be a quick fix. "Then why don't you bathe and wash your hair."

It didn't feel like we should return to life as normal, but I couldn't think of anything else to do. What happened at the end of the stories? Nothing, obviously. You had to end the tale somewhere. It was as though the wicked stepmother and stepsister ceased to exist.

I thought I would feel more of a sense of accomplishment. I'd found Ella the best future I could, and thanks to some frogs, I was hopefully going to get a kinder Fanchon, one who would soon be able to afford a roof and enough food. We simply had to last until her birthday. I even wrote a strongly worded refusal of marriage to a certain ancient nobleman. I expected to feel more relieved.

One consequence of expelling Ella was that I suddenly had to cook. My skills were limited to putting slices of cheese in between slices of bread and making stew, although Fanchon probably disagreed. Look, the stew was a little thin, but it's not like I had great ingredients. If I'd had good chicken, it would've been a different story.

On the third day after Ella left, Fan beat me to the kitchen for lunch, where I caught her chopping a tomato and carrots from our garden and putting them on a bed of cabbage. She looked up at me, startled, probably worried I'd be offended. I just thanked her and let her work. The tomato ended up a little crushed, like she'd gripped it a little too hard, but there wasn't blood anywhere, so I took it as a win.

On the fifth day after Ella left, Fanchon ventured out to the market with me. She started out with her head held high, jaw clenched, defying anyone to make fun of her. We both knew perfectly well that news of our fairy misfortune had spread around the countryside. There wasn't a soul in Strachey who didn't know that Fan had been cursed to have frogs fall from the sky when she spoke. Her haughty determination wilted just a bit under the stares and whispers of our neighbors. By the time we actually reached the stalls, she'd balled up her fists in an effort, I thought, not to burst into tears.

"Well, they're certainly not making it easy to think kind thoughts, are they?" I said. "I say we practice with the vendors. They're usually nonjudgmental. What's something nice we could say about the cheese seller?"

Fan stared daggers at me as I stepped up and bought my usual wheel of cheese.

"I like that he treats everyone with good cheer," I said, turning my attention to the vegetables. "If his last customer was rude to him, he never takes it out on the next one."

I glanced at Fan to see her response, but her attention was drawn elsewhere. Two young noblewomen walked past; they tittered as they saw Fan and began a whispered conversation. I turned my head just in time to see Fan lunge forward, fists still clenched.

Grabbing her arm, I pulled her in close to me. "They're not worth your time," I said quietly. "Not worth the time you'd spend on an insult."

Fan still smoldered with fury. *She's only ever learned to go on the attack,* I thought. *You've got to teach her how to defuse.*

"But if I had to have a kind thought about those two," I said, "I could say, well, isn't it in style to be small right now? Small waist, small feet? They're even small-minded!"

Fan cracked just the tiniest shadow of a smile.

"I want you to appreciate that I'm doing this with you, Fanchon. It's very difficult for me to have nice things to say, and I'm old and set in my ways. All right, vegetables."

As I began haggling over cabbage, I saw Fan cringe and slink away. I turned to look for her when I'd finished, but I didn't see her in the stalls. That didn't surprise me. While she could have pointed at an item she wanted to buy, she didn't have any money, and I didn't think she could mime "Put it on my credit."

Outside the market, I scanned the street. Shoppers had stopped in the road to chat, blocking the way for a poor coach driver, who inched his horse forward while shouting at everyone to get out of the way. As the people finally scattered and the coach pulled through, I caught a glimpse of the grassy hill on the other side of the road.

I almost missed Fan; she had her back to me, and she was facing two smug-looking young noblemen—I'd hardly expected her to be conversing with boys. Then I saw her fists, still clenched at her sides, and the way every inch of her body suggested that it wanted to back up. I quickened my pace.

". . . Belinda says she's too embarrassed to have you at her party, so she's uninvited you. Is that true?" I heard one say. Was that Oliver Quincey?

"Tell you what, if you just say nothing, we'll assume the answer's yes." And Liam Windham, his doublet laced obnoxiously open to display a little tuft of chest hair. They chortled at their own wit.

"Wait, I've got one, I've got one," Oliver said. "I heard that you're kissing any poxy sod who will give you a few sovereigns, and that onion-breath Alfie is your best customer. Is that true? If you say nothing, we'll just assume that's a yes."

Fan tried to back away, but Liam grabbed her wrist. "I think she should give us the same deal. Come on, doll."

The minute his hand touched her arm, I felt a plume of flame ignite between my ears. Fan attempted to yank her arm away, but naturally, he wouldn't let go. She started trying to peel his hand off her arm, so he reached for her with his free hand. The moment I came within reach, I lunged forward and seized his wrist.

"Take your hands off my daughter," I said. If I could have lifted him by his wrist, I'd have dangled him in the air. Despite my best attempt at a vise grip, however, he broke free with a sharp tug.

"Now, this is all a misunderstanding!" Liam said. He pulled Fanchon toward him and put his arm around her. "We don't mean any harm," he patronized.

"Right! She hasn't said a word of complaint," Oliver added. They fought back laughter.

"I told you to leave her alone." I shoved Liam Windham, aiming right for his shoulder, to knock his arm off my daughter.

"Whoa, madam," he said, letting go of Fan and taking a step back. "We're just having fun here."

"Fun?" I shouted. "Do you think my daughter's having fun? Are your little jokes making her laugh?"

"Umm, madam, I think . . . ," Liam began. He raised his hands and began making small pressing motions. I recognized that gesture. It was the universal sign for calming down hysterical women. Something in me snapped.

"You have never thought a day in your life!" I stepped up so I could shout in his face. He made one more calming gesture, like he was going to push me away, so I slapped at his arms. His look changed from amusement to bewilderment, and he shot Oliver a glance of growing panic.

"You're out of control, madam," Oliver said as he grabbed me by the arm.

I wheeled on Oliver, tearing my arm out of his grip with a flailing jerk. "I have had enough of you and your friend's swaggering, self-important, insolent pretentiousness. You are terrorizing my daughter! You're not funny, you're cruel!" I yelled and shoved Oliver.

"Hadn't we better get guards?" Liam said, scanning the market wildly as Oliver staggered back.

I felt Fan tug at my dress. She was probably embarrassed, and I know I should have been, but I just couldn't take it any longer. I was so furious—furious that I'd lost Henry and Ella now, furious that I'd had to stoop so low to take care of my daughters, when any one of these people could have helped. I think I was even furious at Husband #1, and if I was conflating these little twerps with my abusive late husband, well, too bad for them.

Oliver shot forward, his face a few inches from mine. "Did you just shove me, old woman?" he barked.

In response, I reached out to shove him again, this time with both hands. He was ready for me, deflecting my hands with his forearms, but I kept reaching for him, forcing him to parry my barrage of elbows and grasping fingers.

"Oh my God, she's insane!" Liam hissed. "Guards!" he shouted a bit half-heartedly, as though he wasn't really sure he wanted any authorities seeing this.

I ignored Liam's call for help and Fan's silent, insistent pleas for me to back down. I finally got past Oliver's guard and seized the lapels of his doublet.

"If I even see you look at my daughter again, I will—"

"What?" Oliver said, shoving me slightly as he disentangled his clothes from my grasp. "You'll tell our mums?"

Before I could add to the list of my increasingly poor decisions, suddenly someone grabbed Oliver's collar from behind and pulled down hard, pinning Oliver's arms to his sides. Then Oliver began to topple backward, revealing Ethan Kingsley neatly sweeping his legs out from under him. Oliver hit the ground with a thud.

"Kingsley, you pillock!" Oliver shouted.

"You leave Fanchon and Madam Radcliffe alone," Ethan demanded.

"This is definitely not all our fault," Liam said.

"Get over here, Kingsley," Oliver said. He had picked himself up off the ground and was now marching toward Ethan.

I saw Liam glance from Oliver's clenched fists to my face. I must not have looked any saner—he grimaced in alarm and rushed to intercept Oliver.

"It's not worth it, mate," Liam said, putting his hand on Oliver's chest and pushing him away.

As the two of them stomped off, the rush of anger drained out, leaving me exhausted and horrified. If Ethan hadn't shown up, I'd have started a fistfight with two twenty-year-old men. What was wrong with me? For some people, grief just manifests in crying jags. Apparently, it spurs me on to humiliating brawls I couldn't possibly win.

I took a deep breath and put my arm around Fan. She nestled against me, wiping tears on her sleeve.

"Thank you very much, Ethan," I said. I felt Fan nod.

"M-my pleasure," he said, suddenly shy.

I resisted the impulse to explain why I'd started such a disaster. Fortunately, Ethan kept talking.

"If you need anything while I'm here on break, I'm happy to help. I could walk with you, next time you've got to do the shopping," he said.

"That's very generous of you, and I will take you up on that offer. I suspect, however, we'll be lying low for a while." An understatement. I'd need to lie really, really low after this.

He nodded in understanding. "Have a good day," he said.

We said goodbye and turned toward home. Fan cried the whole way back. I kept my arm around her, and she didn't let go of me.

Fan and I celebrated her birthday a day late, after the paperwork arrived turning her inheritance over to her. She paid for a birthday feast that included both ham and chocolate cake, which probably cost more than I'd spent on food for nearly a year.

The following day, our first creditor knocked on our door. He was lean, with a beady stare and eyes a fraction too close together. He was accompanied by a burly giant, who stood there cradling a solid wooden club in his folded arms.

"Good day, madam. I'm here to collect what your daughter owes me," the shopkeeper said.

"Indeed. And how much does she owe?" I replied.

"Six hundred and seventy sovereigns, even."

"Hmm. May I see the itemized record, please?"

"What? Well, you see, ma'am . . ."

"You didn't keep track?"

"Look, madam, I know how much your daughter spent! If she refuses to pay what is owed—"

"What do you sell?" I interrupted.

"Ladies' goods," he said. "Handkerchiefs, stockings, gloves—"

"My daughter did not spend six hundred and seventy sovereigns on stockings."

"Do you mean to cheat me?" he snarled, his lip quivering in anger. "I will be satisfied! If that girl doesn't pay her due, we'll seize what's ours! I'll let Flint here have a look around, maybe he can convince her to pay!"

Flint tapped the club on his bicep. The shopkeeper glanced behind me, flashing a toothy grin. I followed his gaze and saw Fanchon standing there, wide-eyed and white as a sheet. I kept a firm grip on the doorknob, just in case I needed to slam it in their faces.

"Sir, setting aside your extremely illegal threats, I'm not saying my daughter doesn't owe you money. I'm saying six hundred and seventy sovereigns is obscene."

"Well, see, some of that is interest. I'm not explaining interest rates to a couple of women, so—"

"No, please don't. In that case, may I see the contract my daughter signed stating the rate and the principal?"

"You are testing my patience, woman! You are withholding my due, and I will see your daughter in debtor's prison! Are you saying I can't calculate my own business dealings?"

"No. If there was neither contract nor record of the loan, you cannot claim interest. I will give you one last chance to name the actual amount my daughter owes you, or I will report you for extortion."

His eyes gave a brief flicker of frustration before his expression settled into a grimacing pout.

"One hundred thirty-eight," he grumbled.

That sounded reasonable. I turned to Fan. "Why don't you write a check, love."

They weren't all such bullies, but that also wasn't the only threat of debtor's prison. It certainly wasn't Fan's largest debt. By the time she'd finished paying all her creditors, she'd spent most of the money in her account and we couldn't fix the roof until the next deposit from her father's company came in. So I extended the life of our tight budget.

A few days after her birthday, I noticed a book missing from my shelf. I had to hide my grin when I caught her reading Davenport's *Treatise on Economy: Wealth, from Homes to Nations*. Even I wouldn't choose to read an economics textbook from cover to cover, so I bought her *A Beginner's Guide to Budgets.*

I'm not sure whether it was staring down men like Flint that motivated her or viewing her bank account bleed out as she wrote check after check, but she also began to clean. She worked out a schedule for doing the laundry, sweeping, dusting, and scrubbing the bathroom, so when her next deposit came in and I asked her if she wanted to hire servants, she shook her head vigorously and pointed to herself.

I did want to encourage frugality, so I didn't argue. I made a mental note, however, to talk her into hiring a cook eventually.

About a week later, I again responded to a pounding at the door, only this time, it wasn't a creditor. It was Maribelle.

"Oooh, Evelyn, I'm so angry at Cora and Delia!" she fumed as soon as I opened the door. Before I could even say hello, she marched past me into the house, still ranting.

"At tea, they were saying the nastiest things about you, and Fanchon, and Ella, and I told them to stop being rude, but they just laughed, so I stood up and said I would have nothing more to do with them, and I came straight here! I brought treats." She dropped her basket on the living room table with a little more force than was necessary.

"Um," I stalled, a bit stunned. "Maribelle, I really don't care what Cora and Delia say about me."

"I know, but they were saying it's embarrassing that you had to have your life sorted out by fairies, but there's nothing embarrassing about fairies! It's so beautiful, and I love fairies, and Cora and Delia really wind me up!"

"Well, I appreciate that you stood up for me. And Fanchon and I will definitely eat your treats."

"Wonderful!" she cried, clasping her hands. "They're fondant cakes!"

Normally, I would have tried to get rid of Maribelle rather quickly, but to my astonishment, I found I was glad of her company. Some part of my inner self must have watched in horror as she and Fanchon and I sat down to try her little cakes.

Mostly, however, I was filled with the realization that I hadn't had an actual friend since Henry died. And I missed it. I missed him, of course, but I'd forgotten just how nice it is to have another person who cared.

Now it appeared I'd have two. If only there was a way to average out how much they both talked.

About two and a half weeks after the fairies had descended upon us, the queen announced the wedding of her son to the beautiful Ella Radcliffe. Fan and I were in the marketplace when the herald read the proclamation, watching as the crowd erupted into a cacophony of astonishment.

"Well, that didn't take long," I muttered.

Fan looked at me as if I'd sprouted horns.

"What?"

She waved her arms frantically, pointing at the herald and tugging on her ear; she was so animated, I thought she might start jumping up and down. She insistently held her arms out toward the herald.

What on earth? I thought. I mean, it was exciting news that Ella was marrying the prince, but—oh, damn. I was the only one who knew Ella had met the prince.

My eyes widened in horror. You cannot tell Fan there were no fairies, my mind insisted. Luckily, Fan only nodded, encouraging my epiphany, as though I'd finally figured it out.

"You mean . . . our Ella?" I went with it.

Fan nodded and gripped her head, grimacing as if in pain.

"Are you all right?"

She stamped her foot a little and paused to think. Then she put up her fists, almost in front of her face, and shook them back and forth.

"What?"

This time she bent over and stuck her head out, and then flopped her hands, which she'd raised level to her head.

"Fan, I don't suppose, since you've been really nice to me, you might consider talking to me? Only to me, if you're not ready to talk to other people. I really don't think frogs will fall if you're talking to me."

She scrunched up her face. Please, I thought, I can't take much more of these charades. Finally, she grabbed my hand and dragged me into an alley away from all the shoppers. She stood on her toes and whispered in my ear.

"If Ella's the princess, she could put us in jail!" she hissed.

"We didn't do anything illegal, Fan," I replied. "You weren't always nice to Ella, but you didn't break the law. I'm sure if you sincerely apologized, she'd forgive you. Actually, that could be a good use of your first words. I bet you're about ready to speak again."

Was I ever wrong about that. Mortified, Fan shook her head vigorously.

"I know you're nervous, but the fairy did say the curse could be lifted. And I think you're ready for some better luck."

Fan just kept shaking her head. Inwardly, my spirits sank, and my stomach fluttered in panic. Had I actually trained my daughter to be seen and not heard? Had I accidentally taught her to keep her opinions to herself? It ought to be time for her to talk, my mind insisted. I tried to reassure myself. Fan can't stand to stay silent forever, I thought. She's willing to talk to you. Be patient, Evelyn.

As we walked home, quietly, another thought hit me.

"Are you jealous of Ella for marrying the prince?"

She stopped so she could reach my ear.

"Not really," she whispered. "I never had a chance of marrying the prince anyway."

"Well," I said, "I think you had as much a chance as any young woman in the kingdom. But no, mathematically speaking, given the number of noblewomen in the land, your odds were slim."

Fan held out her hands in a classic "That's life" gesture.

"Besides, I don't think you'd have enjoyed being a princess."

She looked up at me quizzically.

"I don't think you'd be happy with all the restrictions. Not being able to go wherever you like, and never leaving without a guard. Even as a child you were independent. And always curious. I chased you all over the place."

I caught the tiniest self-satisfied smirk on Fan's lips.

"Believe it or not, we may have it more interesting than Ella does."

As if to illustrate my point, the royal carriage was waiting for us when we got home. The wood was painted a deep, luxurious red, and every edge and piece of trim was gilt, probably with real gold. And it was parked in front of my house.

Adding to the elegant spectacle, Prince Aiden jumped down from the carriage and held his hand out to Ella. Instead of simply helping her step down, however, he put his hands on her waist and lifted her down, letting the skirts of her soft pink gown whirl around her feet. She looked happier than I'd ever seen her.

Fan, on the other hand, was frozen like a statue, eyes wide and mouth gaping open. She made a choked noise as Ella descended from the carriage, sort of a "hrk" sound. I curtsied as the two approached us, but Fan was in a world of her own.

"Going to have to curtsy, Fan," I muttered.

She jumped into action. The prince bowed to us and bid us rise. As Fan stood up, I saw her put her hands to her cheeks—she was trying to look like she was just astonished, but I noticed her fingers kept drifting in front of her eyes. This must be the part of the story when the stepsister has her eyes gouged out, I realized.

"Madam Radcliffe, Miss Envers. I am Prince Aiden. It's a pleasure to meet you. Ella's told me a lot about you," the prince said, without a trace of irony.

Fan looked very skeptical, and I had my share of doubt. I couldn't imagine Ella had anything to tell that would make it a pleasure to meet us. Still, I knew my manners.

"It is an honor, Your Highness."

"We'd hoped to be the first to tell you, but if you've been in town, then perhaps . . ." He trailed off.

"We heard the news a few moments ago. Congratulations, darling!"

Fan nodded in agreement and moved her hands enough to show a smile.

"I want you both to come to the wedding, of course," Ella said. "It's going to be here in Strachey, at the summer mansion."

"We'd be honored, dear. And if there's anything at all we can do to help . . ."

"Well . . . ," she started, shyly.

"What do you need?"

"Well, I know since Fan has her inheritance, you don't really need to stay here, but I was hoping maybe you would? Since I did grow up here, but I won't be able to take care of the house, and I would like to know it's still here . . ."

"Ella, I'd also like to know it's here. I wasn't planning on going anywhere."

She breathed a sigh of relief. "Oh, thank you, Stepmother! And Aiden said he would have the roof fixed right away!"

"Your Highness! That's very generous of you both, but I should be honest—Fanchon can afford to fix it."

"I know, but I want to," Ella said.

I felt my heart heave as though it were breathing a sigh of relief. It was the one last thing I'd hoped for. Financially speaking, I didn't need Ella to forgive me, now that Fan wouldn't cut me off. My soul, however, needed it badly. My guard now officially lowered, tears rushed to my eyes.

"Then thank you," I said and held my arms out, without thinking. It took Ella a second to decide, but she eventually stepped forward and put her arms around me. I hugged her tightly for a moment. "I'm glad you're all right," I said.

"Thank you, Stepmother," she said, stepping back.

"Do you need to gather any of your things?" I asked, trying to sniffle inconspicuously.

"No, we'll send someone for them, if that's all right. We just wanted to tell you about the wedding."

"Of course. We're glad you came," I said. Fan nodded in agreement.

"Then . . . I guess we'll go now. We'll send you invitations!"

"Until later, darling."

Fan waved at Ella, but as Ella turned to go, Fan suddenly started waving both arms frantically and hitting me on the arm.

"Ow! What is it, Fan?"

Ella turned back around and Fan rushed forward. She's going to do it, I thought. She'll apologize, she'll speak, and it'll be the happiest ending anyone could imagine.

"What's wrong, Fan?" Ella asked.

Fan stuck out both hands to the side like stop signs, closed her eyes, and took a deep breath, all in mental preparation. Here it comes . . .

She pointed to herself. Then she held her left arm out in front of her, rounded, while the right arm made circles . . . oh, stirring. She was holding a pot and stirring it. I tried very hard not to sigh.

Ella just stared. She had that intent stare that told you she was thinking, so Fan went for more detail. She grabbed a handful of air and threw it in the pot. Then she mimed a little salt shaker and sprinkled some in the mixture before she went back to stirring.

"Oh!" Ella said. "Are you cooking?"

Fan nodded and pointed to herself insistently.

"You're doing the cooking now? Good for you, Fan! That's very impressive."

Fan pointed to Ella, then put her palms together and flapped them open and shut.

"Oh, a book! How many words is it?"

Fan shook her head. She pointed to Ella. She stirred the pot. Then she opened and shut the book.

"A cooking book!" Ella exclaimed, delighted. "Oh! I do have a recipe book! Here, I'll get it for you."

Ella and Fan ran into the house, leaving me standing outside with the prince. I knew I ought to say something, but I wasn't sure what. I couldn't think of anything that wouldn't inspire a response like, "Well, after you threw Ella out of the house . . ."

Luckily, the prince broke the silence. "I can't express how grateful I am to have met Ella. She never says anything bad about anyone, does she?"

"She gets that from her father," I said.

"It's incredible. We need that. Court needs that kind of positive energy. She's going to change the world."

I wouldn't have said that about Ella, and I suddenly felt a bit guilty. Why couldn't she change the world?

"I don't think it was a coincidence that we met," he continued. "I'm certain fairies led us right to that spot." He laughed. "My old schoolmates would definitely have a go at me for believing in fairies, but once you've met Ella, how could you not? She's perfect."

"You're a lucky man, Your Highness," I said.

He smiled wide and nodded. When I first saw him, I'd assumed he was shy, but I could see now I was wrong. He was sure of himself. Probably comes with being a prince, I thought. Although Henry had been quite the opposite, there was still something about the prince that reminded me of him. Ah. Sincerity, I realized. I didn't think the prince could be anything but genuine.

I heard Ella's voice as the girls left the house. "And see, I've made notes on some of the recipes of changes I made, and I've written in what you can substitute if you can't find some of the ingredients."

Ella closed the book and handed it over to Fan. Fan smiled and gave a little bow. Then suddenly she threw her arms around Ella's neck.

"Oh!" Ella exclaimed, but she returned the embrace.

Fan stepped back, bawling, but she held Ella's gaze fiercely for a good while. Oh, say it, Fan, I thought.

But she didn't need to.

"It's all right, Fan," Ella said. "I forgive you." Fan started crying even harder, and Ella gave her another hug.

"Would you—would you like to be my maid of honor, Fan?"

Fan's jaw dropped and she pointed at herself incredulously.

"It's just that . . . some of the other young women at court have come to meet me, but I think they're all very jealous, and they aren't very nice at all, and I don't want to be all by myself at my own wedding!"

Now Ella had started to tear up, but Fan wiped her eyes, put her hands on her hips, and nodded firmly.

"Oh, thank you!"

A few tears ran down my cheek as Ella and her prince rode away. Oh, hold it together, Evelyn, I thought. Maybe this was why these fairy tales were so popular—Maribelle's type of fairy tale, of course, where the wicked are forgiven, and everyone lives happily ever after. So here we are, I thought. This is how a happy ending feels.

CHAPTER ELEVEN

"ALL RIGHT, FAN. You can do this. Remember what we've talked about."

Fanchon's lips were shut so tight I was surprised she could breathe. The musicians played a stirring waltz as noble couples whirled around the dance floor. The prince and his radiant new bride greeted a throng of well-wishers. Young women who both hated and loved Ella threw themselves at the next tier of noblemen. Nothing like a wedding reception to make a lasting match. The maid of honor and stepmother of the bride huddled in a corner.

"Remember what the fairy said. When you're nice to others, you deserve good luck yourself. As long as you have something nice to say, you don't need to worry. And I think you've got nice things to say, sweetheart."

She still stared at me with fearful big brown saucer eyes.

"Fan, I'm going to teach you my three steps to introductions. First, shake hands firmly—not too limp, not too strong. Next, pay a compliment. Finally, ask a question. With any luck, they'll just keep talking, and you won't have to say another word. All right?"

Fan nodded slowly.

"Sweetheart, you look beautiful. Now you've just got to show that you're beautiful on the inside. I know you are," I said, and I did. Wasn't that the point of being her mother? Because only I knew that somewhere deep inside was the little baby I'd held, and I'd never,

ever seen anything that beautiful again. "You've just got to prove it to everyone else."

I pointed her toward the party and scanned the crowd for a gentle first target. "Look. There's Ethan Kingsley. He's not very popular, so you won't have competition. And he rescued you from those bullies in the marketplace. He won't mock you."

I pushed her forward. She drifted over to Ethan, who waved hello. Fan stuck her hand out stiffly for the handshake. He said something. Fan nodded. Silence. Compliment, Fan. Compliment. She eyed his vest. She clenched her jaw and made up her mind. I watched her mouth open. Words came hesitantly out. She cringed ever so slightly, waiting for the frogs. Then the grin broke from ear to ear. Full of confidence, she followed up with a question immediately. Now he smiled, probably because people rarely asked him to dance.

As Fan practically skipped to the dance floor, she flashed me a beaming smile. I returned a look that said "I knew you could do it," and turned to face the party. It was a sea of people I didn't recognize. I drifted past a few conversations, some on Ella's choice of wedding dress or flowers, others on the current quail population or ways to rid a garden of snails. People are dull, I thought as I settled into a portion of the room a little less occupied than everywhere else.

The decor in the summer palace was sumptuous, to say the least. The walls of the ballroom were painted to resemble a cloudy sky, and gold trim lined every visible edge, making it appear as though they'd captured the noonday sun. It was overboard for my middle-class tastes, but more tasteful than some. At least there weren't pineapples, which had never been regarded as a symbol of beauty and therefore didn't belong in a grand ballroom.

This is exactly that type of moment, I thought, and for a second I could almost hear Henry's voice. "Lord Whitcomb is certainly enamored of the pineapple motif." I felt a lump in my throat. Here I was, in a massive crowd of people, surrounded by the thickest, darkest cloud of loneliness I'd ever experienced.

This isn't a happy ending, I thought. I don't know why it had never dawned on me that the girls would be gone. Not completely, of course, and sure, Fan wasn't married yet, but they were grown-up, and they weren't mine anymore. The stepmother does get the raw end of the deal, I thought, although that wasn't entirely true. I'd received a new and improved Fan and excellent financial security. Between the two girls, I'd be cared for well into my dotage—which would be wonderful, if I were getting ready to die. What could I do all day besides sit in the house and think about Henry?

Although, perhaps a little grieving wouldn't be so bad. I'd hardly had time to think about him, I'd been consumed with the girls. Time to stop putting off the pain. I sighed.

"You said what?" A woman's voice broke my reverie.

"Look, it was rash! I'm not saying it was smart," said her husband, presumably. I glanced at them—definitely husband and wife. She glowered at him, arms folded, and he waved his arms around, as if that would impress upon his wife his sincerity. It didn't.

"Glory be!" she griped. "There's lights on inside after all! Not smart? That's so far past dumb it's in the next county! You not only told Lord Piminder a lie, you told him a ridiculously stupid one!"

I didn't recognize them, but their clothing suggested they were minor nobility, barely a step up from me. His pants showed signs of mending, and her dress was from a previous year's catalogue. Lord Piminder, however, was probably richer than the queen, and the type to make you lick his boots. If he'd lied to Piminder, no wonder his wife was furious.

"I know! I just thought . . ."

"What? That our daughter actually could spin straw into gold? That she's just not been applying herself?"

"I was just trying to get us this marriage, Lilla!"

"If she could spin straw into gold, we wouldn't need to beg Piminder for his son's hand!"

"Lilla, please calm down . . ." She fixed him with a smoldering glare. "All right, look. Maybe her fairy godmother will show up, like in the stories!"

"Fairy godmothers don't happen every day, Pate."

"What about the new princess?"

"Ella Radcliffe? Our Clarrie is sweet, but she's no Ella. If that's the fairies' standard of virtue, we're sunk. You'll have to tell Piminder the truth."

He blanched. "You know I can't do that. He'll demand payment on the loan, and we haven't got it!"

Spinning straw into gold. Harder than making diamonds fall from the sky, I thought. You couldn't afford real gold, obviously. You could make fake gold, but the minute Lord Piminder took it to get it valued, he'd know he'd been defrauded.

Unless he never got that far, I thought. If his son proposed to the girl in front of a crowd of people right after she spun straw into gold, the town would practically riot if Lord Piminder tried to stop the wedding. The fake gold could just disappear.

I was halfway through planning how I would fool Lord Piminder when I started to question why I cared. It's not your daughter, I thought.

But look how concerned they are! How much would they pay for the fairies to fix this?

That's a horrible thought, Evelyn, I told myself, but my mind wouldn't quite let go.

People want the stories to happen. They feel more comfortable when they're following the bread crumbs of a fairy story. Maybe sometimes they just needed a . . . consultant. Someone to put them on the right path. It could even benefit society! After all, weren't the fairy values of kindness and forgiveness ultimately good for us? As long as you got results, did it really matter if the fairy's miracle was more mundane than magical? Or that your parents paid a very reasonable fee to ensure fairy cooperation? It couldn't be any more of a fraud than business consulting usually was. If you knew what you were doing, you wouldn't be paying someone else.

And come to think of it, this might be the one business where a woman would be preferable. Plus, I had real, first-hand experience. There'd certainly be a market for it. With Ella's story making the rounds, there'd be a rush of young women looking for their princes and parents setting impossible tasks for prospective suitors.

The more I thought, the more excited I felt. The old Evelyn, the one who'd worked her way through Furnival's and advised her husband's trading company—that wasn't really me anymore. She wasn't gone, of course, but I'd grown out of her. I was a mother, and a stepmother, and a widow now, and I couldn't go backward. But this, a consulting godmother, this was maybe a way I could go forward.

"Excuse me," I said as I walked up to the squabbling couple. "I couldn't help overhearing."

The wife appraised me suspiciously, her narrowed, slit eyes glaring at me from her round, reddened face.

"You look familiar," the husband said.

"Mother—stepmother of the bride."

"Right, congratulations!" he said. "Good on you, and all that."

The wife rolled her eyes.

"Thank you. I just—well, it seemed as though your daughter is in need of a fairy godmother, and since I have some experience with that . . ."

"You know how to get them to show up?" he asked in astonishment.

"Well, I know what Ella did, and I know how the fairies tend to think."

"And you'd just help us? Out of the goodness of your heart?" the wife said.

"Well, perhaps we could consider it like a business consultant. If you achieve the desired results, you pay me a modest fee."

"This is a very good idea," the husband whispered.

"We'll consider the offer," said the wife.

I gave them my most reassuringly winsome smile.

"I look forward to hearing from you. I'm Evelyn Radcliffe, by the way. The Fairy Stepmother. Incorporated."

PART 2

CHAPTER ONE

"I REALLY OUGHT to cancel the paper," I muttered, tossing the *Strachey Times* to the side.

I'd just sat down to breakfast—porridge, bread, and a little cheese. I'd tried to read the newspaper, although the preponderance of advice columns and lifestyle articles made that difficult. Could I get a Capital paper delivered? Surely they had to send subscriptions to Strachey.

"Morning, Mom," Fanchon said as she bounced into the room.

"Good morning, dear. What—um—what have you got planned for the day?" Fan had come in wearing some of Ella's old rags—the hem on the skirt was fraying, the muslin shirt had elbow patches sewn on, and the apron had turned light gray from accumulating so much dirt. She'd twisted her hair up and tied a wide cloth around her head. If she was planning a massive cleaning project, I wasn't getting roped in.

"Gerta's coming in early and she's going to give me a cooking lesson!"

Whew. Gerta was our cook, the first and only servant Fan had allowed me to hire. "Well, that sounds exciting."

"I thought it might be kind of messy, so I got out Ella's cleaning clothes."

"Good thinking."

"Is there honey?" she said from the kitchen doorway.

"In the cabinet."

"Yes! Only thing that makes porridge edible." She entered the kitchen, then immediately ducked her head back out. "In general, I mean. Not your porridge specifically. And I'm very grateful we have porridge to eat. It's really not that bad."

"No offense taken, Fan. And I think mixed feelings about porridge are pretty normal."

She breathed a little sigh of relief. In the months that had passed since Fan began speaking again, we'd had blessedly few close calls. After all, I no longer stashed frogs in the rafters, so the fairies weren't about to punish any particularly wicked blurts. We'd had a rough go when one of Fan's former friends told her she was too low-class to associate with anymore. And she and I had almost had a row when I let slip a criticism of her father.

In neither case did I remind her of the fairies and their frogs. I don't actually want her holding all her frustrations inside; I just hoped she might consider being a bit nicer. She should feel free to express her opinions. I didn't even think about the fairies until Fan gasped and started backpedaling, which has quickly become a tradition in our household. She was trying to decide just what constitutes speech deserving of good luck, I suppose. At the moment, that seemed to exclude criticism of any kind.

Fan returned and sat down with her breakfast. She picked up the paper I'd discarded and went straight to the lifestyle section.

"Ooh, that looks tasty. I wonder if Gerta can make it. Maybe she can show me. Although I'm sure I have to start with the basics. I don't know how hard this is."

"Mm-hmm," I murmured, only half listening.

"Oh my! They're saying hemlines are going up this year. The trains will be so short! And sleeves won't be so open? How are you supposed to tell the difference between fancy dress and regular clothes, then?"

I bit back a number of sarcastic replies. "Quality of the fabric, maybe?"

"Oh, that would work. Silk and satin are definitely not everyday wear."

"You'll have to update your wardrobe."

Fan nodded and gave a noncommittal shrug. I was just about to assure her she could afford it when there was a knock at the door.

"I'll get it," she said.

I heard a man's muffled voice, to which Fan replied, "Thank you very much. Here you are." Then the door shut, and she bounded back into the room.

"It's a letter from Ella!" she cried. "I only sent her a letter a few days ago—she responded so quickly! But look, it's got the royal seal and everything!"

I raised an eyebrow. I would have said it was definitely too soon for Ella to reply, but I couldn't imagine any other reason for us to get royal mail.

Fan rushed out of the room.

"Where are you going?" I asked.

"Where do we keep the letter opener?"

"In the top drawer of my desk."

"It's not—oh wait, never mind."

The letter had been sewn shut with embroidery floss. When Fan returned with the paper knife, she stuck the blade under the floss and pulled upward, trying to slice the threads.

"Careful!" I said, flinching as she tugged the opener toward herself. "Normally I point the blade away from my face."

She removed the floss and seal and set the letter opener on the table.

"You're going to put that away, right?"

"Mm-hmm."

She wasn't, I thought as she unfolded the letter. She'd read no more than the first few sentences when her mouth gaped open and she dropped the parchment like she'd been burned.

"Oh holy—mother of—poxes and plagues and—frogs!" she exclaimed. Cursed? Cursing seemed to be off the table for Fan, although harmless words said quite loudly weren't.

"What's wrong?" I said, reaching for the letter.

"The queen wants to give me a title! And for me to be presented this Season!" she shrieked.

"What? Why?"

"I don't know!"

I read the entire letter. "She says that since you and Ella have grown close, she wants you to feel like you can visit and not be self-conscious about your station." I frowned. I hardly knew the queen, of course, but my instincts said she was the one self-conscious about Fan's station.

Fan took the letter back from me and read it through, biting her lip in worry. I wondered what could be bothering her. I would have expected her to be shrieking in joy and excitement, not fear and anxiety.

"Do you think . . . ," she said in a small voice. "Do you think this is the sort of thing I could refuse?"

"What? Fan, you've wanted to be part of the Season ever since you were a little girl! I know it'll be expensive, but you really can afford the wardrobe. Why don't you want to do this?"

She shifted uncomfortably. But just as she opened her mouth, we heard the back door open.

"Miss Fanchon?"

"Hello, Gerta! I'm coming!" She turned to me. "Gerta's here," she said unnecessarily.

I looked at the clock. "And I've got to go to an appointment. But we're not done with this. When I get back, we're talking about this letter."

Fan nodded and snatched the newspaper page with the recipe, then ran off toward the kitchen.

I sighed and began clearing the breakfast things. I knew Fan had been embarrassed by the frogs falling, but in the last month or so, she'd started seeing friends again. I thought she was back to attending parties and having fun. I thought she'd want to be part of the Season. She'd always loved high society. She'd enjoy it. Truth be told, even I had enjoyed parts of it, although the small talk was deadly.

Besides, no, this wasn't the type of thing one could refuse. We were going to attend the Season this year.

The Season took place every summer, when the nobility from the Capital descended upon us for hunting excursions, horse races, and fancy-dress balls. This was primarily because the Capital was overcrowded and beastly hot in the summer, and our country estates offered more space to enjoy the weather.

Husband #1 had always wrangled invitations to a few events each summer, despite his lack of a title, because he could always find some friend who would bring him along. After he died, no one wanted me there anymore, which was fine with me. My enjoyment of a good garden party had been soured by the number of liaisons my husband had accumulated in the hedge maze. Now, I only had to tolerate the increase in traffic, the women stopping you on every corner to ask for directions, and the sudden jack in prices.

Except this year. This year, I'd be back at the parties. Oh God, I'd be back at the parties.

Now, Evelyn, I told myself as I returned the letter opener to the desk drawer, this could be a good thing. You'll be able to meet people. Reintroduce yourself. You might make new friends, which would be good because it's getting a little boring around here.

Today, however, just might be the start of something exciting. Last week, a few months after we'd met at the wedding, Patrick and Lilla Babcock had written asking for my advice. Apparently, Lord Piminder had believed Patrick's lie about his daughter's ability to spin straw into gold—or perhaps he'd decided to call Patrick's bluff. Either way, the Babcocks needed a fairy godmother, and I'd declared I could get them one. It remained to be seen whether I was as foolish as Lord Babcock.

I dressed my most professional and set out for the Babcock estate. The Babcock family had been nobility for hundreds of years, but they'd never been more than small fish in a very large pond. Naive investing strategies meant they'd never increased their land holdings—and with that, their station. Previous generations had paid tribute instead of collecting it, always living under someone else's thumb. Now, it appeared, they were beholden to Lord Piminder.

When I arrived, their servant showed me into the sitting room, where both Lilla and Patrick waited. He shot up out of his seat as I entered.

"Ah, Madam Radcliffe! Thank you so, so much for coming!" he said, wringing my hand.

Lilla stood stiffly and nodded her greeting. Clearly, hiring me hadn't been her idea.

"I'm happy to help," I said, rescuing my hand. He gestured to a chair, and we all sat down. "Perhaps you can tell me exactly what's happened."

"This fool told Lord Piminder our daughter could spin straw into gold."

"Lilla, we've been over this!" Patrick Babcock was, at first glance, an ordinary middle-aged man. His pleasant face wore the laugh lines of a proud father, and he had the slight paunch common to men of his age. When he became animated, however, his whole body seemed to quiver, as if he were moments from jumping out of his skin.

Lilla threw her hands up in mocking resignation.

"And why did you promise this?" I asked.

"I panicked! It was all I could think of! I was nervous—" He couldn't seem to speak without waving his arms around.

"Yes, that much I understand," I said, hopefully stalling another domestic dispute. "It's how you got yourself into such a situation that I'm having trouble with."

Patrick sighed and stroked his graying goatee. "Right, of course. My father, God rest his soul, took a loan from Piminder's father—"

"And I'll tell you exactly where his soul's resting," Lilla spat.

Patrick winced. "Anyway, my father accepted horrible terms, but then old Piminder died before he could collect, and I don't think his son knew about it right off—I certainly didn't. But eventually the man realized we owed him, and now interest had accrued, and we'd never paid a bit of it off."

"And that foot-licker wouldn't agree to renegotiate!" Lilla said. "Even though we've got no chance of paying it back. So I said, he's trying to put us in debtor's gaol, so he can take our land! And then Pate said—"

"Why not give him our land," he finished.

"So you tried to arrange a marriage between your daughter and his son?" I prompted.

"They're the same age, and they even fancy each other," Patrick said. "She's our only child, so whatever we've got would go to Piminder's son. We thought it was a perfect solution."

"Not for Lord Piminder, I take it," I said.

"No, he said our Clarrie wasn't good enough for his son," he replied. "And here's where I went wrong, I suppose, but she and I'd just been talking, and she'd told me how she wished she had a special talent like the girls in the stories, like spinning straw into gold, and so I just—"

"Blurted it out," Lilla said.

"And did Lord Piminder give you a deadline?"

"He said he'd give us until the end of the summer—pay the loan in full or prove Clarrie could spin straw into gold, or he'd turn us in to the moneylenders." Patrick sort of slouched in his chair, his nervous energy completely drained. He looked utterly defeated.

I fought back a sigh of disgust. Lord Piminder was toying with them: offering them a glittery ray of hope on a debt they couldn't hope to pay off, while he bided his time until he could collect their property and marry his son to someone more valuable. The weasel. Well, I would enjoy seeing his face when fairies dumped a load of gold-covered straw on his porch.

"Well," I said, "the good news is, I think your story is definitely the sort the fairies are drawn to." And not just because a certain one of them likes to see arrogant noblemen get their comeuppance. As far as I could tell, these stories all seemed to feature a sweet young woman who'd fallen near destitution.

Patrick breathed a sigh of relief. "Is there something we ought to do?"

This was the part I'd thought most about, ever since I'd impulsively volunteered to help the Babcocks at the wedding. I knew I could help them; I was quite confident I could fool Lord Piminder into believing the fairies had chosen his new daughter-in-law—and I didn't really feel guilty about doing it. He was ruining these people to feed his own greed. He deserved what was coming to him.

Of course, I'd have to lie to the Babcocks as well, because the more people you let in on a ruse, the more likely it is to fail. And that was where I started to feel a pang of conscience. As soon as I'd heard the Babcocks speak, my instincts said I had a potential consulting firm on my hands. But it's the very definition of fraud to charge someone for a service you won't—and can't—provide. On the other hand, I could give them a fairytale ending; I just couldn't do it with magic.

And now that I'd heard the full story, there wasn't a chance I could stomach minding my own business. Lord Piminder had to be stopped, and the fairies could do it without filing an expensive and contentious lawsuit or selling off most of the Babcocks' belongings. If you can help, you should. Right?

"Our primary goal is to prepare Clarrie," I said. "We must make sure she's the kind of heroine the fairies like to help."

This was the heart of my business plan. As I'd thought about how much Fanchon had changed over the last few months, I'd had to reluctantly admit that perhaps all these fairy stories did have a purpose. They instilled values in these girls. It's true, I wasn't crazy about some of them, like "women are meant to clean the house until they are rescued by a prince," but others, like "be kind and considerate," are hard to criticize. What if I were able to help a few young women become sensible, good human beings?

"What would you consider your daughter's main flaws?"

"Well, she's a bit on the clumsy side," Patrick said. "She does know how to spin and stitch and all, and she valiantly puts in the effort, but all her creations end up a little lopsided."

"Can hardly get through a doorway without smacking the side of it," Lilla added.

"Yes, she does run into things, doesn't she?"

"All right," I said. "But she's kind and hardworking?"

"Oh yes," Patrick said.

"She is quite a sweetheart."

"That's what the fairies like to hear. Is Clarrie home? May I meet her?"

"Of course! I'll go get her!" Patrick said. He leapt up and hustled out of the room.

Lilla sighed minutely and for a moment let her tightly woven mask slip; the dark circles under her eyes deepened, and the corners of her mouth fell. She must be exhausted, I thought, and I understood the feeling completely.

"Madam Radcliffe, may I present our daughter, Clarice?" Patrick reentered with the young lady in question.

Clarrie looked like her mother, with a round face and a small turned-up nose, a dark complexion and a fountain of curls. She gave me a tiny wave and reached out to shake my hand.

"Nice to meet you!" she said.

"Clarrie, Madam Radcliffe is going to help us find your fairy godmother, so she can help you spin straw into gold!" Patrick said.

Clarrie's eyes widened.

"In my experience," I said, "fairies tend to help young women who have tried everything they possibly can. They become offended if you sit back and expect them to do all the work for you."

"Do you mean I should try spinning straw into gold?" she asked skeptically.

"Not yet. First, we must be sure we've exhausted every possible alternate means to persuade Lord Piminder to let you marry his son."

The color drained from Patrick's face. "I—I did talk to him . . ."

"I know," I said. "But your primary concern was your loan, correct? Have you ever read a fairy story about refinancing loan payments? Fairies like to help true love. They won't arrange a marriage because it's convenient for you. They'll only do it if Clarrie truly loves this young man."

Particularly because I wasn't going to push any young woman into a marriage she didn't want.

Luckily for her parents, Clarrie nodded her head enthusiastically. "We've been friends ever since we were small. We're just right for each other. And he's furious his dad won't let him make his own choices."

"See, that's the kind of story the fairies like. We need everyone to know that Lord Piminder is keeping these two young people apart."

"Everyone? Like everyone in Strachey?" Lilla asked. "I thought we were looking for a fairy godmother, not the gossipmongers."

Oops. "Fairies aren't omnipresent. We must make sure that our actions are noticed." I scrambled authoritatively.

In truth, I really had meant everyone—at least, every noble here in Strachey. This campaign needed the court of public opinion to turn on Lord Piminder, and no one was better suited for the job than Clarrie Babcock. She was, in a word, adorable, which was probably her blessing and her curse. She wasn't gorgeous like Ella, and she was too sweet for many to take her seriously. But it would be impossible to dislike those dimples. If Strachey knew she was a star-crossed lover, they'd turn on Lord Piminder in an instant, making it that much easier for me to manipulate him.

"It makes sense, Mom, if you think about it. Fairies surely don't follow Dad to every meeting he has. They've got more important things to do. But if word spreads, they'll have to find out!"

Bless you, Clarrie, I thought. "What we need is a public proposition, ideally from one of you," I said to Patrick and Lilla.

"But—surely I can't ask him again. He'll be even harsher!" Patrick said.

"That's why—"

"Well, I can't do it," Lilla interrupted. "I'm her mother! How embarrassing would it be if her own father won't negotiate for her hand!"

Actually, the more pathetic the better, I wanted to say.

"But he's already given me his terms," Patrick said before I could interject. "I've got nothing new to offer. Have you met Lord Piminder, Madam Radcliffe? He might demand payment now! He could take me to court on the spot!"

"Which is why we're making this public. He may be rude, but I don't think he'll dare prosecute you in front of the entire nobility."

"You think, or you know?" Lilla demanded.

Oh, rookie move, Evelyn. Thinking loses negotiations. My instructors would have laughed me out of town.

"There's got to be another way," Patrick said. "I just don't see how we can talk to him again!"

Clarrie's face fell, and she looked at me hopefully.

I pursed my lips. "It'll be difficult, but I'll see what I can do."

"Thank you," Lilla said haughtily.

"I'll look into a few things, and I'll be in touch," I said, rising to leave. They shook my hand and showed me out, and I walked back to the road cursing myself.

Really, Evelyn? I still had to get this to take hold—I had to have some leverage over Lord Piminder. Now I'd have to hope that spreading rumors could cause enough of a stir he'd start to feel worried.

Two slips of the tongue in one meeting. That wasn't like me at all. You're probably rusty, I told myself. You'll pick it back up. At least, I hoped I would. What if I'd lost my touch? What if, after all this time, it turned out that I really couldn't consult?

Stop it, Evelyn. These were first-day jitters, that's all. There would be wrinkles to iron out. Besides, I wasn't even sure I wanted to make this an official gig. I didn't know if it was viable. Or if I would like it. I needed to calm down and see how it went.

When I came home, Fan was sitting at the dining room table, her arms crossed on the table and chin resting on her forearms as she stared down a dish of what had to be shepherd's pie. I noticed the queen's missive sitting next to the pie.

"Do you want some?" she said as I walked in. "It turned out pretty well."

I sat down opposite her, picked up her fork, and ate a mouthful. You have to do this with children; my mother had explained this to me when I was pregnant with Fan. You have to take what they offer you, and be happy about it. I'd only had to turn Fan down once to know my mother was right.

"Well done," I said. "You're really coming along! Was it very difficult?"

She shook her head. "No, I think I could make it again without help."

"Excellent!" I said. She smiled faintly and continued to stare at the dish. I waited.

"I can't turn this down, can I?" she said finally.

"Fan, if I thought this would be bad for you, I'd fight the queen until she had to banish me. But this is an opportunity you can't really argue with."

She sighed and put her head down.

"It doesn't have to change a thing about how you live your life. We just have to get through this summer. And honestly, it'll be worse for me. You can be your beautiful, charming self and enjoy the parties and make friends, and I'll be stuck talking to boring old people. If you're worried, we can have a signal. You tug on your ear and then scratch your nose, and I'll know to come rescue you."

She lifted her head back up, and I caught a little grin.

"But I have to be sponsored," she said. "I don't know a single noblewoman who would do that. The queen would have to make someone, which is so embarrassing. And I have to make sure I dress properly, and no offense, but I don't think you're the best person to help with that."

"Well, you're right on the last count, but that's why we hire a dressmaker. I'll just make sure they don't overcharge you. And the first part is easiest of all. Maribelle will be so excited to sponsor you she'll probably try to sew you a new wardrobe. And the queen will be pleased with her, since her husband is such a good friend of Aiden's."

Fan sat up and nodded, forcing a smile. "Maribelle's nice," she said. "I suppose I should respond to the queen." She stood, picking up the letter, and turned to leave the room.

"You'll be wonderful, sweetheart," I said as she left. I knew her confidence had taken a hit after the frogs fell on her, but maybe the Season would be just the boost she needed.

I covered her shepherd's pie and returned it to the kitchen. It hadn't been bad actually. It probably would have tasted better hot, and it wasn't what I'd choose to eat in the late morning, but all in all, at least she had more ability than I did.

I was just heading toward the study to research the best way to put a gold coating on something, when I heard a knock at the door.

"Miss Babcock!" Clarrie Babcock stood on my porch, hands tightly clasped. "Come in," I said.

She shook her head. "That's all right, Madam Radcliffe. I just wanted to ask, could I do it? Could I ask Lord Piminder to let me marry his son? Because I will. If Mum and Papa won't, I will."

I stared for a moment in surprise. Apparently, I'd underestimated Clarrie. I wasn't expecting her to have guts.

"Yes," I said. "But you do know this will cause a stir, right? And he will not be kind to you."

She swallowed hard and nodded. "Yes. But a stir is what we need, isn't it? For the word to spread. And I know he'll be mean, but if people see him rejecting true love, I think they'll be on my side."

That was, in fact, exactly my point.

"Besides," she continued, "I was thinking about what you said about fairies liking young ladies who do their best. And if I didn't try this, well, I wouldn't be doing my best."

"You're very brave, Clarrie. You've got to pick your moment carefully."

She nodded. "People have to see it, so that the word can get out."

I reached out to shake her hand. "Good luck."

CHAPTER TWO

"THIS IS LIKE a practice tonight, right?" Fan asked nervously as I tugged on the laces of her corset.

"Oh no," Maribelle said. "It's a real ball!"

Fan blanched. "But I thought you said it was practice for the garden party!"

"Everything is practice for the garden party!"

"You told me this was a fancy house party," I said.

"Oh, silly Evelyn! It can't be a house party because there's no dinner!"

"So it's a full-on ball, dance floor, everything," I replied.

"Dancing?" Fan said weakly.

"No, well, the Courtenays don't have a huge dance floor, so it's not really a ball-ball—more like a partial ball . . ."

"How much dancing is there going to be?" Fan interrupted urgently.

"Not as much as a whole ball-ball," Maribelle said, drawing a huge circle with her hands. "But the boys do like to ask girls to dance, so if this is a real ball"—she drew the circle again—"then tonight is like a tiny mini-ball." She made a little circle with her hands. "Well, maybe not that tiny . . ."

"Can I avoid it? Can I just stand somewhere so I don't have to dance?"

"Oh, but if someone asks you, you can't say no!" Maribelle's eyes widened in horror.

"But I can't actually dance!"

"Wait a minute," I interrupted. "You went to the prince's ball—there was dancing there. And I saw you dance at the wedding!"

"Yeah, with Ethan Kingsley! Who happens to dance . . . no better than I do. And I'd have been willing to dance with the prince if my legs were broken!" She looked like she might hyperventilate.

"All right, now calm down. There's nothing we can do about it tonight, so you'll just have to do your best. But I promise we'll have dancing lessons—starting tomorrow, if you want."

Fan nodded and took a deep breath.

"Oh, don't worry, Fan! It's going to be just magical, you'll see!" Maribelle said, removing Fan's dress from its hanger.

"Remember," I whispered. I tugged on my ear and then scratched my nose. Fan gave me a faint smile.

"Now, let's get you ready to charm the world!" Maribelle gushed.

As it happened, Fan really couldn't dance.

I was concerned she would hide behind me and Maribelle all evening, but when the first suave young nobleman complimented her porcelain skin and asked her to dance, she blushed appropriately and took his hand.

Her biggest problem was her arms, I thought as I watched them. Instead of with a graceful bend, she extended her arms rather more like they were fused at the elbow.

"Her forearms look like blades," I muttered.

"Hmm?" Maribelle said. "Doesn't she look lovely? You must be so proud of her!"

I was proud of her. She was delightful, sensible, and feisty. I also couldn't help but notice that she wobbled when she spun and stepped on her partner's feet when she came out of a turn.

"Maribelle Frandsen!" A Capital noblewoman approached us as I cringed at Fan's last spin.

"Oh, Lady Nicola! It's so good to see you! Let me introduce Madam Evelyn Radcliffe. Evelyn, Lady Nicola Dumond."

We curtsied. I tried to keep watch on Fan out of the corner of my eye, but Lady Nicola's hair was just slightly too high.

"Evelyn's daughter is being presented this Season! I'm sponsoring her. It's so very exciting!"

"Oh, congratulations! My daughter Odetta was presented last year. There'll be a husband in it this year, for certain," she murmured conspiratorially.

Maribelle gasped and oohed. I tried to give my traditional fake smile, but it felt unnatural on my face and rather similar to my bad-taste-in-my-mouth expression. Good heavens, was I rusty at this, too?

I heard the music wind to a finish and caught a glimpse of Fan curtsying to her partner as a new song began and new couples took the floor. She bounced back over to us, a sizable grin on her face.

"Oh, here she is now!" Maribelle said, and we were all introduced again.

We were in the midst of exchanging pleasantries when Lady Nicola's daughter approached. "Mother, who have you found now?" That triggered another round of names.

"Is this your first year?" Odetta said, shaking Fan's hand. "How precious." She was slim and dainty, with a little pouting smile. "You must feel like a little lost sheep. I remember exactly how I was last year. Here, why don't I introduce you to my friends."

Fan shot a quick glance at Maribelle to make sure she was allowed to do this, but Maribelle just clapped her hands and cooed, so Fan let Odetta take her arm and steer her away. She hadn't looked for my approval, so she missed my tight-lipped glower. Who exactly did Miss Odetta think she was? She'd been through the Season once! That didn't give her the right to mock Fan to her face.

I exhaled and practiced my fake smile. "Oh, I just saw someone I recognized. So nice to meet you." I nodded goodbye to Lady Dumond and escaped to cool my heels.

It is not a good idea to hover around Fan, I told myself.

But I just want to know where she is, I replied. What if they haze the new debutantes? I'll just locate her, and then I'll go somewhere else.

I wandered around the mansion, trying to look interested in the house's decor and not like I was lost. I spotted Fan among a group of girls giggling in the billiards room. No hazing, it seemed. I tried to hover inconspicuously in one of the adjacent rooms, wondering how long I could get away with doing nothing.

"The Courtenays certainly have an impressive collection of stained glass." I heard an elderly male voice behind me. I turned around to see who he was speaking to and realized it was me, of course.

I must have had a blank look on my face because he pointed behind me at a stained-glass window I hadn't realized I was staring at, probably because I was trying to spy on Fan out of the corner of my eye.

"I hear they import it from Turmurel. They say the craftsmen there complete a ten-year apprenticeship before they are allowed to sell their creations."

I gave my charity smile again. Already it was feeling more natural. He was quite tall and thin, with long arms that tremored only slightly, despite his age. He was considerably older than I was, with white hair and a bald pate and purplish circles under his eyes.

He stepped up next to me and gestured toward my empty glass. "Shall I take that for you?"

His voice was grave, and most importantly, his accent was exceptionally well bred, which meant he wasn't a servant. He was trying to impress me. I immediately felt a little flutter of panic. He wasn't unattractive and had an undeniable upper-class magnetism, but I didn't want attention. Not that kind of attention. I missed Henry, and I wanted everyone to give me at least three feet of personal space. I was tempted to explain all of this immediately, but my more rational side interjected. Probably, I thought, if you simply don't encourage him, he'll just leave you alone.

I did hand over the glass. Couldn't really get around that. Then I snuck a glance into the other room to see if I could use Fan as an excuse to get away. She was still surrounded by Odetta and friends, who were laughing and chatting merrily while Fan stood there quietly with a blank grin. Well, that couldn't be helped by having your mother intervene.

"Ah, I ought to introduce myself," said the elderly nobleman as I was watching Fan. "Hugo Piminder." He gave a slight bow.

My eyes lit up. Sorry, Henry. "Evelyn Radcliffe," I said, offering my hand. I immediately turned on the false smile I'd always used for impressing my first husband's clients. It was part royalty, part shark, and all charm. This one, somehow, hadn't rusted with disuse.

"Ah, you were quite the local celebrity last year."

"Yes, I'm the wicked stepmother."

He chuckled. "How fortunate that everything worked out for you. I'm afraid word did get around of your family's predicament. But your stepdaughter's wedding was quite lovely. And how clever of them to hold it here in Strachey. Have you visited your stepdaughter at the palace?"

I shook my head. "Not yet, although I imagine my daughter will receive an invite soon. She's being presented this Season."

"Well, I do hope you are able to see the place. It's quite marvelous. I had the opportunity to visit—when I was much younger, of course. Some sort of honor for my service in the wars, I think. Regardless, the interior was positively magnificent."

Goodness, this wasn't a name drop; he'd dropped an entire building on me. I imagined myself crushed under the weight of a few tons of marble and gold and expensive furniture, and gave an involuntary little snort. Obviously, he didn't know why I found his anecdote so funny, but after a brief moment of internal debate, he seemed to take it as encouragement.

"One expects, of course, to see gold leaf finishing on nearly every surface. Not so. Rather, they have simply allowed the dark cherrywood to speak for itself . . ."

I stifled a guffaw. Oh Lord, Evelyn, don't lose it. Furniture finishings! He was describing furniture finishings to me! I took a deep breath and tried to get a grip. Send your mind out, I thought as I bit back giggles. You're working here.

He certainly didn't seem as bad as the Babcocks had intimated. He was pompous, sure—an opening gambit featuring the royal palace and him as a war hero!—but not in a malicious sense. He was simply very wealthy and always had been, and he'd been raised with an innate surety that he was better than most everyone else. What he was doing to the Babcocks was downright cruel, and it didn't seem to fit. Perhaps, I thought, there was more to this story. I was fairly certain I could get it out of him, if I could steer him away from the home furnishings department.

I was about to stop him from moving on to porcelainware when out of the corner of my eye I spotted Clarrie Babcock peeking through the doorway. I gave a tiny shake of my head and held up a hand behind my back, hoping she would catch on and wait. The party was a good choice for her confrontation, but she needed a room full of people. Well, I could help with that. His reaction was something I'd very much like to see.

"Do you know, I've wanted very much to get a look at the Courtenay's fortepiano," I said, gesturing toward the drawing room, where a young man clearly attempting to impress a young woman played and groups of nobles chatted. "Shall we?"

He made to offer me his arm, and immediately I felt a flush of heat run through me. I pretended not to notice and took myself into the drawing room. He ought to chase you a little bit, I thought. But I don't want to be chased, and I definitely don't want to be caught. I want to go home, I thought, and suddenly, I wanted to cry. Instead, I tried to push it all out of my head. Use the smile, I told myself.

I found a spot to stand near the fortepiano and tried to look fascinated by it.

"Do you play?" he said, coming up behind me.

"Oh no. I'm not particularly musical. I am fascinated by how it works, though. Have you ever seen the inside of one? All the music comes from little tiny levers and strings."

"I can't say I have, although I did have the opportunity to go to a concert given by a well-known viol player at the Royal Opera House . . ."

Oh, stop! Now I'd been hit by an opera house! I glanced toward the archway leading toward the ballroom and pretended I'd seen something.

"I am so sorry to interrupt, but I think my daughter is trying to get my attention. It's her very first Season; she's an absolute nervous wreck."

He smiled knowingly. "Ah, yes. Young women do get worked up over the silliest things."

I could have slapped him right then but gave a tense false smile instead—not my best work—and cleared out to make room for Clarrie.

I entered the ballroom but circled quickly out before Maribelle caught sight of me. I took up a position outside the drawing room where I'd be able to see Lord Piminder's face and hopefully be able to hear him and Clarrie too.

Clarrie crept in tentatively, hands clasped in front of her and shoulders a bit hunched. She straightened herself up and approached Lord Piminder.

"Excuse me, sir." She curtsied.

"Yes, young lady?"

"Um, I'm Clarice Babcock, sir."

"You don't seem that certain."

"Oh," Clarrie squeaked. Her eyes weren't quite focused, and she looked like she might run away without another word.

You can do this, I thought. People are paying attention. Lord Piminder's piercing bass had cut through the room, and one by one, conversations were coming to a halt. This is your moment, Clarrie.

"Did you need something, Miss Babcock?"

I was sure she'd decided to flee, but instead she swallowed hard and raised her voice.

"Lord Piminder, I beg you to reconsider your decision regarding your son and I—" Clarrie started, undoubtedly rehearsing words she'd prepared beforehand.

"Reconsider my decision? Did you think I wasn't serious?" Piminder interrupted.

"No, I . . ." Clarrie was flustered but rallied valiantly and tried to continue her speech. "I just wanted you to know that we truly love each other . . ."

"Ah, so you thought you could say a few magic words about true love and I'd have a sudden change of heart? That I'd somehow forget how woefully inadequate you are as a match for my son? That you'd convince me this wasn't a ploy of your father's?"

"But it isn't! I really love Terence!"

Piminder smiled in a way I recognized far too well, although I hoped I looked more charming and less ghoulish. "And in my benevolence, I've offered you a chance, young lady. Spin enough gold to pay off your father's debt, and I shall give my blessing to your nuptials. From what your father implied, that shouldn't be too difficult. Were I you, I'd spend my time spinning, not dancing."

Clarrie burst into tears and fled, and Piminder simply walked away as if nothing had happened. In my direction. I hurried toward the ballroom and had just rejoined Maribelle and Lady Dumond when the girls reentered.

"I think it's time for us to go, Fan," I said.

"Did you see what happened to Clarrie Babcock?" Fan whispered.

"It was humiliating, Mother," Odetta was saying, practically laughing in glee.

"Hmm?" I said noncommittally. "Maribelle?" I motioned toward the exit.

"Ooh, I'm not quite sure where my husband went," she said. "You go ahead."

Fan had already started toward the front door. I turned to follow her and just caught Odetta's voice.

"Lady Frandsen's new girl is hopeless. Absolutely brainless, Mother."

I clenched my fists and fought the urge to turn around. Fan was waiting for me at the door with my coat. I tried to quickly hide my scowl.

"That wasn't so bad," Fan said. "Those girls were nice. I was a little shy, but I think I can get used to this. I can get dancing lessons, right?"

I could only manage a nod. If I'd opened my mouth, I'd have screamed.

May Odetta Dumond have the luck she deserves, I thought.

Don't curse people, Evelyn, I reprimanded myself. Save your anger for Hugo Piminder, who, I noted, had utterly, utterly failed to impress me.

I should have known he hadn't believed Patrick Babcock. He was teasing them with this spinning-straw-into-gold line, and he was enjoying it. Anyone who could so persecute sweet Clarrie Babcock deserved to be taken down.

Although as I listened to some of the conversations buzzing around us, I began to hope that Clarrie might not need much help from the fairies.

"Can you believe him? The poor girl!" women muttered around me.

At least one thing had gone right tonight. I smiled, finally for real.

CHAPTER THREE

"MOM?"

Fanchon found me in the study the next morning, reading one of my father's manuals. He was a proud chemist, not an alchemist, and as such, he thought it was ridiculous and pointless to attempt to turn any sort of metal into gold. It was not pointless, however, to occasionally put a shiny gold-like coating on something. Looking back, I suspect my father walked a fine ethical line.

I closed the book as Fan entered. Brass was probably the cheapest solution, but it would still be easy to spot as a fraud.

"How are you, dear?"

"Um, I'm fine. I was wondering how I would go about finding a dance instructor. It's just that I don't think I want everyone to know I'm taking lessons."

"Oh! That's right. Well, that's not a problem. I can teach you."

Fan started, openmouthed and wide-eyed, like a giant gust of wind had almost knocked her off her feet.

"You can dance?" She was so surprised, apparently, she didn't even notice the fairies might have construed that as rude.

"You're looking at a proud graduate of Ms. Arbuthnot's School for Charming Girls. Besides, your father and I used to go dancing quite often. I don't actually mind dancing."

"But aren't we going to need someone to do the man's part?"

"You're looking at a very tall graduate of an all-girls school," I said. "Now, I think if we move some furniture in the living room we'll have the space for this."

Fan followed me into the living room, and we pulled the armchairs to the edges of the room and carried the center table to the hallway.

"I think that'll do." Besides, since I would be leading, at least she couldn't ram my shins into the corner of the table. "One issue I noticed about your dancing is that you're very stiff. We want everything to be more fluid. When we put our arm out, for example—see how mine has sort of a bend in it?"

Fan nodded and tried to mimic my arm.

"Right, I'm not exactly sure how your elbow can go that way . . ." I tried to reposition her arm. "I think *bend* was maybe not the best word. We definitely don't want to see a pointy elbow corner, we want it to look like our arm is curved. That's better."

"That hurts! That's not natural!"

"You have to get used to it. You probably have to build up the muscles. Now let's start with a minuet, and let's try to remember we want to be light and airy, like we're floating around the room."

"We'll start here at this end. Other side of me. Hold my hand. Other arm out gracefully. Ready? Right—Sink. Left—Right—No, don't sink yet—Left, now sink. Now right—"

"I'm on my left," Fan interrupted.

"What? We must not have sunk correctly."

"I did sink!"

"Right, but I think it wasn't on the correct foot. Or possibly beat," I said.

"I never understand the minuet count," she admitted.

"You do a whole minuet step in two three-counts. It goes, 'One, sink, three; one, two, sink.'"

"Yeah, I never do that right."

"Well, let's try this. Let's get the pattern down first, no sinks." We reset at the end of the room. "So let's go. Right foot—feet together. Then left, right, left, together. Repeat. Right, together. Left, right, left, together."

Fan and I minuet-walked the length of the room several times.

"Was Dad a good dancer?" she asked.

"He was excellent."

"Did you like dancing with him?"

"I did," I said. Right up until I realized he used every partner switch to seduce new lovers. I didn't tell Fan that. "All right, we're not going to add in the sinks yet, but let's try to get the tiptoes correct. The first step is a flat foot. Then when we come together, let's just tap our foot, like this. Then left tiptoe, right tiptoe, left flat foot, tap. The flat foot isn't so much a stomp. You can toe-heel."

We were so intent on tiptoeing across the room, we both missed the knock on the door—until it had turned into a rather angry pounding.

"Is that the door?" Fan asked.

"I think it must be," I said, climbing over the table we'd set in the hallway.

I opened the door on an impeccably dressed woman with a very sour, tight mouth and cat-eye spectacles that only accentuated her pinched glare. Her hair, piled in a knot on her head, must have been colored with some mix of henna and indigo, for its hue was far too close to magenta to be natural. She carried a black carpetbag with minimal white accents, its sides bulging—the only evidence of untidiness about her entire person.

"Hello," I said. "Sorry we—"

"You must be Madam Radcliffe. I am Roompilda Stidolph. I'm here to prepare Fanchon for her Season. My letter of reference."

I started to say we hadn't asked for a consultant, but then I saw the seal on the letter she'd handed me.

"The queen sent you to help Fan?"

She looked at me over the top of her spectacles with an expression that said, "My, we are quick, aren't we?" Even her face was dripping with sarcasm.

"May I?" she said, gesturing toward the house.

"Oh. Yes," I said, turning and immediately cracking my shin on the center table. "Ow. Fan, help me move this back."

Fan and I reset the furniture, Roompilda trailing along behind us, casting a disapproving eye on everything from the color of my drapes to my lifting technique.

"I was just giving Fan a dance lesson." We put the armchair back in place and offered it to our visitor.

She hid her skepticism about my dancing abilities better than Fan had, but I'd still caught that raised eyebrow. Although, to be fair, one of Roompilda's eyebrows always seemed to be raised.

"Good. Dancing lessons are certainly high on our list of priorities."

"What other lessons do I need to take?" Fan asked.

"Comportment, etiquette, conversation, to name a few."

"I can do those things!"

"Can you? This is the Season. You are not merely trying to impress Strachey. The Capital is here. If your behavior varies even slightly from that of the other girls, everyone will notice."

"In terms of etiquette, of course. We don't want all you girls to seem like you were made from the same mold," I said, less to reassure Fan than to inform Roompilda. I'd been to finishing school. I wasn't giving her free rein with my daughter.

Roompilda gave a dazzling fake smile that put mine to shame. "The queen simply wants you to be prepared before you attend your first fete."

"Oh, I already went to the Courtenays' party! It went really well."

Roompilda's already icy countenance dropped a few degrees. "You've already been out?"

Fan nodded. "It was lovely!"

"Without any instructions, without any training. Ugh." Roompilda shook her head in disgust. "Now we'll have to add damage control on top of the rest. Still, nothing I can't do . . ."

"Damage control?" Fan cried. "But I didn't embarrass myself! Everyone was really nice to me!"

Roompilda tipped her head and gave Fan a rueful smile that fairly obviously said, "Bless your heart."

"That's because they're well bred."

"But—"

"Do you know what they said about you behind your back? With no training or skills on your part, I can guarantee it wasn't a wall of compliments."

Fan deflated. I, on the other hand, bristled. Exactly how mean to my daughter did she need to be? Could she not have convinced Fan she needed lessons without making her feel like an embarrassment?

"I don't think it's necessary—" I snapped.

"Can you honestly say you are certain this was an unparalleled success?" Roompilda interrupted. I opened my mouth to interject, but she kept going. "Are you certain that you gave no little darts to the gossipers?"

She gave me a pointed glance. My objection died in my throat. I knew, of course. And I knew stupid little Odetta wasn't one of a kind. I knew Fan had mildly embarrassed herself, and while I wouldn't have pointed it out to her face, I'd still have done something. I'd—well, I'd have hired a consultant. I stayed miserably silent.

"I—I guess not," Fan said, eyes welling up. "I thought if I was just a nice person, then . . ."

"Only fairies care about that. This is court. Shall we begin?"

Fan nodded.

"Excellent. Madam Radcliffe, if you wouldn't mind?"

She glanced at the door. I made it out of the drawing room with poise, but I definitely slammed the door to the study. Dismissing me from my own living room? How self-important could a person be?

I kicked the ottoman in frustration, which did nothing but hurt my toe. I knew I should continue reading my father's herbal, but I'd never be able to concentrate now. I'd probably get it into my head to start eavesdropping on the lesson, which would lead to meddling, which would only cause trouble. Fan needed help, and I couldn't give it—my social skills were rusty and outdated. Roompilda may be condescending, I thought, but she was probably very, very good at her job.

You'd better leave the house, I told myself, or you won't leave them alone. I found my purse and walked into town.

I knew it would be futile to try to get a little shopping done. The day after a ball, the brunch traffic was always brutal. But there was at least one shop that wouldn't be packed, and it had a shopkeeper I very much wanted to speak with.

When I finally reached the apothecary, I pushed the door open and nearly walked right into a noblewoman and her daughter.

"Do you have any of those, what are they called, Aroma Elixirs?" the woman asked. "You inhale the good smells and they replace the bad humors."

"I don't think that's a medically sound treatment," said our apothecary, Milburn Kent. "I have some headache medicine, if you'd like that."

"No, no, none of that works for my daughter. Only the aromas help."

"Well, I'm not sure I have that specifically, but I do have scented candles."

"Oh, heavens no! It's the special blend of oils Aroma Elixirs uses that cures the headache."

I rolled my eyes and leaned back against the wall, arms folded. Milburn caught my expression and suppressed a grin. "Well, let me see what I've got in the back," he said. "Does the young lady have a scent she prefers?"

"Lemongrass and lavender," the young woman said.

Milburn nodded and disappeared into the back room. The older woman turned and fussed over her daughter, asking where the pain was. The girl rubbed the bridge of her nose and her forehead; her mother reached out and started rubbing her temples. I had trouble imagining how those strong-smelling oils didn't make her headaches worse.

After a few minutes, Milburn came back carrying a small vial. "I regret to say I do not carry Aroma Elixirs. However, and I probably shouldn't tell you this, I did recently catch word of a new formula that should be hitting the market very soon, developed by a new company. I happen to know how they mix it, and I've whipped you up a small amount of your favorite flavor."

Both mother and daughter were suitably impressed. The girl gaped as she took the vial from Milburn. The mother paid without a second thought. I grinned at Milburn as they left the shop.

He raised both hands in a shrug. "If Aroma Elixirs has no qualms about taking their money . . . I don't want to be a charlatan, but I'm afraid all my customers want to be duped. Except you, of course."

I sighed. "If my father were alive, he'd be furious he hadn't thought of this oil business himself."

Milburn chuckled. Milburn Kent was a small man, and every part of him seemed rounded. He himself had large round spectacles, which made him look perpetually nervous. He had a tendency toward perspiration, and when he was concentrating on a mixture, beads of sweat invariably formed on his receding hairline.

"How's your wife, Milburn?"

"Oh, quite well, thank you. What can I do for you today?"

"I'm sure you're familiar with the gold penny trick," I said.

"Of course! Coat a copper penny with zincum filings and fire it. The copper and zincum make brass, and it looks like you've got a gold penny. I showed my kids that trick. Were you going to do it with Fanchon? I imagine she's a little old for that, but it is fun."

"Actually, I have some copper candlesticks I dislike and thought I might try it. I found an outline of the process in my father's notes, but he isn't as thorough as I'd like. Can I do this at home?" This was only half-true. Of course, I had no such candlesticks, but my father really had left out what I thought were some essential details: how much zincum to use, how long to leave it in the oven, etc.

"As long as your oven gets quite hot, you should. You can mix the zincum with lye to help it coat the copper, or if you have a big enough crucible you can simply use that."

"And what ratio do you use to get the right color?"

"Well," Milburn began, "some say the best imitation gold is seventy-five percent copper and twenty-five percent zincum . . ."

I took notes as he laid bare the mysteries of brass. If I could get thin copper threads, I could add the right proportion of zincum to give them a brass coating. This could work. At least, I hoped so, because then I'd be stuck with paint or gold leaf—the former of which would look embarrassingly fake, while the latter would be barely affordable and beyond tedious.

"I might have zincum in stock. Would you like me to check?" Milburn asked.

"Let me estimate how much I'll need, and I'll get back to you," I said. "Thank you, Milburn."

"Anytime! Have a wonderful day!"

Now I'd have to know the amount of the loan, I thought as I left the shop—and then the volume of gold equal to that amount, so that I could order the copper. It would be wonderful if I could somehow get Piminder to come down on the amount of gold Clarrie needed to spin. I didn't want to coat a whole barn's worth.

"Madam Radcliffe!" I turned to see Clarrie herself waving me down.

"Hello, Clarrie. How are you this morning?" Not particularly well, if her puffy eyes were any indication.

She shrugged. "Mama was furious. Papa was terrified. Even Terence was a little cross with me."

"Terence?"

"Lord Piminder's son. He thought I'd embarrassed myself. But it is going to work, isn't it? Do you think the fairies will hear what's happened?"

"Absolutely," I said.

"I'm just really worried what he'll do to Mum and Dad. They don't have family members they can go live with. I mean, I can go into service, can't I? I don't need to be proud; there's a lot of people who suffer worse things. But I don't know what Mum and Dad can do! So I've got to fix this."

I swallowed down a lump in my throat. I'd been in exactly this position just a year ago, only I'd had two daughters to worry about, not two parents. And until the diamonds and the frogs, I'd had the same last-ditch plan: marry someone, whether I wanted to or not.

"Clarrie, I have no doubt the fairies are going to help you and your family. You do want to marry Terence, right?"

She nodded, but with less conviction than she'd had a few days ago. "No, I do, I really do. We just had a bad day today." She set her jaw and changed the subject. "What do I do next?"

Give me time to make some gold, I thought. "At this point, we will undoubtedly have to be patient. But you must take any chance to impress Lord Piminder."

Clarrie grimaced.

"I know. He's unpleasant. But it's the only way you can try to solve your problem yourself."

She sighed, and nodded in resignation.

"Think of it as though you're giving him a chance to stop being the villain," I said. "And the more unpleasant he is, the more he simply digs himself in. All right?"

"All right. Thank you, Madam Radcliffe."

"I'm happy to help, Clarrie. Chin up, and have a nice day."

I watched Clarrie stride off into the marketplace. I probably should have told her to pretend not to know me, I thought. I wouldn't get anything out of Piminder if he knew I was working for Clarrie. Ah well, she was a sharp girl. Hopefully she would think of it herself.

I started back toward home, dodging carriages and nosy tourists. I was almost halfway there when I remembered why I'd left in the first place. I groaned.

This was exactly why I needed Henry. You'd think a person who always thought on the bright side would be insufferable, but he wasn't. The mental gymnastics he went through trying to find something nice to say when I was furious were downright hilarious. And he knew it, too. The Season when we were married was the best one I'd ever suffered through.

I could picture him walking next to me, hands in his pockets, ready to reassure me that things couldn't be as bad as I thought they were.

"What would you say about Roompilda?" I asked him.

"She just rubbed you the wrong way, Evie. You're actually very similar!"

What.

"No, well—" his image broke off, just as he always had. Whenever he floundered, he would hem and haw, starting and restarting his sentence, always with a pointed finger or openhanded gesture. "What I mean is," I pictured him continuing, "she may not have your interpersonal skills, but she's still a consultant, just like you. You try to get girls ready for the fairies, she has to get them ready for the court. You're just not used to someone else being the expert and bossing you around. Not that I'm saying you're bossy, of course, um . . ."

No, it's all right. Point taken, Henry, I thought to myself. I manipulated people with honey; Roompilda seemed to do it with a slap in the face. Still, she was just trying to do her job, and I knew exactly how that felt. Perhaps, just perhaps, I needed to accept that she knew more than me.

She knows more than you do, Evelyn, I admitted to myself. See, that wasn't so hard! I gritted my teeth and tried not to sneer. Let the woman do her job.

Roompilda was just leaving as I approached the house.

"I will be returning every day this week at precisely nine o'clock," she said abruptly. "We have considerable ground to make up, but it would be inadvisable to refuse callers at this point. Please make yourself available during calling hours."

"Wait, what callers?"

She looked at me as if I were a particularly slow child. "I won't know who they are until they call, but I imagine they will be nobles who want to meet Fan."

Who would want to meet Fan? The Season had hardly begun, and she'd barely made a splash. Well, her stepsister is the princess, I thought. Great. We'll have a house full of desperate nobles hoping to curry favor with the royal family.

"You ought to have tea prepared. It would be better if you had at least one more servant, but I suppose that can't be helped."

Don't get riled, Evelyn, I told myself. She knows what she's doing—and she's right. You ought to have someone to open the door. You just don't like being told what to do. I took a deep breath.

"Good day," she said, and walked away, carpetbag in tow. What did she keep in there? Books to balance on Fan's head?

I found Fan collapsed on the couch, rubbing her eyes. "Oh God, Mom, you would not believe how many mistakes I made last night. There are so, so many rules. I so should have gone to finishing school." She suddenly looked up at the ceiling in alarm. "Sorry, I didn't mean to be critical. I'm sure you didn't think it was a good thing for me . . ."

"No, I tried to send you," I said, sitting in the armchair across from her. "Your father didn't want you to go."

"Wait, what? But Dad ate this kind of thing up! He'd be thrilled I was doing this. Wouldn't he?"

"Oh, absolutely. But your father never believed anyone was really qualified enough to teach you. I managed to persuade him to visit the school I went to, and I had to hear dissertations on all its flaws for weeks. I didn't dare visit anywhere else, he might've tried to shut them down."

Fan grinned.

"Then I insisted we find you tutors, but he demanded to see their lesson plans every day and ordered them to make changes. If they didn't quit from the nervous strain, he usually found a reason to fire them after a month or two. After he passed, I couldn't afford to keep it up."

"Why not? We weren't poor," she asked.

I hesitated. I really needed to stop running my mouth, or I was going to accidentally say something Fan didn't need to hear.

"No," I began cautiously. "But the allowance your father left was meant for you, not for both of us. And his will didn't actually let me access your balance, so while we had plenty, all I had to work with were the allowance payments."

Fan frowned. "That's a big oversight. I wouldn't have thought Dad would make a mistake like that."

I just shrugged. It wasn't a mistake. I changed the subject before Fan could realize that her father hadn't intended to provide for me at all.

"How was Roompilda's lesson?"

"Oh, I learned how to stand up perfectly straight, and what to do with my hands, and how to walk like a lady. She says tomorrow we're going to practice what you can talk about, since people will be coming to see me."

"I wouldn't worry too much. You're charming and delightful."

She smiled weakly and nodded.

"You don't seem like you believe me. Do you want to talk about something? Is something bothering you?"

She shook her head. "No, I'm fine, Mom. Thanks. I'm probably just nervous because it's all new. I'm sure it'll go fine." She tried to smile a little brighter.

You've got a lot to learn about fake smiles, kid, I thought.

"All right. You let me know if you need something," I said, which was an inadequate response in every way, but I didn't know what else to say. I never had known. I'd been just fine when she cried because she was either tired or hungry, but as soon as she got old enough to have all these complex reasons for being upset, I was lost.

I walked out of the room, feeling a little like a coward. You can't force her to talk to you, I thought. But it would be nice if she did.

CHAPTER FOUR

"HAVE YOU WORKED in a house before, Mina?"

"Sometimes I take care of all the Cutler babes," the young woman said. She was Gerta's younger sister, and no more than fourteen. She was all I could get on short notice.

"Hmm, well, this is a little different. I've only got two main jobs for you, though, all right?"

"Yes, ma'am," she said eagerly.

"First, I need you to answer the door. The maid, or footman, or whoever knocks, will tell you who's calling and give you a card. You'll bring the card to me, and then I'll send you back to the door to say, 'Madam Radcliffe and Miss Envers would be delighted to see . . . ,' and then you say the name of whoever called. Clear?"

"Madam Hradcliffe and Miss Henvers hwould be deeeelighted to see Hugh," she repeated, adding a pretentious *h* to the beginning of any word she could. I assumed she meant *you*, not a nobleman named Hugh. I hoped. "How was that?" she asked. "I've been practicing talking like a nob."

"Right, well, you don't actually need to. You can just talk like yourself. We're going to need to get you something that looks like a uniform. Fan?" I shouted. "Rats, she's still in her lesson. Well, when she's done we'll find you something to wear."

Mina's eyes were dancing with glee.

"The other thing I need you to do is carry in the tea. Gerta will give it to you when it's time, and you'll just carry it into the drawing room and place it on the table. I'll pour, so you don't need to worry about anything else. Just bring it in the room."

"Do I need to curtsy when I go places?"

"Not while you're carrying a tea tray."

She nodded but dipped into a little curtsy anyway. There was a definite bounce in that bob, and I made a mental note to watch the tea carefully when she came in. With hands at the ready.

"If I need anything else—and I don't think I will—there's a bell pull in the drawing room that rings a bell in the kitchen. If you hear the bell ring, come into the room and see me. But I don't think I'll ring it."

"I'll be very helpful, ma'am! If you need anything, I'm at your service!" Mina solemnly put her hand over her heart.

"You behave yourself, missy," Gerta said as she came out of the kitchen and thwacked Mina with a dish towel. "Do you know how many people'll be coming, ma'am?"

I sighed. "A Lady Rundle announced her coming this morning with her son and daughter. So, three, I think. I hope."

Gerta nodded and returned to the kitchen. I barely had time to turn around before Roompilda came marching out of the sitting room with Fanchon in her wake. Roompilda gave Mina a condescending eye—the girl was still bobbing up and down, muttering greetings filled with superfluous *h* sounds.

"Fan, take Mina back and try to find something of yours or Ella's that could look like a uniform, please."

Roompilda gave me a tiny haughty smirk as Mina skipped away. I tried to smile blankly. She was right that I needed another servant. I wasn't too proud to admit it. Well, only in my head. I was definitely too proud to say it to her face.

"Good luck," she said and left.

I hustled into the sitting room to tidy. It had been cleaned, of course, so really I just rotated a vase a few degrees and moved the clock over an inch. I hadn't entertained since Husband #1 died, and I was nervous. Visitors were how you acquired a reputation.

You needed people to talk about you. You needed them to judge you—favorably, of course. I hated it, but I'd become good at it, for the sake of my husband's business. Now, of course, I'd do it for Fan.

She eventually joined me, and we sat there in silence, listening to the clock tick. She sat on her hands. I picked at my nails.

When we finally heard the knock on the door, we both sprang to our feet.

"No, Mina's got it," Fan said as we both took a step toward the door.

"Right, right," I said, sitting back down. I listened for Mina's voice. "Does she have it?"

"Probably?"

I waited a few seconds. "I'd better go—"

"Wait, are those her footsteps?" Fan said as I stood up. I paused.

"Hgood hafternoon," I heard Mina say. I sat down and rubbed the bridge of my nose.

"What is she doing?" Fan whispered.

"Sounding fancy," I groaned.

Fan watched the doorway with a stricken expression.

"Hright this hway," we heard after a few moments. We stood up, and I put on my most dazzling smile.

"Lady Rundle," I said as she entered the room. "So wonderful to see you!"

"Hevelyn Radcliffe," she said. Apparently, Mina's affectation was right on target. "I've heard so much about you, I can't believe we've never met!"

Really? I could.

"It is surprising, isn't it? Please, my daughter Fanchon," I introduced. Lady Rundle grasped Fan's hand and gushed over how precious she was.

"This is my son Damian. He's the newest councilor to the minster of the Treasury!"

"It hasn't happened yet, Mother," he said, "but I do think my chances are quite decent." He feigned a humble smile.

"Ooh, you're too modest. And this is my daughter Carmindy." Carmindy curtsied and smiled sweetly, dimples beaming. She couldn't have been much older than Mina.

"It's simply a pleasure to meet all of you," I said. "Please, have a seat."

"How have you found Strachey so far?" Fan said, her voice a little stilted, as if she were reciting from a script Roompilda had given her. Which, I considered, was likely.

"Oh, we just adore Strachey. Don't we, children?" Lady Rundle said. Carmindy nodded.

"Strachey has such an old-fashioned feel," Damian said. "Almost like time has moved on without it. Such a nice break from the bustle of the Capital."

"And you have the most stressful job!" Lady Rundle exclaimed.

Fan had a blank look, like she was trying so hard to listen she'd forgotten to think of a new question.

"Tell us about your work," I filled in.

"Well, at the moment," Damian said with a bemused look at his mother, "I'm a senior assistant to one of the Treasury councilors. But my superior is retiring, and—not to brag, but I'm what you might call an obvious replacement."

"Oh, how exciting!" Fan cooed.

Damian shrugged modestly. He was moderately handsome now; however, he had a thickness in his neck and chest that in my experience meant he would only widen with age. I imagined his neck visibility wouldn't last very long. Rather like Husband #1, actually. He had been downright beautiful when we first met, but then the more money he got, the more potbellied he became.

"What does a Treasury councilor do?" Fan asked.

"Oh, I'm sure you wouldn't be interested. I'm afraid that's the less exciting part. Important, of course. Essential, even. We give advice on spending, budgets, taxes, you know. Awfully complex for a lady."

I saw Fan's lips purse, but I couldn't react fast enough to stop her.

"Taxes?" she said. "Are you recommending the new import tax? Because I don't think that will solve anything. It'll just get passed on to the consumer."

Oh, Roompilda would kill me if she heard about this. I'd explained tax burden to Fan a while back—she'd been curious about the protests over the new tax—but I didn't expect her to use it as an opening salvo. Damian looked a little taken aback, while his mother frowned at Fan's forwardness. Carmindy just smiled vacantly.

"Well, you two will have to discuss this sometime!" I said cheerfully. "Carmindy, is this your first Season?"

"Oh, I'm not old enough to go to all the balls. I wish I could! I've heard that at the garden party they have a hedge maze taller than your head so that you can't find the way out!"

"Do you know Lord Allenby employs thirty gardeners to prune it every day?" I said.

Carmindy's jaw dropped.

"You think it can't possibly be worth the money, but once you're in that maze, you can see it was all worth doing!" Lady Rundle said, chuckling. I mentally exhaled—the tension had passed, although Fan looked a little pale, like she was struggling between fury and embarrassment. I offered her a second chance at the conversation.

"Fan, you'll have to give Carmindy some ideas of things she can do while her brother goes to balls."

"Do you like the outdoors very much? It's very pretty to go down by the river. A lot of girls like to take watercolors and paint there. And you must have tea at Tea Rose Cottage and try the biscuits from Hornbow's Bakery. They are the best biscuits you will ever eat."

Speaking of tea, in came Mina. She brought the tray over to the table. As soon as I saw her knees bend, I shot up out of my chair and reached for the tea tray, just managing to hold it steady while Mina bobbed up and down.

"Thank you, Mina," I said, setting the tray on the table myself.

Mina practically skipped out of the room. Lady Rundle gave her a faint, puzzled smile.

"She's new," I said as I poured. "How do you take your tea?"

We made it through the rest of the tea without any more faux pas. Lady Rundle did make Damian drone on a bit about a very important project he'd worked on for the Crown, the details of which he wasn't supposed to tell us about, which made me wonder how he managed to spend so much time talking about it. Luckily, the topic of taxes didn't come up.

I was still trying to figure out what they wanted from us as they left. If Damian was courting Fan, he was doing it subtly. I had visited a number of Strachey's eligible bachelors the previous year, and their mothers had been anything but subtle. On the other hand, he had mentioned his promotion often enough—perhaps he simply hoped we could put in a good word. Either way, this was clearly more of a scouting mission. Laying the groundwork, so to speak, for the big conquest.

Sure enough, as we bid them farewell and I showed them to the door—Mina was nowhere to be found—Damian took Fan's hand and kissed it.

"It's been a pleasure, Miss Envers. I hope I may call on you again?"

"I would be delighted."

"Excellent. Perhaps we can go riding. I will send my manservant around with a card."

The instant I shut the door behind them, Fan let out a huge breath. "I'm not going to apologize," she said defiantly. "I'm not sorry about it at all!"

"Sorry about what?"

"What I said! I thought he was extremely rude. No one wants to talk about stupid taxes and budgets. They're dull! It has nothing to do with being a girl."

"Oh. I don't think you have to apologize."

She just stood there with her fists still clenched and mouth all screwed up. I could all but hear the "but . . ." hanging in the air.

"But you think you should?" I asked.

"Aagh!" she wailed. "It was so embarrassing! I don't know why I said that! It was totally the wrong thing to say. Roompilda would be furious! But I still meant what I said!"

"I think the one mistake you made was that you came on a little strong. I probably would have made a joke out of it. I might have said, 'Oh, I don't know. Are there very many gentlemen who find budgets truly interesting?' That way it doesn't seem like I'm attacking our guest."

Fan's eyes widened in horror and she clapped her hands over her mouth. "All right, I'm sorry! I'm sorry! Oh God, the frogs are going to come back. All this Season stuff makes me so nervous I don't think before I speak!"

"Whoa, Fan—"

"But one mistake can't mean I deserve bad luck, right? I wasn't trying to be mean, I just wanted to stand up for myself. But I see what I did wrong, and I'll learn from my mistake. I think as long as I'm trying to do better, it should be okay, right?"

"I would have to think the fairies care about whether you're actually trying to hurt people. Surely, being a little bit confrontational doesn't deserve bad luck."

She breathed a sigh of relief and marched off to her room.

The next day, we had Lady Farthingbras and her son Justice. Fan started out the picture of propriety.

"I do hope you're enjoying Strachey," she said as we sat down.

"Yes, thank you, Miss Envers," Lady Farthingbras warbled. She had aged to the point of being rather crusty, with wrinkled folds of skin hanging from her neck and arms. She looked down her sharp hooked nose at us, even though we were at eye level.

"Oh, wonderful," Fan said.

Silence.

"Umm . . . ," Fan stalled.

"And what do you do, Justice?" I volunteered.

"Justice is a lance corporal in Her Majesty's cavalry," his mother answered. Justice gave a quick nod.

"And at such a young age," I said. "You must be very proud."

Lady Farthingbras smiled, basking in the superiority of her son. Justice maintained his stony silence.

"Have you been to many foreign places?" Fan asked.

"Justice has ridden the deserts of Mornubia and traversed the plains of Gelgravitz," Lady Farthingbras pronounced.

Fan looked sort of puzzled, her gaze going from Lady Farthingbras to Justice. The thing about Fan is that the spinning gears in her mind are practically transparent. You can more or less see her thinking. Right now, she was wondering if he was mute.

"My, how exciting," I said.

Fan nodded, trying to turn her attention to Lady Farthingbras; unfortunately, her curiosity won out, and she continued to give Justice surreptitious glances.

"Although I'm sure it's rather worrying for you," I continued.

Lady Farthingbras sighed and dramatically put her hand to her heart.

"We humbly make the sacrifices the Crown requires of us," she said.

Well, I wasn't sure about humbly, but Justice at least was serving the Crown, so I had to give them credit for that.

As I thought about that, I noticed Fan startle, ripping her eyes away from Justice to stare fixedly at Lady Farthingbras. I stole a glance at Justice just in time to see him running his gaze over Fan, like he was examining her from head to toe. I could just picture him thinking, Yes, yes. You'll do. Except apparently his mother would have to say it for him.

Well, not in my house.

"How noble," I said, returning to my conversation with Lady Farthingbras. Now, however, I stooped to her level of communication—simple sentences, no questions.

She was probably expecting me to continue speaking, but instead I merely smiled serenely into the silence.

"Umm," Fan mumbled. "What are your plans for the Season?"

"We always look forward to attending the parties," Lady Farthingbras said. She looked expectantly at me, as if returning the question.

"As do we," I said.

"I've never been to any of them before," Fan said, "but the balls all seem so delightful."

As soon as Fan stopped speaking, the room fell quiet. Fan shifted her gaze between me and Lady Farthingbras, a look of panic spreading across her face as she realized she had nothing left to say. Even Lady Farthingbras began to show her discomfort, but I simply continued to smile. I will outlast you, I thought.

Sure enough, after a few seconds of dead silence, Lady Farthingbras said, "Well, we don't want to take up too much of your time."

"It was so lovely to see you," I said, rising to my feet so that no one would get the impression I was sad that they were leaving.

"The two of you will have to associate sometime," she said to Fan and Justice. Fan smiled nervously as Justice leaned over to kiss her hand.

"Goodbye!" I very nearly slammed the door after them.

And that, I wanted to tell Fan, was how you win a fight without ever going on the attack.

"Okay, that was weird, wasn't it? I mean, it wasn't just me, right?" Fan said, wiping her hand on her skirt.

"Yes. That was weird."

"I'm not trying to be rude. But he didn't say a word! And it wasn't like she was interrupting him so he couldn't get a word out. He just never said anything!"

"No, no, he didn't."

"And he was just staring at me! I mean, I've had guys look at me before—but, like, right before they come talk to me! He was just inspecting me, like—like I was fresh produce!"

"Just so you know," I said, "I think the saying is 'fresh meat.' But yes, that was bizarre and inappropriate, and if he does ask you out riding or anything, I'll make an excuse for you."

Fan nodded. "That's . . . probably a good idea. Is this usually how it goes? That you're visited by boys and their mothers? I guess I just figured more girls would come."

"Well, I'm afraid knowing you isn't that useful to young women. But it could be very useful to young men."

"Because I could marry them," she said flatly.

I nodded. She looked irritated—was that it? That she was mostly useful as a wife? That's what would have irritated me, obviously, but I knew better than to assume she thought just like me.

"I guess that means we're going to have a lot of strange boys visiting," she said.

"I imagine so."

She huffed. "This is a stupid system. If a boy wants to find out if he wants to marry me, he shouldn't bring his mother around to talk to mine. Oh gosh, sorry, that was kind of hostile." She sighed and scrunched up her face, trying to think positive thoughts, I suppose.

"I'm sure that everything will be lovely," she said. "At least this will be a great way to meet some people before the next party. These are just introductions, really."

She didn't look like she'd quite convinced herself, but she smiled like she had and turned to leave the room.

"And I really, really hope tomorrow's not as weird," she muttered.

"Hmadam Hradcliffe hand Hmiss Henvers hwould hbe hdelighted hto hsee Hugh." By day three, Mina had gone utterly overboard. Each sentence sounded like she was hyperventilating—and like she had an imaginary friend named Hugh.

"Good morning, Lady Relish," I said as Mina led Lady Relish and her son into the room.

"Oh, Madam Radcliffe, Miss Envers, it is such an honor to meet the two of you," Lady Relish gushed. She was tall and spindly, with large round eyes that protruded from her skull.

"You're too kind," Fan said with a demure curtsy. Lady Relish simpered. "Won't you sit down?" Fan said.

"Oh, I must introduce my son, Heribert," she said, gesturing toward the young man.

He bowed and shook hands and remarked upon how nice it was to meet us. He took after his mother, particularly in regard to the eyeballs.

"I do hope you're enjoying Strachey," Fan said, sticking to her script.

"We love Strachey!" Lady Relish said.

Heribert nodded enthusiastically. "It's a lovely place. We come every summer."

"Yes, we always come see our friends—do you know the Paynes?"

"Somewhat," I said. I knew they were richer than ninety percent of Strachey.

"Lord Payne is quite a good friend of my husband's. We always enjoy coming to see them. They're just so marvelously elegant. But I can't imagine what it's like being the stepsister of a princess!" she said, briefly grasping Fan's hand. "Have you been to the palace? Is it unbelievable?"

"I haven't actually been to the palace. They had the wedding here, so . . ."

"You went to the wedding!"

"Um, yes, I was Ella's maid of honor."

"The maid of honor!" Lady Relish looked like she might pass out from excitement.

"Yes . . . um, it was lovely."

Lady Relish made a noise that was somewhere between a sigh and a squeal and fanned herself. Fan was starting to stare, her expression a mix of concern and disbelief. I moved the conversation away from Lady Relish.

"Tell us more about yourself," I said, turning to Heribert. "What do you do?"

"Ah, I'm a junior partner at Curtis, Easom, and Gibbs. It's one of the largest shipping magnates in the kingdom. You probably haven't heard of Norbert Easom," he said.

"I have, actually. He was one of my late husband's main competitors."

Heribert looked surprised, although you could only tell that from his eyebrows. His eyes were permanently surprised.

"Oh! Well, yes, of course. Envers Enterprises. Not as thriving nowadays as it used to be, but still a power player, certainly. Easom's my mentor. You should see the things he's done at CEG. Just last year, he discovered a brand-new lane to the East! If you're as obsessed with jewels from the East as Mother is, I'm your man," he said.

Lady Relish chuckled and put her hand on Fan's again. "Now that's the only part of all this I understand! He goes on and on about work, and I can't comprehend a word of it."

"You're happy as long as I bring you jewelry!"

"And I'm very proud of what my boy has accomplished. Norbert Easom, imagine!" This time, as Lady Relish reached out, Fan instinctively jerked her hands back, so Lady Relish patted Fan's knee instead.

Fan's attempt at a polite smile instead looked strained and weary, and it was directed mainly at Lady Relish's hand. I was smiling falsely, but I was fairly certain it was the one Henry called dangerous. He used to say that whenever he saw it, he'd run away from the blast zone.

It wasn't just that the two were egregious name-droppers—that wasn't usually enough to provoke outright hostility from me. No, I was on edge because I smelled a plot. Was Norbert Easom still after my husband's holdings? Did his overeager little protégé want to impress his mentor with a coup?

My inner voice broke in. It's not like you to be so defensive over anything about Husband #1, I thought. No, I told myself. This is about Fanchon. And I'm not giving my daughter to someone who considers her a piece in an acquisition that ups his winter bonus.

As I opened my mouth, a part of me warned, Don't do it, Evelyn, but that voice was accustomed to being ignored.

"So, Heribert," I started.

"Please, Herb," he said.

"Herb. What—"

Fanchon's eyes lit up. "Herb?" she said. He nodded. The corners of her mouth danced. "Herb . . . Relish . . . ," she whispered.

Oh no, I thought. She was going to start giggling. I'd have to investigate Easom's interests later.

"What do the two of you have planned for the rest of the summer?" I asked quickly.

"Oh, we're hoping to do some riding," Lady Relish said.

"We'll be at the garden party, naturally. Will you be there?" he asked Fan, who was in the middle of gulping a deep breath.

"Of course! Everyone goes to the garden party," she said.

"I certainly hope I get to see you there."

"Oh!" Lady Relish exclaimed. "We'll be going to hear Isabella Trembledina sing! Have you heard of her? She's such a tremendous, world-class opera singer, and she'll be here in Strachey! My daughter got us tickets—she knows her from school." Lady Relish merely waved her hand and Fan flinched and rotated her knees toward me, trying to keep them out of Lady Relish's reach.

"And I'll be testing my mettle in the gird and cleek tournament," Heribert said.

"Wait, what?" Fanchon exclaimed, with a sudden broad smile. "Did you just make that up?" She immediately tried to wipe the smile off her face, but the corners of her mouth kept twitching, and her lip had started to quiver.

"Oh," Herb began, "you probably know it as hoop and stick. True traditionalists, however, use the original, historical name—"

"Hoop and stick?" Fan interrupted. "Like the children rolling their hoops?" She was starting to titter. I put a firm hand on her shoulder, hoping she would calm down. We can laugh at how ridiculous he is later, I thought.

"It is a child's pastime, but the sport is anything but," Herb said. "You've got your races, plain and simple. Then you've got your agility courses. Imagine a sort of winding track, right, and periodically you've got pairs of rocks, no more than a few inches apart. Then you, as the athlete, have to roll your hoop through each pair of rocks—we call them gates—without touching either of the rocks."

"Well!" Fan managed. She was trying to force herself to take deep breaths, but each time a chuckle started to rise to the top, she had to hold her breath until it passed, which made her sound like she was wheezing. I patted her back. Keep it together, sweetheart.

"Then you have my event, the duels."

"Duels?" Fan said weakly.

"One-on-one, two girders—again, using the historical name—charge at each other, each one using his hoop to try to knock the other fellow's hoop over. I would say it's easily as much a mental challenge as a physical spectacle."

Fan snorted and started, quietly shaking with laughter, but Heribert wasn't paying attention.

"They sort everyone into brackets and make a giant tournament of it. By the quarterfinals, the matches are pretty intense. They call the whole thing the 'Battle Royale.'"

Fan lost it. Finally, completely lost it. She shrieked and dissolved into tittering convulsions.

"I'm sorry," she gasped. "I'm so sorry. Sorry . . ."

I put my face in my hands.

CHAPTER FIVE

THE NEXT DAY, Mina came bouncing into my study. "There's three cards today!" she exclaimed.

I almost wept. "Thank you, Mina."

Three visitors? You couldn't have them all at once, could you? Not if they were all mothers and sons, I was pretty sure. You'd have to have some other girls, and I certainly didn't want to host a whole luncheon. I'd have to reschedule two of them. That was all right, wasn't it? I briefly considered asking Roompilda, and then laughed at myself for thinking of it.

I leafed through the cards. A Lady Corbyn and her son. Never heard of them. You probably won't have heard of any of them, I thought. I'll have to pick randomly. Close my eyes and point. Or throw darts. Did I have darts somewhere?

I looked at the next card. Oh, forget randomness. Lady Francesca Kingsley and Ethan? Absolutely. The Corbyns were a no. They could come at the beginning of next week. And this last card . . . I stopped suddenly as I read the name. Hugo Piminder.

Why did he want to visit me? Men didn't do visits. I could tell him I had to entertain Fan's visitors, at least. I turned the card over.

Perhaps you would like to join me for dinner tonight? it read.

Dinner. No, no, I wouldn't like to. I didn't like him at all. He shared at least one trait with Husband #1: he was sweetly charming to anyone he wanted something from, and utterly awful to those who didn't matter. I didn't have to like him just because he was nice to me, not when he'd been so cruel to Clarrie. After all, as I'd learned from Husband #1, as soon as you weren't useful anymore, you could change categories quite quickly.

I did need to talk to him, however. I had to know how much the Babcocks' debt was, and most importantly, I needed him to make this a bigger deal. I needed all of Strachey to anticipate the day Clarrie Babcock would spin straw into gold. And the only way I could get him to set parameters would be to speak to him, despite how badly I wanted to ignore him.

I took a deep breath and wrote my responses on the cards. Then I gave them to Mina to deliver and prayed they'd all arrive at the correct destination. Fan should be happy Ethan's coming today, I thought. Surely, she would have an easier time being "proper" around someone she liked.

I walked by the drawing room where she was having her lesson and put my ear to the door.

"Your spine should be perfectly straight. Imagine a string attached to the top of your head. If someone tugs on it, it will pull you upright. No, that is not straight. If you arch your back, you are simply making your rump look even larger." I heard Roompilda sigh.

"Now suck in your stomach," she said.

"Ow. I can't stand like this."

"You've practiced your atrocious posture for too long. You'll build up the strength eventually. Shoulders down. Now, we have no interest in seeing your neck, so tuck your chin. It's more ladylike."

"My neck feels like it's on fire."

"You'll get used to it."

No wonder so many women had back problems. Perhaps I'd have to tell Fan not to follow Roompilda's posture scheme too carefully. What, me, subvert Roompilda's lessons? Never! Ha.

When they finished, finally relinquishing my sitting room, Roompilda left with no more than a disapproving once-over. Fan sat down and rubbed her neck.

"It's important to stand up straight, but I don't think what Roompilda is telling you is good for your spine," I said.

Fan shrugged miserably. "But I can't look like I'm a slouch." She changed the subject before I could argue. "Who do we have coming today?"

"Oh, good news! Ethan and his mother!"

"Really?" Fan's eyes lit up for a moment, but then she quickly bit her lip in worry. "She sort of terrifies me."

"Yes, I suspect she aims for that. But at least Ethan isn't . . ."

"Weird," Fan finished.

"Right." Apparently, the last few days had been so bizarre, Fan could say so without worrying about the fairies. I felt even the nicest fairy would have to admit the last few boys weren't the top of the lot.

For a few minutes, Fan helped me tidy the living room. Then, when I imagine she hoped enough time had passed, she said nonchalantly, "Do I look all right? I didn't really put in a lot of effort this morning."

I hid a smile and said, "I think you look lovely."

"But you would have to say that. I'll just go check. I'm not being vain, I just don't want to embarrass myself," she added with a quick glance upward, probably for the fairies' benefit.

"Whatever you want," I said.

When the Kingsleys arrived, I just tried not to listen to Mina. Fan and I stood up as she led them into the room.

"La—"

"Hthe Hkingsleys, hmadam," Mina said, sounding a little like she was preparing to spit. Apparently she'd decided to announce our guests.

"Thank you, Mina. That will be all."

Lady Kingsley raised an eyebrow as Mina flounced out of the room, full of importance. She didn't comment.

"Evelyn," she said.

"Lady Kingsley, it's good to see you," I replied.

"Didn't I tell you to call me Francesca? Regardless, you should."

"Won't you have a seat?" Fanchon said.

"Fanchon, darling, how are you?" Lady Kingsley said as she sat down. She was a surprisingly small woman, easily mistaken as frail right up until she began speaking.

"I'm doing well, thank you. How are you?"

"Oh, well, I'm alive, aren't I?"

"Good to see you, Ethan," I added.

"Thank you, Madam Radcliffe," Ethan stuttered shyly.

Lady Kingsley swatted him on the arm. "Now see, what did I say about mumbling?"

"Um, how are . . . you enjoying the Season?" Fan said. Well, she couldn't ask if they were enjoying Strachey, so she'd flipped it around.

To my surprise—well, to my mind Francesca Kingsley was always a surprise—she gave the biggest eye roll I'd ever seen. I burst out laughing.

"Do you not like it?" Fan asked.

"Come on," Francesca said to me, "you can't tell me you're not annoyed every year."

I shook my head, still laughing.

"There's not a single one of those people I want to see," she said. "And all they do is complain that they can't have everything they want."

"But you do always get a lot of donations for your foundation," Ethan said.

"Yes, well, that is the only good thing to come of the whole extravaganza."

"Is it really so bad?" Fan asked. "I thought the Courtenays' party was quite nice. I mean, the balls are all right, aren't they?"

Francesca sniffed. "I suppose if you're a young person, they might be fun. But Balser and I are hardly going to go dancing, are we?"

Mortified, Ethan gave Fan a wide-eyed grimace. She stifled a giggle.

"I'm an old woman," Francesca continued, "so instead of all the fun parts, I'm stuck with the other old women."

"And the sudden exorbitant prices. If you had to do the shopping, you'd be annoyed, too," I said to Fan.

"Ugh, it's obscene!" Francesca exclaimed. "It's a forty percent markup at least."

"At least," I echoed. "Not to mention the traffic."

"Carriages everywhere! If you've got a house at all close to the main road, you don't get any peace from the hooves."

"It's like no one from the Capital has ever heard of walking," I said.

"I don't think they have."

"They cram all those carriages into the city center and then get fussy that the traffic's not moving!" I said. "It makes me want to scream!"

Francesca nodded. "Seasonal Irritability Disorder. I get it every summer."

"You've hit on one of Mother's favorite subjects," Ethan said to Fan, leaning conspiratorially toward her.

"I'm so sorry—" Fan began, leaning in over the table toward him.

"Don't worry about it," Ethan said with a grin. "She likes to complain," he whispered loudly.

"I'm just surprised!" Fan said. "I mean, I knew my mom didn't like it, but . . ."

"I'll stop, I'll stop," Francesca said. "Don't want to grouse. There, change the subject."

There was silence as Fan thought for a moment and then frowned in panic. "Umm . . . I didn't really have anything else to talk about!"

"How's school, Ethan?" I said.

"Oh, I graduated!"

"Congratulations! What are your plans?"

"Well . . ."

"That's what I keep asking," Francesca said.

"I've been looking for jobs, of course."

"He's had some good offers in the Capital."

"That's excellent. In shipping?"

"Mostly, yeah. I'm not particularly a fan of trading shares. That feels like you're just selling people packets of air."

"Often you are," I said.

"I really like to figure out the best way to get things from place to place. From the people who make them to the people who need them, you know? That's what—for my final project, I worked out the best way for Mother's foundation to ship the relief aid to people in other kingdoms."

From my limited interactions with him, it seemed to me that Ethan Kingsley was an immensely genuine young man. After all, who went to a pretty girl's house and spoke to her mother about organizing shipping routes? No one putting on an act would choose to be a bit dull.

"Interesting," I said. "I suppose you'll be moving to the Capital, then."

"You're going to move?" Fan said suddenly, her face falling. "Permanently?"

"I don't really want to," he said. "I'd like to find a job in Strachey, but . . ."

"But there's not as many opportunities," Francesca said. "So, we'll see."

"I hope you don't have to move," Fan said, pouting.

"I hope not either," he said, and I think I caught him blushing.

We talked for a few more minutes—Fan and Ethan couldn't seem to think of anything to say, so Francesca and I traded a few Season anecdotes.

"You'll be at the garden party, won't you?" Fan asked Ethan as they were leaving.

"Of course," he said.

"Oh good! I'll see you there."

No sooner had I closed the door than Fan spoke up.

"Mom, could I get Ethan a job with Dad's company?"

"Well, probably, but—"

"Yes! What should I do? Probably write a letter. Do we have stationery?"

"Yes, but hold on, Fan. You—"

"What? He needs a job. I can get him a job!"

"You realize that he'd still have to move to the Capital, right?"

Fan visibly deflated. "Oh."

"Plus, you might want to ask him first."

Fan made a flat, tight-lipped pout and had her hands on her hips, and she looked like she had just enough self-control not to stomp her foot.

"I'm not saying it's a bad idea. I'm just saying it's probably polite to talk to him."

"Oh, fine. But if he needs my help, I am going to solve this for him!"

I pursed my lips to avoid grinning, but I'm fairly sure my eyes were dancing. I remembered back when—what did she call him? A weenie? Well, it's remarkable how you change when you really need people to be nice to you.

"Good for you," I said.

She nodded firmly and started to leave.

"Oh, I forgot to tell you—I'm not going to be home tonight," I said.

"Where are you going?"

"I've been asked to dinner by Lord Piminder," I said, trying not to sound as tense as I felt and undoubtedly failing.

Fan raised her eyebrows in surprise. She opened her mouth to reply, but instead stood for a few seconds weighing her options. Apparently, she thought better of all of them. "Okay," she said.

"Yep."

"Right then." She nodded and hurried off.

I sighed. This is work, Evelyn. Remember all those parties you went to with Fan's father, and how many dull conversations you had just to make a charming impression on his superiors? This is that. You're just going to work.

CHAPTER SIX

HE SENT A carriage for me. It had plush velvet cushions and embroidered curtains to pull across the glass. I pulled them. I didn't particularly want word to get around.

It was obviously an exceptionally nice carriage, and I'm sure I was supposed to be impressed by it. The carriage brought me through his front gates and right up to his front door, where a servant met me to usher me into the house.

I should have insisted on hiring my own carriage, I thought. Then I'd be free to leave early.

If it's that bad, Evelyn, you can walk, I told myself. It's summer. You'll be fine.

The Piminder mansion was . . . well, an architectural marvel. The servant led me into the sitting room, where one wall seemed to be made entirely of panes of glass, offering a view of a garden in full bloom. While the windows were reminiscent of an atrium, the ceiling reminded one of a church. It had those semitriangular things that I thought were called vaults and that, if I wasn't careful, Piminder would explain to me.

Lord Piminder stood when I entered the room and bowed gracefully. "Good evening, Madam Radcliffe. I am glad you came," he said, "particularly given the haste of my invitation."

"I'm afraid haste is how I run things these days. I am entirely at the mercy of my daughter's social schedule. And naturally I'm always the last informed."

He chuckled. "Dinner will be ready momentarily. Would you care to see the grounds?"

"I would love to."

The door to the courtyard led out onto a deck. We walked down the steps to a cobblestone path, which led into the garden.

"How charming," I said. A marble young lady poured water from her urn into a fountain surrounded by terraced flower beds, which contained only the very brightest flowers. They were, I thought, all bulbs—which, based on the gardening budgets I've approved, were by far the most expensive.

"Yes, you might be surprised to know that this has always been my pet project. My late wife insisted on a yew garden. But I always thought it was much more relaxing to sit among the flowers. Here."

He beckoned me to follow down the path along the side of the mansion.

"How old is this place?" I asked.

"About two hundred years, I should think. My great-grandfather built it, I am told. Much of this is the original masonry, with some repairs, of course."

"Is that a gargoyle?" I said, looking up at the roof.

He laughed. "Ah, you've found Bruno!"

"Bruno?"

"Yes, my father and his brothers named him. He's kept four generations of Piminder children tucked quietly in bed all night."

"Were you a rambunctious lot?"

"Our nurses latched onto the symbol of Bruno the Child-Eating Gargoyle with singular desperation. Or so I'm told."

I couldn't help laughing. We continued along the path to his wife's yew garden, an arrangement of bright green trees pruned into boxes, spheres, and ellipses, all popping their heads up above a manicured hedge. In the center of the garden stood a gazebo. I followed him through the gate in the hedge and into the gazebo. He gestured to me to sit.

"It's very . . . nice," I finally said after we'd stared at the trees for a while.

"It puts me on edge," he said. "Did even when she was alive. Could never put my finger on why."

"Well, I can't say it's my favorite garden ever. I think it would get to me not being able to see out."

"Yes, I've always assumed that was the problem. Seems like a waste of a good gazebo to be hedged in here."

"Although there's something about the geometric shapes. It's almost too perfect."

"You know, I believe you've hit on something. But how else would you shape the trees?"

"Well, I'd be sorely tempted to turn some of those bushes into lions."

He chuckled—I couldn't tell if he thought I was joking. I wasn't.

"I'm sure dinner is ready by now," he said. "Shall we?"

He rose and offered me his arm. I took it without thinking.

"Perhaps I'll tell the landscaper to leave a few stray leaves," he said.

To my surprise, we ate at a small table in a little nook off the kitchen. I was certain he'd try to impress me with the grandeur of the great dining hall, but we didn't even walk through it. He pulled out my chair for me and apologized just in case the meal wasn't to my liking—and then apologized for it being too boring, since he'd gone with standard fare because he didn't know my tastes. He seemed genuinely worried, as though my approval of him hinged on this one detail. I reassured him as profusely as he apologized, amused at how suddenly I was the one putting him at ease.

He told me stories, of his apparently wild youth and not at all about interior decor. He'd outsmarted an angry horse merchant abroad, making off with a horse for a third of its value in a ruse that involved not one but two chase scenes. He once made his way across the border of Gelgravitz disguised as a washerwoman in order to smuggle out a ruby the size of his fist. He was a charming storyteller, and before long I found myself telling him about business school—a topic I rarely bring up, as men find it so off-putting, but he seemed only intrigued.

It wasn't until dessert that I realized I hadn't got what I came for.

"Oh!" I said, in what I hoped was a smooth transition. "I've been meaning to ask. What was that young woman on about at the Courtenays? I missed most of the scene while I was looking for my daughter, but it's all anyone will talk about."

He waved his hand dismissively. "Just a stupid girl. Her father owes me money, and he thinks everything will be solved if she marries my son."

"How much does he owe you? Sorry, that was rude. But surely it's easier to just pay you back!"

"He does owe me some twelve thousand crowns," he said. "I imagine that's as much as his estate is worth."

More, I thought as I choked just a little on my strawberries. I wouldn't have valued the Babcock land at anywhere near that.

"Good Lord," I said. "What will you do if he cannot pay you?"

"I shall have to take him to the courts. The loan has been overdue since my father was alive. We have been lenient for a very long time."

Because you didn't even know about the loan, I wanted to shout. My distress must have shown on my face because he continued to rationalize.

"As a businesswoman, surely you understand—I must be consistent. I loan large sums to many individuals. If I were to relieve Patrick Babcock of his debt—or even to restructure it—how many of my business partners would expect the same leniency? And if I did it for everyone, I would be ruined very quickly."

He said it so calmly, so coolly. Not even a hint of empathy for the Babcocks, who he was about to chuck out on the streets.

"And your son . . . doesn't want to marry her?"

Piminder shrugged. "He is infatuated and thinks he is in love. In a year he will see he was foolish and that he could do better. You don't care for my reasoning," he said, responding to my pursed lips.

"I'm too far on the side of true love, I suppose." Which didn't really cover my position accurately at all. I was for people making their own choices and for generally not being an ass.

"If I thought this were true love, I might see it differently."

"Hmm. Well, that is a much less interesting story than I'd been led to believe. By the time it got to me, that young woman was supposed to be spinning straw into gold."

He laughed. "No, that part is true. Well." He waved his hand, acknowledging that we both knew Clarrie Babcock couldn't really spin straw into gold. "Her father said she could. God only knows what came over him. I offered to let her spin gold to cover the debt. Hopeless child."

"You're kidding. How does a person think his daughter can do that?"

"I have no idea!"

"When is her deadline?"

"Oh, I just said the end of the summer."

"No, you have to have a date! Everyone's going to want to see this. You have to let the anticipation build!"

"But surely, everyone knows she can't do it."

"She might have a fairy godmother," I said.

"Ah yes, just like your Ella."

"And now everyone in Strachey thinks that way. You've got to give the people what they want. Call Patrick Babcock's bluff."

"Hmm." He sat back and grinned, hands crossed in his lap. "Set a final date. At which point the girl will fail. Or cheat, which would make them look even worse. I won't be the villain of the story because I gave the girl a chance. And if the Babcocks thoroughly embarrass themselves, who will care if I take them to court?"

Wrong! I wanted to shout. The correct answer is "Oh no, I don't want to make a public spectacle out of completely ruining them."

Instead, I just said, "You might even lower the value she has to spin. She won't really be able to, so why not say you'll accept just five thousand crowns' worth?" Particularly because I might actually be able to pull that off.

"Oh, a magnanimous gesture! I will have to consider that," he said, chuckling. "You have quite the devious mind, madam. I suspect your husbands did not fully appreciate it."

I felt a surge of pride, a tingle of pleasure at the compliment, and immediately hated myself for it.

"I suppose I should be getting home," I said. "My daughter . . ."

"Of course. Although I will be sorry to see you go. Let me summon my carriage."

I almost said I'd walk, but I shook it off. Don't be ridiculous, Evelyn. It's dark, just take the carriage.

He walked me to the front door, and we waited for the carriage. As it pulled up, he turned to me and swiftly and gracefully took my hand.

"Thank you ever so much for coming . . . may I call you Evelyn?"

I nodded. "No, thank you," I murmured.

"Good night," he said, and gently kissed my hand.

With a wobble, I climbed into the carriage as quickly as I could, narrowly avoiding hitting my head. My entire arm felt like it was on fire, and the space just behind my ears throbbed. As the carriage took off, I couldn't help rubbing my hand on my skirt, over and over.

That was awful, I thought.

No, it wasn't, I replied. You actually enjoyed yourself, Evelyn, right up until you remembered he was a self-serving bloodsucker.

I really wanted to apologize, but to whom? Henry? I'm sorry, I thought. I'm so sorry for enjoying myself. But it didn't help. Was it really so bad to have fun? To make a connection with someone? I mean, in this case, obviously, Hugo Piminder had questionable morals at best, but in general, in theory, wasn't it good that I could feel things? Now my head was just generally starting to ache. Maybe I'd had too much to drink.

The carriage stopped, and I stepped out in front of our house, a dignified one-story with a bay window and a cheery paint job and gardens tended lovingly but without much precision. The roof had shingles now, but I still pictured it with thatching, because that's how it looked when I imagined Henry coming home. I burst into tears. I'd definitely had too much to drink.

I entered the house quietly, assuming Fan was asleep. I started a little when I saw her lying on the couch, trying to read with her book inadvisably close to her candle.

"Hi, Mom," she said.

"Hi, sorry, sweetheart. I didn't think you'd be awake."

"I waited for you. Are you all right?" she asked as I heaved a little sobbing breath.

"Hmm? Yes, I'm fine . . ."

"Mom, are you crying?"

"What? No, it's just . . ." I was obviously crying, I realized. My voice was all choked, and I couldn't stop sniffling.

"Mom, what's wrong? Sit down." She made room for me on the couch.

"Oh, don't worry—"

"Mom, I have never seen you cry in my entire life."

I sat down next to her and dug a handkerchief out of my purse. Fan looked at me like I'd grown a second head.

"Mmm, I'm just tired, and . . ."

"Did it not go well? Mom, you don't have to see him again."

"I just miss Henry," I said, knowing full well I was dodging the issue.

"Mom, that's okay. You can tell people, 'Sorry, my husband died, and I don't want to do this.' You're allowed."

"You know if Ella hadn't married the prince, and—and all that, I was this close to marrying some slobbering, ancient museum relic. He'd have turned you two into scullery maids, but he'd have kept you fed."

Fan flinched a little. "Yeah, well, none of that's a problem anymore. You don't have to save anyone, because I'm taking care of you. If Lord Piminder gives you the creeps, or if he's rude, or if it isn't enjoyable, Mom, you get to say no."

"I didn't hate him," I said, wiping my eyes. "It wasn't unenjoyable."

Fan watched me blow my nose. "Do you feel guilty?" she said finally.

Did I? Honestly, I didn't know a thing at this point. I sort of shrugged in hopelessness.

"Because I know I didn't know Henry that well, but I'm like one hundred percent sure he would say you should be happy."

Well, if he were here to say it, it'd be a moot point, wouldn't it? I thought crossly. But Fan was right, of course. You'd say I should be happy—wouldn't you, Henry? If I wanted—if I liked Hugo Piminder—

But I don't, I thought. He's loathsome. And charming. And I genuinely, genuinely liked him, and he's a horrible person.

I don't think this is about me, love, I could hear Henry say.

"I can't trust myself," I said, sobbing. "I don't trust that I'll make a good choice."

"What?" Fan said.

"You have no idea how much I loved your father when we got married," I blurted out.

Oh, idiot, I thought. Couldn't a fairy drop a load of frogs on me before I said stupid things?

Fan sort of cringed, her hand hovering near my back where she knew she probably ought to keep patting me though she mostly just wanted to run away.

"I'm sorry, sweetheart. I know you don't—it's not your job to solve my problems."

"No, if you need—" she started, knowing the right thing to say but not at all sure she wanted to say it.

"No. I'll feel better in the morning. You're right. I didn't like it that much, and I don't have to see him again. It's that simple."

She nodded, then leaned over and put her arms around me. I kissed her on the head.

"Get a good night's sleep, sweetheart."

She stood up, taking her book and candle.

"And be careful with that candle."

CHAPTER SEVEN

I THOUGHT WE would get a little break from the Season, after a week of both Roompilda's morning lessons and afternoon callers. I don't know how I got this impression—wishful thinking, probably. I was so very wrong. The next day, Roompilda arrived to chew the two of us out.

"Well, I hope the two of you are happy. Having received the reports, I can now decisively say last week was an unmitigated disaster. You," she said to Fan, "have either learned nothing from me or possess a severe deficiency in self-control."

"I know!" Fan wailed. "I'm sorry! I was nervous and those visits got so weird!"

"Wait, how are you receiving reports on us?" I said.

Roompilda just ignored me. "Those were peers of the realm, and you have the audacity to consider them bizarre?"

"In Fan's defense, one of those boys didn't speak. He silently leered at Fan for the better part of an hour."

"And the others? The one you accused of not paying taxes? The one you mercilessly mocked, for God knows what reason?" Roompilda's questions were the very epitome of pointed. She never broke eye contact, glaring at Fan over her cat-eye spectacles until I thought Fan would melt. She didn't even raise her voice.

"I didn't say he didn't pay taxes!"

"Are you asking them exactly what Fan said?"

"And you." She turned to me. "How on earth did you think you could refuse Lady Corbyn?"

I should have pressed her on how she knew all this, but now that the cat eyes had turned on me, I was compelled to defend myself.

"First, I tried to reschedule her. It's not my fault she couldn't find any other morning to come. Second, I'd also received a card from Lady Kingsley. I couldn't refuse the Kingsleys."

Roompilda sniffed in disgust. "No Strachey noble is as important as one from the Capital."

"Then why does the prince—"

"Tomorrow you will be attending the Finleighs' ball." Roompilda turned back to Fan. "The Allenby garden party is in little more than a week. All eyes will be on you, and if you fail to impress, you will never gain your standing back. You will be a drain on your stepsister rather than an asset. It is my hope that you will redeem yourself this weekend; therefore, in today's lesson I will give you a script to follow. I had assumed you had the sense to choose your own topics of conversation, but since you do not, we will not leave it up to chance. That will be all," she said to me. "We are ready to begin."

You can't just send me away! I wanted to shout. Unfortunately, I still had a headache from the night before, and I was short on comebacks, so I just stormed out.

I was about to retreat into my study and go back to sleep when I heard something drop through the mail slot. As I bent to pick up the folded note that had fallen to the floor, the pressure in my head stabbed like a dagger in my left eye. I hissed in pain and read the letter with my good eye.

It was a brief note from Clarrie.

"He's picked a date—the twenty-first, right before everyone goes back to the Capital. And he said I only had to spin seven thousand crowns' worth!"

The exclamation point had a heart instead of a dot. I breathed a sigh of relief. Last night's emotional wringer had been worth something after all.

The next day I ordered spools of thin copper wire and zincum filings. I went to two separate merchants—an inconspicuous seller of odds and ends (who made regular trips to the Capital) for the wire, and Milburn for the zincum. Not that I imagined anyone would see Clarrie's gold straw and think, "Say, wasn't that Radcliffe woman in here buying the ingredients to make brass?" But I really didn't want to take a chance.

I considered Milburn's explanation of the process. I could use lye, which was disgusting and would leave a noticeable odor in my kitchen, or a crucible, which seemed imminently preferable. He very kindly sold me one, and I went on my way.

When it came to performing the actual alchemy, I would have to find a time when Gerta, our cook, wasn't here, I realized when I got home. I would have to use the kitchen stove, and I didn't want to be seen. I could give Gerta the day off—and Mina, who would be far more curious—and I'd have to wait until Roompilda was gone, as well as get Fan out of the house. Or, I thought, I could simply work in the middle of the night.

I had only just settled down in my study with a book when Mina came and found me.

"Hmadam Hradcliffe, Hlady Hfrandsen his here to hsee Hugh."

"What?" I said. I didn't wait for Mina's explanation. I just went to the door to see for myself.

"Yoo-hoo, Evelyn!" Maribelle called out. "It's time to get ready for the ball!"

"Come in, Maribelle," I said. "Already? Thank you, Mina."

"Where's Fanchon?"

"Fanchon?" I called.

"I love your new maid! She's adorable!"

"Mm-hmm."

"I couldn't really understand what she was saying, but she looked like she takes her job so seriously!"

"Hi, Maribelle," Fanchon said as she entered.

"It's time to start! The Finleighs are so much more important than the Courtenays. I know that's an awful thing to say, but that's how the Season is!" She giggled.

I really should have anticipated that Maribelle would be cripplingly indecisive. We spent at least an hour trying on all of Fan's gowns. Just when I thought we'd narrowed it down, Maribelle would have Fan retry a dress. Then, when we'd finally settled on an ensemble, Maribelle began to dither over painting a little rouge on Fan's cheeks.

"Mom, I think my bodice needs to be tighter," Fan said when Maribelle had finally stepped back from her face.

"What? No, it doesn't."

"Roompilda said it has to be too tight to fit your fingers in underneath."

"That's ridiculous. You're supposed to be able to fit two fingers."

"Ooh, not anymore," Maribelle said. "Not for the young women."

"Fine." This was probably going to lead to Fan passing out, but apparently, she was going to have to make this mistake herself. "Hold on to the bedpost."

"Now, we have to decide what to do with your hair," Maribelle said as I gave the laces a massive tug. Fan gasped. Don't inhale, I thought. You won't be able to breathe out.

"But I did do my hair!"

"Oh, I'm sorry, love!" Maribelle cried. "But for something like this, it's got to be more complicated than piling it on your head."

"I can't do anything more complicated! Not to myself. Can you do hair?"

Maribelle froze, cringing.

"Well, what do I do?" Fan asked in a panic.

"Ooh, I'm so sorry! Here, I can . . ." Maribelle fretted, hands hovering over Fan's head. I noticed no one asked me.

"I can do hair!"

I turned around to see Mina's head peeking around the door. She'd been eavesdropping shamelessly, I realized. Oh well.

"Can you?" I said, more skeptically than was polite.

"Oh!" Maribelle laughed. "I can't believe you forgot you had a ladies' maid!"

That's because I don't, I thought.

Mina pranced into the room, grinning with pride. She looked at Fan's reflection in the mirror and tapped her chin.

"I think we shall do . . . a half-twist Winsom knot chignon with a triple tuck."

I just covered my eyes and whimpered.

Well, as much as I was sure Mina was just stringing random words together, she could, apparently, style hair. Not even in my wildest imaginations had I pictured us getting out the door, but somehow, we found ourselves at the top of the stairs leading into the grand ballroom of the Finleighs' massive estate.

"Ooooh!" Maribelle squealed. "I just love this! The first real ball of the Season! Isn't it exciting? The lights are so beautiful, all the people are so beautiful! Even the smells are beautiful! And just imagine, the garden party will be ten times more beautiful!"

Fan looked out at the crowd and turned a little green.

"Now, this gentleman is going to introduce us, and then we get to go in. I wonder if my husband already went in."

"Can't I just sneak in?" Fan whispered.

Maribelle giggled. "Of course not! Excuse me, did you already introduce Lord Frandsen? Oh, you probably don't remember. Hmm, I didn't really look for him in the foyer."

Maribelle wrung her hands, craned her neck, and started spinning around much too quickly to spot her husband—even as he approached us from where he'd undoubtedly been waiting in the foyer.

"Maribelle! Maribelle," he said, waving at her. I put an arm on her shoulder and pointed.

"Oh!" She burst out laughing. "There you are!"

"Here I am? I've been waiting for you for an hour."

"Oh no! Well, it's actually a funny story . . ."

He took her arm and strode toward the steward, while she practically had to run to avoid being yanked off her feet. She still didn't stop talking.

"Lord and Lady Frandsen," the steward announced.

I motioned to Fan to follow. She reached tentatively for my arm, but I shook my head.

"Miss Fanchon Envers," the steward said as she walked down the stairs. "And Mother."

Well, I've had worse introductions.

"Ooh, now there are so many people to introduce you to, I can't decide where to start!" Maribelle was telling Fan as I reached the bottom of the stairs.

"Urrnggh." Her husband let out a strangled grunt and walked away, giving Maribelle a half-hearted wave.

"I think . . . no, maybe—do we want to meet people in the ballroom or people by the punch?"

"Regardless, I think we shouldn't block the bottom of the stairs," I said.

"Oh yes. Evelyn's so sensible."

Maribelle shuffled us toward a corner and we surveyed the ballroom. I swear I really was watching the crowd, but I was still surprised when a familiar figure emerged.

"There you are," Roompilda said. Good Lord, the woman was a cat! I wouldn't have thought a woman with such vibrant red hair could somehow hide from notice, but she managed to fit right between servant and noble—too drab and uncharismatic to be important, but poised and self-assured enough that no one would dare ask her where the toilets were.

She looked Fan up and down. "Satisfactory," she said. "You will go into the hall, that way, and immediately enter the room to your left. The young ladies there will introduce themselves. You will remember what we spoke of and say only the things I told you to say."

Fan nodded. Roompilda pointed toward the hall. Fan swallowed hard and set off, giving me a shy wave. I tried to smile encouragingly, fighting the impulse to kick Roompilda in the shins. I wouldn't have had a chance anyway. She melded back into the crowd as soon as Fan left.

"Who was that?" Maribelle ventured.

"A tutor," I said. "The queen sent her."

"Ooooooh . . ."

I spent most of my time hiding in a corner. I couldn't help imagining what this would be like if Henry were here. He would have made me be sociable, and then I would have tried to make him laugh, which was altogether too easy. Without him, I just stood there.

It wasn't until I caught sight of Hugo Piminder that I was suddenly inspired to move. I didn't think I could pull a Roompilda, so I pushed through the crowd into the hallway. I peeked into the room on the left but saw no sign of Fan. She could be dancing. We'd kept up our dancing lessons, and I think she'd improved some. She wouldn't be stepping on toes, at least.

I wandered through the Finleighs' parlors and halls, hoping Lord Piminder hadn't spotted me. I seemed mostly invisible to everyone else. I had no reason to be there, unless Fan needed me, at which point I would suddenly pop into existence. As I considered this, I came to a shocking realization: I'd spent most of my life being someone's wife.

It was how I'd always looked at myself. For years, I'd been the hated, unhappy wife of Bertram Envers. I'd been Henry's behind-the-scenes partner-wife. But neither of those identities were current, and so I'd latched on to being Fan's mom. And now she was very nearly grown-up, and I didn't know how to just be me.

I was so lost in my thoughts, I forgot to keep moving, and when you're trying to avoid someone, standing still is sudden death.

"Evelyn! I wondered if you'd be here this evening," Lord Piminder said, bowing as he approached. Drat.

"Yes, I'm here with Fanchon."

"I took your advice."

"Oh?"

"Yes, I told Miss Babcock that I would consider it sufficient if she spun a much lower sum of gold."

"Ah. That is more sporting of you," I said.

"Can you believe she is here trying to impress me tonight?"

In fact, I could, since that's what I'd told her to do. Well, I actually wanted her to impress everyone else, but neither of them needed to know that.

"Impress you how?"

"Manners, I think. She's the very picture of polite conversation."

"Maybe that's just how she is," I said.

"And somehow, in an estate full of people, her conversations always happen to be within earshot of me."

"Well, she's in love with your son. She wants to prove she'd be a good wife."

"Have you met her? She's so utterly ordinary it's dreary. Even if her father wasn't trying to get out of his debt, I wouldn't allow the marriage. Can you imagine her in my family home?"

I was stung by how superficial his response was. First of all, Clarrie wasn't ordinary or dreary; she was independent and brave and charming. Furthermore, she was the type he ought to imagine in his estate, as she was too sensible to squander his fortune. That aside, he was judging her solely on some first impression. She hadn't dazzled him with wealth or beauty, so why should he spend any more time on her?

He must have noticed I was offended. "It's all a moot point, anyway. She's not in love. The Babcocks are money-grubbers. You may put your delicate mind at ease." God, I was so glad he was showing his true patronizing colors so quickly.

"But you're sending them to the poorhouse! That's cruel!" I said, not listening to the inner voice telling me not to engage.

"Ah, yes. Women always choose mercy over justice. Am I really supposed to reward their delinquency? When they've had years to pay their due?"

"But you didn't even know they owed you!" I exclaimed. The second the words were out of my mouth, I realized my mistake. I wasn't supposed to know that.

He looked confused, and it was only a matter of time before the dissonance resolved itself.

"That's what you said the other night," I lied. "You didn't realize your father had extended the loan until years later. Under such circumstances, couldn't you afford a little mercy?"

"But . . . I don't see how the length of time . . . ," he stuttered, part of his mind still insisting that he hadn't told me any such thing. If I could just make my escape quickly . . .

"Um, excuse me, madam?" A young woman approached me and curtsied, halting our debate before it got started. "Are you Fanchon's mother?"

"Yes. Is everything all right?"

"She said she needed help and to come get you."

"Where is she? Sorry," I said to Lord Piminder. I didn't pay attention to his response; I just followed the girl. If Fanchon had sent someone to hunt me down in a ballroom this crowded . . . well, it didn't have to be serious, but that's where my mind immediately leapt.

"She's in the ladies' washroom," she said, giving me directions.

When I reached the toilets, I had to push my way through the line of affronted women.

"I'm not cutting, I'm not cutting. Fan?" The Finleighs had taken your standard wooden bench with holes and separated them into little individual seats, surrounded by curtains. A clever way to add some privacy, but it meant I couldn't see Fan.

"There's a line, you know," one woman complained.

"Fan?"

"Mom?"

I hurried toward her voice. She held the curtain open an inch for me.

"I don't think I'll fit in there with you, sweetheart." Here we came to the main flaw of the washroom's design: there wasn't really room for women's skirts in the cubicles. They'd probably been designed by a man. "What's wrong?"

She tried to step back, wedging herself into the stall without tripping over the bench. I fit most of my right side in and assessed the situation. She looked paler than usual, her eyes wet.

"Sweetheart, what happened?"

"Every one of those boys asked me to dance. Damian, Herb, and Justice. And I really liked dancing with the first two. They were really polite. But then Justice wanted to dance a waltz, so he had his hand on my waist, and he kept . . . he kept moving it down to my—my hip."

Fan started to cry. I, on the other hand, had developed a taste for blood.

"And when it was done, I told Rena—she's one of the girls—and she said it meant he liked me, but it made me nervous, so I ate like three eclairs, and I forgot I wasn't supposed to eat that much. So then, I know that some girls when they eat too much they make themselves gag and throw it back up, so I came here to the toilets, and I tried, but my bodice makes it so I can't bend over, and I made a mess, and I think there might be sick on my dress, but I can't bend over to see it! And I'm really embarrassed and my ribs hurt."

You've got to take care of Fanchon before you can behead anyone, I told myself.

"All right, sweetheart. You're all right. I'm going to find a damp cloth for you." She'd tried to clean up after herself with her handkerchief, but that had only gone so far. I wet a cloth and wiped her face. Then I examined the front of her dress, dabbing at a few spots.

"I think you're all right, love. It's not as bad as you think." There was a spot on her shoe of—look, the lighting was dim and I didn't examine it that carefully. I wiped it up.

"It was really bad before you got here. I was worried May wasn't going to be able to find you."

"I wish I'd known you were in trouble, darling. I'd have said three eclairs weren't so bad."

She cracked a small smile amid the sniffles.

"Do you want to go home?"

She nodded.

"All right. Well, you're all cleaned up. Let's go find Maribelle and have her get the carriage."

We worked our way back to the ballroom. Fan kept her head down, and as we hit the mass of people, she tried to hide her face in my shoulder. My instincts said Maribelle would be at the punch bowl and dessert table, and sure enough, she was. I told her Fan wasn't feeling well, and before long, we were sitting quietly in a carriage, riding away from the hubbub.

Fan had nestled up against me, still crying. I, on the other hand, was imagining hunting Justice Farthingbras down. When I got my hands on that little—

No, Evelyn, I stopped myself. This is your fallback. It's where you always go when you're heartbroken. Sure, he's a scumbag, but feeling angry is just putting off feeling devastated for Fan. How could a few parties be such disasters?

"Shh," I said, rubbing her shoulder. And then I remembered one more question. "Fan, why were you worried about how much you ate? You're very healthy."

"It's in style to be really skinny. Roompilda said I had to lose weight."

This time, no inner voice tried to calm me down.

CHAPTER EIGHT

"HOW DARE YOU tell my daughter to lose weight?" I shouted.

As usual, Roompilda had arrived for Fan's lesson in the morning, brushing past Mina and into the sitting room. I was waiting for her.

Roompilda exhaled sharply in a way that said she was disappointed to have to explain this to me.

"That's dangerous!" I said. "It's dangerous for her to be purging, and it's dangerous for her to starve herself! Not to mention she's perfectly healthy!"

"I am simply doing my job, which I'll remind you is to make her attractive at court."

"No, it isn't! Your job was to help her learn how to present herself."

"Surely I don't have to tell you that physical appearance matters in your presentation at court? Your daughter is slightly too thick to be considered attractive, and—"

"Enough! Just get out. Get out!"

"May I remind you who sent me?" Roompilda said in understated indignation.

"You may. Is the queen really going to force a tutor on my daughter? Doesn't she have better things to do? We're done. I never should have accepted your 'help' in the first place. You've done nothing but browbeat my daughter into someone she's not! We are done with your meddling. Go."

I thought I caught a smirk on Roompilda's face as she marched out the door. I chalked it up to her supercilious self-importance.

Fan met me in the hallway after I'd slammed the door on Roompilda. Her eyes were puffy and a little red, like she'd been crying again this morning.

"I'm so sorry, sweetheart. I should have known from the beginning. I never should have let her in the house."

Fan shrugged, which I hoped meant she wasn't blaming me.

"I'll get you out of this. If you don't want to keep this up, I'll write the queen and tell her . . . I don't know, but I'll make something up."

Fan thought for a second and shrugged again. "I can keep going. For Ella."

"And you don't need lessons. You've always known how to be popular. You used to work a party so well, I'd send Henry to follow you around and make sure you didn't get into trouble. You're probably rusty. God knows I am. All those fake smiles and gabbing about hairstyles—I haven't done it in ages. We both just need to warm up."

She looked at me with tear-filled eyes. "But I can't do that anymore. It's all gossip and making fun. No one actually liked me then, either. No one really likes anybody. It's all talking behind someone's back, and I don't . . . I don't really want to deserve that kind of luck."

Oh, those stupid frogs! For a brief moment, I wanted to tell her there were no fairies, and she didn't need to limit what she said. But that wouldn't help her feel better, I thought. What would I tell her—that the frogs were an accident and that she can gossip and backstab as much as she liked? That wouldn't be a relief. She'd still feel like a terrible person.

"But I figure, it doesn't really matter if people like me," she continued. "I just need the title so that I can visit Ella. I'll muddle through."

She turned to leave, then stopped and said, "Thanks for yelling at Roompilda, though."

"Anytime, love. My pleasure."

My copper and zincum arrived a few days later. After Fanchon had fallen asleep, I sneaked downstairs to the kitchen. I poured a bed of zincum filings in the crucible, wound some of the copper wire on top, and covered it with more zincum.

With my crucible prepared, I turned to the oven. I started the fire and let it burn for a few minutes to heat the bricks. Then I scraped out the coals, mopped the floor of the oven to create a little steam, and stuck the crucible inside before the bricks had a chance to cool down.

Then I waited. My mother had tried to teach me to bake when I was young; among the many reasons I had failed was that I couldn't stand waiting. I'd try to peek at my creation every few seconds, which only released all the heat. I was only marginally better as an adult. After several very long minutes, I opened the oven door, turning my face as the heat hit me, and realized I didn't have a way to remove the crucible from the staggeringly hot oven.

I searched the kitchen, which had been sensibly furnished by Gerta. Leaning against one wall was our peel, a rectangular board attached to a long handle. I grabbed the peel and used it like a broom to push the crucible out of the oven. I hadn't prepared a bucket of water like I was supposed to, so I grabbed two potholders, took the lid off the crucible, then ran and dumped the contents in the basin of dirty dishwater.

Coughing and spluttering, I had to stagger back as the steam enveloped me so that I could take a breath. When the air was finally clear, I used a set of tongs to remove the copper wire from the dishwater. I'll admit, my heart leapt when I saw a golden gleam. I sort of wanted to squeal. This could work, I thought. This could fool people. It wouldn't fool Lord Piminder, but he wasn't really my target.

I breathed a sigh of relief. Experiment successful. I couldn't do the whole batch now—I needed a better system, obviously, or I was going to light myself on fire—but I knew it would work, and it might even look good. I cleaned up the kitchen, with the exception of the dishwater. I'd have to dump that down the drain in the floor, and knowing me, I'd do it so loudly it would wake up Fan. I took my gold straw back to my bedroom and went to sleep.

It wasn't until the light of day that I noticed the patches: copper patches, specifically. The gleaming brass was mottled with reddish spots, where the zincum apparently hadn't bonded to the wire. It was with considerable annoyance that I hoisted that basin of dirty water and tipped it over into the drain. That meant I'd have to try it with lye, which would stink to high heaven and require thick gloves and a set of pans and basins that could never, ever be used for food preparation.

I bought lye from the lady who makes soaps, and tins and gloves and a new basin in the market.

"Is that a new basin?" Fan said when I arrived home with my purchases.

"I thought the old one was looking a little shabby," I said.

"Did you walk home with all that?"

"Yes." Which, coincidentally, might explain why I'd come home so cross.

"You should have hired a carriage!"

"This time of year? None available."

"Mom, do you know what's happening with Clarrie Babcock? At the ball the other night, I heard someone saying she was going to spin straw into gold, like in the stories."

"Ah. Well, Clarrie and Terence Piminder want to get married, but Lord Piminder won't agree to it. Lord Babcock, in trying to persuade Lord Piminder, said that Clarrie could spin straw into gold. Now Lord Piminder has said he will allow the marriage if Clarrie can prove it."

"Is that why you didn't like him very much?"

"I found him to be quite kind and gallant to me and borderline cruel to the Babcocks. So, yes."

"It's not fair that he's planning on humiliating her. It's not her fault her father lied. I've heard how the girls are talking. She's going to be a laughingstock!"

"Unless her fairy godmother shows up."

Fan scrunched up her nose. "That would be the last story I'd want to have happen to me."

"Why?" Oh God, did this have a bad ending? Weren't these all about young women who had fairies come in and solve their problems? The fairy turns the straw into gold, the end. Right?

"The girl is locked in the tower or cellar or whatever," Fan explained. "And she can't spin the straw into gold, so she's crying and this little man shows up and says he'll do it if she gives him things."

"Wait, what?"

"I know, right? This little tiny man just appears in the cellar with her."

"What, exactly, does she have to give him?" Oh Lord, this could go so, so wrong.

"The first two are jewelry, like her ring and her bracelet or something."

"And then?"

"The last time she promises him her firstborn child. But then she gets it back because he gives her three chances to guess his name, and I think she figures it out by eavesdropping or something."

I—well, I didn't quite breathe a sigh of relief. But it certainly could have ended so much worse.

"Well, I certainly hope Clarrie doesn't get a—is he a fairy? I hope no bargaining little men show up in her spinning room."

"I know, right? Um, Mom, also while you were gone I got an invitation to go to the derby with Herb . . . um . . . and I accepted."

"Oh!"

"I thought I should give him another chance. Since I wasn't that nice to him."

"If you want to go, sweetheart, that's fine with me."

"I do. He was very nice to me at the ball. He was interesting to talk to—he knows so many important people! And I would like to go out."

I didn't think it was a good idea myself, but no one had asked my opinion, so I kept my mouth shut. It was the hardest balance for me to keep. I so wanted to protect her from making bad choices, but I couldn't always tell her what to do. At least Herb hadn't struck me as particularly dangerous. He was an ambitious name-dropper with an eye on acquisitions, but a rather transparent one.

"Well, I'm sure you'll have fun. The derby is exciting."

She nodded and went quietly back to her room. I sighed. Even when she wanted to do something, she wouldn't let herself get excited about it. She'd lost nearly every ounce of cheer or vibrancy since this whole thing started. We'd just worked back from a total loss of self-confidence, and as soon as the summer was over, we'd have to start all over again. And here I'd thought this would be harmless.

Later that night, I snuck back down to the kitchen. This time, I opened the window before I started, I pumped water into the old basin and set it next to the stove, and I kept the peel at the ready. I'd also filled a smaller tub with water so that I could dissolve the lye. I strapped on the gloves, and—oh, I probably should have worn some sort of spectacles to protect my eyes. Well, I'd have to be very careful not to splash.

Milburn had said to swirl the zincum in the lye solution and heat it gently, so I started the oven while the lye dissolved, then let it cool as I stirred the zincum filings into the lye. I let the mixture warm for a minute or two, then pushed it out of the oven with the peel and put my strands of copper wire in the tub. Then, unfortunately, I had to wait.

It was too dark for me to read. I had a lantern so I could see what I was doing, but that was hardly enough light to see a book. I didn't dare go to sleep, as I'd just wake up in the morning with a tub of lye at my feet. I fidgeted for a few minutes, checking my wire every few seconds until it had changed from reddish-brown to silver.

Now it was time to let the fire roar. I lit another fire, scraped out the coals, and immediately inserted a flat pan with my silvery wires.

I waited nervously until it was time to push the pan out of the oven with the peel. With a set of tongs, I plunged the wires into the basin. When the steam had settled, I examined a wire in the lantern light. It certainly looked gold to me. Fingers crossed, I thought. I cleaned up and went to bed.

As soon as the sun was up, I grabbed the gold wire from my nightstand. My pulse quickened as I searched the wires for imperfections, any red or silver giveaways that would ruin the spectacle before it got started. I found none. I had a lovely, gleaming gold sheen on a piece of wire that sure, didn't look much like straw but would to a crowd of people longing for a fairy miracle. I wanted to shout for joy, but I contented myself with a whispered cheer.

I was remarkably cheerful all morning for a person who'd hardly slept the last two nights. If I just did a small batch of wire every night, I'd easily have it all finished. In fact, Lord Piminder had given Clarrie enough time that I could probably give myself a night off now and then.

Now I needed to work out where Clarrie would spin the gold. Fan had said that in the story, the girl was locked in a tower or cellar, which would work beautifully. If we simply spread the word that Clarrie was going to be shut in the Babcocks' cellar, everyone could gather to wait for her to emerge.

Of course, then I'd have to get the straw into the cellar. I didn't fancy my chances of sneaking in armloads of wire while Clarrie was asleep, and I certainly didn't want to play the voice of her fairy godmother. I felt rather lucky my squeaky fairy voice had worked on Ella. One thing I was certain of: there would definitely be no little men bartering with Clarrie. I wasn't exactly sure what message that story sent, but it wasn't one I supported—I was sure of that. Besides, I'd have to resort to puppetry, and that had disaster written all over it.

By late morning, Fan had left for the derby. She'd seemed quite excited—she was quite pleased with her hat, and she gushed about what a beautiful warm day it was—but she stiffened when Herb

Relish knocked on the door. However, as soon as he complimented how exquisite she looked in her outfit, she beamed.

After she left, I headed over to the Babcocks. They'd gone to the derby, so one of their servants showed me their cellar and let me be. As soon as I saw it, I realized the flaw in my plan. Like most cellars, it was simply a small room with only one entrance. Clarrie would have to be practically unconscious not to catch me sneaking downstairs with a sack of brass wire.

I wandered the Babcocks' grounds, looking for inspiration. They did have a barn, I noted, and in addition to the front door, it also had a large back window. I walked around the back of the barn. That window was too high for me to climb through, but I could still lower the bundle of wire in if I had a winch . . .

"Evelyn," I could hear Henry saying, "are you sure you're not going a little bit overboard? It's your decision, of course, but this is a lot of effort . . ."

Well, the Babcocks are in considerable trouble, I thought, but yes, a pulley system is probably too complicated.

The one good thing about a barn, I suddenly realized, was that as a barn, it was probably full of straw. I could hide the gold wire in the straw well before Clarrie entered. I'd need a way for her to discover it, and I'd need the timing to work out, but right now, that seemed like my best option.

On my way home, I also stopped by the booksellers. Perhaps, I thought, it was time to read a few of these fairy stories. They had a lovely selection, a shelf practically bursting with pink. Some books left your hand coated in glitter; others had brightly colored illustrations of cherubic princesses and little ribbon bookmarks in the colors of the rainbow. There were some, of course, that seemed to be for boys and were only about knights, dragons, and animals. And a select few were for adults—preserving the record, I suppose, of how these fairy stories went when they were first written down.

I chose one of these more grown-up volumes and flipped it open. Good God, the stepsisters in "The Little Cinder Girl" really did have their eyes plucked out! As did a prince, it turns out, who fell into thorny brambles. And one stepmother tries to eat her two grandchildren! These stories were much, much more interesting than I'd been led to believe. If the girls at finishing school had mentioned plots like these, I might have read them. But this was never how Fanchon or Ella or Maribelle had told the stories.

Which meant, I thought with a sinking feeling, that this book wasn't exactly going to help my business. No one wants a fairy story where someone claps hot irons on your stepmother's feet and makes her dance. Not in real life anyway. Instead, I chose a pink tome with illustrations and gold leaf lettering on the cover, delicately crafted from hopes and dreams. I could always come back for the gruesome versions, I told myself.

When I returned home, I spent a pleasant afternoon snipping wire and dividing the straws into batches. I'd just retrieved my calendar and was scheduling the batches when I heard a commotion at the front of the house.

"Miss Fanchon, are you all right?" I thought I heard Mina say. I didn't detect a trace of affectation. Oh dear.

I hurried toward the door. Was one success too much to ask? Apparently, yes. I reached the sitting room to find Fan sobbing on the couch, while Ethan Kingsley sat next to her with a hand on her back. He looked—well, he looked intensely uncomfortable, but on the scale of men's reactions to women crying, he fell close to the average.

"What happened?" I asked, sitting across from them on the edge of the center table.

"Some lunatic yelled at her," Ethan said.

"What?"

"I didn't hear what he said," Ethan answered as Fan continued to sob. "I just saw him yelling and went to see what was happening, but I got there too late to hear anything."

"Fan, sweetheart. What happened?"

"He called me Dad's devil spawn!" she said, each word punctuated with giant sniffs. "He said he should have expected Dad to have his own devil spawn running around and that I was just like him because I was trying to elbow my way into the upper class where I didn't belong so that I could leech the life out of everyone in my path."

"Whoa," Ethan muttered.

I was so enraged I was at a loss for words. For at least the third time in as many days, heat seemed to fill my head, putting a stop to all rational thought. The Season, I thought, is not good for my health. I sputtered for a minute.

"I can't—How—Mmmn—How old was he?"

Fan shrugged. "Probably your age, I think."

"A grown man shouting filth like this at a young woman in broad daylight? And he just came up to you and started screaming?"

Fan shook her head. "Herb introduced me to him. I think Herb works with him?"

"And Herb didn't say anything?"

"He—he ran after him. Maybe he told him he was being rude?"

Even Fan didn't believe that. My experience with Herb the name-dropper told me he'd run off to apologize. The disdain on Ethan's face told me he figured the same thing.

"I just don't see why he would do that," Fan said. "Why would he hate Dad so much that he would do that to me?"

Unfortunately, that was a question with some easy answers. The hard part would be narrowing them down. But I'd never seen any reason why Fan had to know all her father's worst qualities. He was good to her, and I didn't think she needed me to ruin that.

"Sweetheart, your father was very successful. That can make people love you or hate you . . ."

"Mom, his face was inches away from me. He looked like he wanted to hit me! He didn't just hate Dad because he was rich. I want to actually know."

I sighed. "Do you remember his name?"

"Yes. Lord Boscomb. I made sure I would remember his name."

Ah.

Recognition must have shown on my face. "So you know him?" Fan asked.

"I—yes," I said.

"Then why does he hate me?"

I hesitated for a moment. I knew I couldn't tell Fan the truth. She didn't need to know everything about her father. But I had to say something, quickly, or she would see right through me. Fortunately for me, Ethan took my hesitation as directed toward him. He had a point—you didn't air this kind of dirty laundry in front of others.

"I should probably go," he said.

"Thank you, Ethan."

"Um, let me know if you need anything," he told Fan.

"Give your mother my best," I said.

As soon as he left, Fan fixed her eyes on me. "What happened?"

"Lord Boscomb's business failed—I suppose you would have been quite young when it happened. There were rumors that your father had caused the business to fail because Lady Boscomb had allegedly passed insider information along to your father in an effort to . . . flirt with him. Apparently, Lord Boscomb believed all the rumors."

As rumors go, those had been fairly on the mark. And *flirt* was a significant understatement.

I expected Fan to call me out, to ask me if the rumors were true. Instead, she latched on to a different part of the story.

"Wait, did Dad cheat on you?"

"I—I don't know," I lied. He did. I knew. "Your father was very public, very charming, and very polarizing. There was an awful lot of gossip flying around. I never had any evidence for any of it."

"Why didn't you do something?"

"You can't stop gossip, sweetheart. If I'd told people to stop, it would only have gotten worse."

"No, I mean why didn't you get a divorce? If you weren't happy, why didn't you leave?"

Her question stunned me momentarily. She'd never asked me this before. I assume she'd always believed that if I wasn't happy, it was my fault. And even though she was starting to suspect that her father might have shouldered at least some of the blame, I couldn't very well dump the full weight of her father's misdeeds on her.

"My father died when you were very young," I said. "He barely left enough money for my mother, let alone me. If I'd left your father, I'd have had very little, and because of that, I was worried that your father would argue—probably successfully—that he should have custody of you. And I wasn't going to let that happen."

I paused. I'd rehearsed that explanation to myself for—well, for nearly twenty years—and I'd always felt so sure of it, like I'd thought everything through and I'd come to the only possible conclusion. Now that I'd said it out loud, it felt hollow. Would I accept this as an excuse from her?

"Anyway, I'm very sorry that idiot took it out on you today. You're not your father, obviously. It had nothing to do with you."

She nodded slowly, her tears finally starting to dry. As she stood up, I opened my arms and she hugged me tightly. She walked back to her bedroom, head down and shoulders a little hunched, and for a really, really brief moment I missed the Fan that would have told me I was stupid.

CHAPTER NINE

THE DAY OF the garden party began bright and early. Maribelle arrived with the gowns we'd had designed for Fan. Maribelle believed every dress was equally perfect, and Fan had lost all confidence that any of them looked good, and since no one would listen to my opinions on fashion, the decision-making process was agonizing.

When we'd finally settled on a gown and I saw Maribelle reach into her cosmetic purse, I opened the door and hustled Mina into the room.

"Just let Mina take care of it," I said. I didn't care if Mina had never touched rouge in her life, as long as Maribelle was outside the chain of command.

"Now, after we get there," Maribelle said, sitting on Fan's bed, "we'll have to wait a little bit, but you shouldn't go very far because Lady Allenby will call all the first-year debutantes to her so that she can present you. She'll blow a big horn—well, she won't blow it, but someone will—and then you'll all gather around, and she'll have you line up, and she'll read your name and your sponsor, and then you'll step forward and curtsy. Then they'll have the debutante dance, where all the first-year girls dance with the first-year boys—and sometimes some second-year boys, if there aren't enough. Or some second-year girls, I suppose, if there aren't enough boys . . ."

The longer Maribelle prattled, the more Fan's brow furrowed and her lips tensed. I waited for Maribelle to take a breath and changed the subject.

"So, Maribelle—how about Clarrie Babcock?"

"Oh my goodness, I know! Can you believe it? I can't believe Lord Piminder is going to make the poor girl try to spin straw into gold! Where would he even get the idea?"

"I heard that her father told him she could," I said.

Maribelle scrunched her nose in confusion. "Why?"

"I think he just panicked. Said the first thing that came into his head."

She nodded knowingly. "It's just so sad. Clarrie's going to be humiliated, just because of true love."

"Well, I'm not sure. I think Clarrie's a perfect candidate for a fairy godmother."

Maribelle brightened, but then immediately frowned. "Ooh, I don't know. You don't think that little man is going to show up, do you? What was his name?"

"I can never remember," Fan said. "I think it might be a different name depending on the book you read."

"That story makes me just a teensy bit uncomfortable," Maribelle admitted quietly.

"I don't think it has to be him," I said.

"If I was that girl," Mina said, "I'd tell him, 'You can't have my child, you greedy bugger. I've already given you my jewelry, now spin me that gold before I bash your head with my spindle!'"

Maribelle was speechless.

"I just think there's no reason Clarrie couldn't get a nice fairy," I said.

When we arrived at the Allenby estate, Fan immediately headed over to the dance floor.

"I'll just wait there," she said. "That way I'm already there when she calls us."

Maribelle flitted away to make idle small talk, and rather uncharacteristically, I decided to make a little myself, although my conversations would be more strategic than idle.

The first woman I found was the mother of another young
debutante.

"Have you heard about Clarrie Babcock?" I asked.

"The poor girl! I always knew Piminder was heartless."

"Do you think she has a fairy godmother?"

"Oh, wouldn't that be wonderful! She might actually spin straw
into gold!"

"I'd almost pay to see that, wouldn't you? See her come out of the
tower or barn or wherever with an armful of gold?" I hinted.

"Ooh, yes. What if we all lined up at dawn to wait for her? Cheer
her on!"

Success number one, I thought.

"I just hope . . ." The woman hesitated. "Well, do you think that
little wrinkled man is the one who will help her? It's just that the
illustrations always make him look repulsive."

Every woman I talked to said the same thing. They'd be eager to
watch Clarrie present her gold, then they'd suddenly remember this
ghoulish little gnome.

"That fairy story is repugnant," an older veteran of the Season
said. "I don't know who that girl was, but she should have rejected
his help and accepted her fate."

"I don't see why he has to be the one to help Clarrie."

"It's unseemly, that's what it is."

"But isn't that all the more reason we should be standing by to
watch the proceedings?" I pled.

A newlywed noblewoman told me, "Oh, short of an actual wicked
fairy, I think he's the worst one to get! Poor Clarrie!"

"But maybe she'll get a good fairy godmother! Who says it has to be him?" I tried to be cheerful.

"I don't know . . ."

"Isn't the girl in the story a little bit lazy? And doesn't her father brag about how great she is at spinning?" The latter was true, the former wasn't, according to my storybook, so I took a little artistic license. "Clarrie isn't a bit lazy! And her father panicked. He wasn't trying to boast. I think they could get a really nice fairy."

"That's a good point. I certainly hope so!"

"I imagine nearly all of Strachey will be there to watch when she presents the gold, just to see if a fairy came!" I said.

"But if it isn't that greedy little man, will it still be a real fairy story?" said a particularly stubborn partygoer.

"Well, Clarrie Babcock can't spin straw into gold on her own, but obviously, if she comes out with an armful of gold, we'll know there were fairies involved."

"But then it isn't the same story," she argued.

"Clarrie isn't the same girl! It's already different."

"I just don't know if it counts if it doesn't go exactly like the story."

Count? Count how? What sort of convoluted logic . . . I sighed.

"Then don't you think we'd better be there to decide?"

Before I could start another conversation about that stupid little disturbing man-fairy, Lady Allenby's horn sounded, although I missed who was actually blowing it.

I wove my way through the crowd until I had a front-row vantage. Lord Allenby's garden wasn't at capacity yet; fashionably late often meant after the presentation of the new debutantes. The crowd consisted mainly of mothers and a few fathers sizing up the new arrivals. Every time Lady Allenby read a new name, some of the noblewomen would lean over and whisper something to a son or daughter, who would respond back with a nod or a shrug or, occasionally, a sneer.

I scanned the crowd for any of Fan's callers. Sure enough, I caught a glimpse of Lady Farthingbras watching Justice. I was still craning my neck to see the Relishes or the Rundles when I heard, "Miss Fanchon Envers, sponsored by Lady Maribelle Frandsen!"

I saw Fan step forward—her knees looked like they were probably shaking—and curtsy. When she stepped back, I quickly surveyed the crowd again. She was getting a few whispers here and there, and I thought I saw some boys nodding to their mothers. A good result. I wasn't going to approve of anyone who would pick my daughter off a menu, obviously, but a moderate level of popularity was for the best. I wanted her to have some hope of making friends, even if the Season had been a modest disaster so far.

Eventually the dance started, and I held my breath for the first few measures. Just don't fall over, I thought. Or step on someone, or get lost and just stand there. Luckily, she'd been assigned a partner even clumsier than she, so by comparison she was like a ballerina. I breathed a sigh of relief.

Since none of the dancers were truly bad enough to get tangled up and pull all the others down, the whole thing started to drag on. I fidgeted and watched the crowd. First, I noticed that hardly anyone paid attention to the dancers. Only a very few of the more sentimental mothers were watching, with tears in their eyes. Second, my eyes eventually caught a glimpse of a blazon of red hair moving through the crowd.

Roompilda. What was she doing here? I'd sent her away. Did she have other clients here? Determined not to let her vanish into the multitude this time, I started following.

"Excuse me, pardon me," I whispered.

She hadn't left the crowd of dance watchers, but she was moving deeper in, past the line of family and dear friends and into the ranks of appraising mothers, many of whom were now grumbling as I bumped into them and blocked their view.

"I beg your pardon!" said an affronted nobleman after I'd run into his shoulder.

"Sorry," I muttered, although I didn't think it was particularly my fault he'd stepped right into my path.

The collision broke my view of Roompilda. I looked in the direction I'd seen her last, but I'd lost her. I started to swivel, examining all the ways she could have turned, but all I found was that an awful lot of people in Strachey have red hair.

Calm down, Evelyn. She can't have gone far. Look systematically—there really aren't that many redheads. No, no, too auburn, too orange, too male, too . . . there.

She'd stopped. I sidled around until I could see who she was talking to: Lady Rundle and Damian. She was explaining something, and they were listening intently. What did she have to tell them? Why was she even speaking with them? She'd told me she had no idea who would be calling, I thought, and then I remembered she'd known exactly what Fan had said to them. These calls were set-ups, I realized, and then kicked myself because it really should have been obvious.

Still, though—why? She'd been trying to get Fan practice, so why was she still chatting with the appointments Fan had botched? As Roompilda moved on from the Rundles, I tried to follow her, but within a few seconds, the music stopped. I turned toward the stage and joined in the polite applause.

The crowd began to disperse across the grounds as the dancers exited the stage. I stood on my tiptoes and looked for Fan. When I caught her eye, I waved cheerfully at her, in a way I hoped was encouraging. She gave me a nervous smile. I watched her tentatively join a group of girls. Please, let her have a good day for once, I thought.

I turned my attention back to Roompilda. I'd lost track of her again, of course, but my instincts said she wouldn't go far. She was here on business, not pleasure. Surrounding the dance floor were tables and chairs, set up for partygoers to enjoy the nearby refreshments. Whatever Roompilda was up to, surely this was where she'd wait. I couldn't envision her playing lawn tennis.

I joined the line for lemonade, the slowest line available, and looked for Roompilda among the seated guests as I waited. I was a few people away from getting my glass when I finally located her. She was sitting at a table on the fringe, reading a book. I received my glass of lemonade and looked around for an inconspicuous spot to spy on her.

Just then, Maribelle spotted me.

"Isn't Fanchon so lovely? Didn't she do so well?" she gushed, approaching me with a plate of pastries.

"She did," I said, maintaining a watch on Roompilda out of the corner of my eye. "I just hope she can finally have a pleasant time at one of these things."

"Oh, I'm sure she will! Everyone has fun at the garden party!"

That was wishful naivety at its finest.

"Let's sit down," I said, directing Maribelle toward a table that offered me a good view of Roompilda.

"How are you, Maribelle?" I asked.

While Maribelle gave me a complete rundown of each of her five children, from their developmental achievements to their eating habits to their bowel charts, I watched Roompilda, of course. Finally, by the time we'd reached child number four's inability to digest beets and I'd run through my repertoire of conversational noises at least twenty times, someone approached Roompilda.

He was obviously a messenger, wearing the uniform of the Pigeon Post Service, which turned a few heads as he drew near Roompilda's table. Pigeon Post was a luxury even the wealthiest used rarely; coach delivery sufficed for all but the most urgent messages and emergencies. Who had the means to send a messenger pigeon to an etiquette coach? I could think of only one individual: the queen.

The messenger handed Roompilda an envelope. She opened it and removed the slip of paper that had been folded and wrapped around the bird's foot. After she'd read it, she shook her head to indicate there would be no response, and the messenger departed. She replaced the message in its envelope, slipped it into her carpetbag, and began walking farther into the garden.

"Why don't we walk around?" I told Maribelle, standing before she could respond.

"Oh! What do you want to see?" she asked, jumping to her feet. "Are we supposed to clean our tables, do you think? I feel bad about just leaving my plate for someone, but I don't see a washbasin . . ."

"That's why they have servers," I said. I put my hands on her shoulders and tried to steer her away from the table.

"Oh, excuse me! Pardon me," Maribelle exclaimed, taking a route through the maze of tables and chairs and brushing past heads as she went. "Lady Blount! Hello!"

I just continued to push her through before she could begin chatting.

"Evelyn, where are we going? Why are we in such a hurry?"

I sighed. I was going to need Maribelle's help. I doubted I could get close enough to Roompilda to eavesdrop without getting caught. With any luck, Roompilda wouldn't recognize Maribelle.

"Do you see that woman up ahead, with the red hair and the carpetbag? She's the one I told you about—Fanchon's etiquette coach."

"The one the queen sent?" she blurted piercingly.

"Yes. Shh. I need to know what she's doing here."

"Isn't she here being Fanchon's etiquette coach?" she whispered.

"No. I fired her."

Maribelle gasped. "You fired someone from the queen?"

"She didn't have Fanchon's best interests at heart! Her behavior has been suspicious, and I need to know what she's up to!"

"Are we following her?" Maribelle's face lit up with excitement.

I nodded. "She just got a message from the queen, delivered by Pigeon Post." Maribelle's mouth rounded into a perfect O of surprise. "That means it's urgent, so whatever Roompilda has planned, it's happening soon."

Maribelle and I walked slowly through the grounds, with our eyes on Roompilda several yards away. She was clearly headed toward the hedge maze, and as we neared our target, I could see why: Lady Farthingbras was seated near the entrance, fanning herself as she watched the line of people waiting their turn.

"She's going to speak to Lady Farthingbras," I said. "I need you to eavesdrop."

"Me?" Maribelle whispered.

"Roompilda doesn't know you. She'll recognize me. I just need to know what they say. I'll wait over here."

Maribelle nodded, hiked up her skirts a few inches, and began tiptoeing sneakily toward the hedge maze. I winced.

As I suspected, Roompilda did indeed approach Lady Farthingbras. I saw Lady Farthingbras greet Roompilda. Come on, Maribelle, I thought. Get in position. Roompilda began to speak just as Maribelle stopped near the line for the hedge maze. Maribelle beamed at me. I held my breath, aching to know what was being said. Then the line began to move.

The Allenby servants were sending in twenty to thirty people at a time, and as they opened the way to the next batch, the crowd surged forward, taking Maribelle with it. I groaned. Maribelle disappeared inside the maze, and Roompilda finished her conversation in secrecy.

"I didn't mean to go in! I didn't mean to go in!" I heard as I trudged toward the hedge maze. "Can I just—if I could just squeeze by. . . This is the entrance, isn't it? How silly, I'm already lost!"

"Maribelle?" I called out.

"Evelyn!" she said as she finally emerged to looks of disgust from the first third of the queue.

"I'm so sorry!" she whispered, clutching my arm. "I didn't actually hear a word they said. The line just started moving!" She looked around. "Is she gone?"

I nodded. With the number of people at this party, any path Roompilda had taken across the grounds had quickly been filled in.

Maribelle clapped her hands over her eyes. "It's all my fault! What is she going to do? What's she going to do to Fan?"

I frowned and tried to ignore Maribelle's wailing. Where would Roompilda have gone?

"Are we sure it's not a good surprise?" Maribelle asked.

I'd seen Roompilda speak to the Rundles and the Farthingbrases. Clearly, she'd be looking for the Relishes. I may not be able to see Roompilda, but could I track down Lady Relish and Herb?

"Gird and cleek," I said suddenly.

"I don't think they serve seafood at the garden party . . ."

"Historical name. Where do they play hoop and stick?"

"Oh! I didn't know they had that one. But lawn games are usually that way."

I took off in the direction Maribelle was pointing, while she flapped behind at my heels. We passed the lawn tennis courts first, and then the croquet wickets, both quite popular. A little way off on my other side I spotted horseshoe pitching. By the time we had passed lawn bowling, liked mainly by men of a certain age, I was worried we were reaching the limits of the Allenby estate.

"Are you sure they're doing hoops?" Maribelle asked.

"There's supposed to be a whole tournament!"

"Maybe it's behind those trees?"

I strode over to a little cluster of trees. Maribelle had been right. Tucked away against the back of the Allenbys' property was the hoop and stick tournament. I saw Lady Relish cheering on Herb, who was battling in the roped-off hoop and stick pitch. Approaching her from along the back hedge wall was Roompilda.

"There she is," I said. "She's headed for Lady Relish. You go that way, I'll work my way around." I saw Maribelle begin to lift her skirts. "Just walk normally," I added.

Although hoop and stick wasn't as beloved as lawn tennis, there were at least enough young men with hoops and a few mothers and young women to surround the large rectangular pitch. I took the long way toward Lady Relish, trying to pass unobtrusively behind the spectators. I just wasn't certain I could get close enough without Roompilda spotting me.

Maribelle, apparently, had a different idea of what constituted unobtrusive. I watched as she scuttled on her toes from the cluster of trees to a lone ash tree. She hid behind the ash for a second, then scampered behind one of the cement columns that held an unlit brazier, still several feet away from Lady Relish. Roompilda had now begun speaking to Lady Relish. Maribelle couldn't possibly hear Roompilda's low tone over the chants of "Relish! Relish!"

I continued to slowly edge around the pitch, while Maribelle scurried over and took a position behind a taller gentleman. Now listen, Maribelle, I thought. As long as her cover didn't start shouting, she ought to be able to hear Roompilda.

"Fault!" I heard from the referee. "Player touched the opponent's hoop with his stick, not his hoop."

"I never!" Herb shouted, and the spectators erupted into a mixture of cheers and jeers.

Lady Relish's attention was immediately drawn away from Roompilda. Her conversation thus interrupted, Roompilda turned at precisely the same moment Maribelle's cover moved toward the pitch to get a better view of the action. Exposed, Maribelle took the—well, I'm not sure it was the only course of action, to be honest. She dived behind a bush.

She was not, in my opinion, very near a bush, but there was one a bit behind her and to her left, so what started out as a dive turned into more of a leap and roll, as she landed partially on the bush and rolled to the ground. I cringed.

Roompilda, who had actually been looking down at her pocket watch, glanced up with a slightly puzzled look, probably feeling the sensation that she'd just missed something really interesting. She turned back to Lady Relish, gave her one more piece of advice or instruction, and took her leave. I hurried over to Maribelle.

"Are you all right?" I asked as I helped her off the ground.

"That was really close!" Maribelle exclaimed. "Did she see me?"

"I don't think so," I said, picking leaves off of Maribelle's skirt.

"Phew! Wait, where did she go? Did I miss it again?"

"I'm afraid so."

Maribelle wailed in anguish. "Where's she going next? I promise I can do it this time! I'll concentrate really, really hard."

I shook my head. "I don't think she's got anyone else to talk to."

"What? Who are these people, anyway?"

I scowled and began leading Maribelle away from the hoop and stick pitch. "Roompilda said she was sent by the queen to coach Fan for the Season. But she's given Fan horrible advice, like telling her to lose weight, and the only callers she's found for Fan are three obnoxious boys and their mothers."

"Oh, I don't think anyone gets good callers their first Season."

"Each one of those visits was a disaster. So why is Roompilda going around this party giving a message to each of the three mothers?"

The wheels in Maribelle's mind began to spin, and her eyes grew even wider as the perplexity seemed to sink in. "Evelyn, wait! We've only eavesdropped on two conversations!"

"She spoke to the Rundles during the debutante dance."

"Oh." Maribelle pouted. "Then what do we do?"

I took a deep breath. "I need the message. I need the message from the queen. I have to get into Roompilda's purse and read that message."

"Evelyn! You can't snoop through people's things! That's not very nice."

"It's not very nice to tell my daughter to stop eating! How else can I know what Roompilda is planning?"

"But how are you going to do it?"

"I have to get her to put down her purse. When would a woman put down her purse?"

"When she uses the toilet," Maribelle declared.

"She'll still take it in with her."

"Oh, right. Do the Allenbys' toilets have curtains that go all the way down to the floor? Because sometimes in toilets the curtains stop a bit above the floor, and then you have to be careful, because someone might snatch your bag! Maybe Roompilda won't be careful, and we could pretend to be thieves!"

"She might not even use the toilets," I said.

"Ooh, good point."

I tried to focus my mind, shutting out the ambient noises of lawn games, music, and Maribelle. Roompilda would have to leave the purse somewhere if she wanted to dance. Could I persuade a nobleman to ask her to dance? Even if I could, knowing Roompilda, she'd probably just refuse.

"Right, I'll just think about myself," Maribelle said. "I put down my purse . . . when I tie my kids' shoes."

What if Maribelle knocked her over, "accidentally"? Don't be ridiculous, I thought. To give you time to go through that carpetbag,

Maribelle would have to knock her unconscious. You can't mug her. Couldn't I? Could I get someone to mug her? Probably not at a garden party.

"Could we get her to drink a lot of lemonade?" Maribelle mused.

I looked around. We had wandered as far as the lawn bowling. In the distance, I could see two couples playing doubles lawn tennis; the women, dressed in their finery, scuttled back and forth, never really reaching the ball before their husbands ran over and swatted it. Who wants to play tennis at a party? I thought. It just makes you sweat, under layers and layers of your nice clothes, while you're strapped into a bodice that's too tight, and no one's dress slippers are remotely comfortable, and—and you have to pile your belongings somewhere!

"A game," I said. "You don't carry your purse when you're playing a lawn game!"

Maribelle gasped. "Evelyn, you're brilliant! And lawn games are so charming, I'm sure she'll want to play."

"I'm not, which is why you're going to have to convince her."

"Oh! Which game are we going to play?"

I thought a moment. If I could just get Maribelle to talk to Roompilda, Maribelle's style of conversation was plenty sufficient to create a distraction. We had to pick a game with ample opportunity for standing around and chatting. That ruled out tennis, thank goodness, and judging by the day's participants, lawn bowling wasn't a woman's game, and if it wasn't proper, Roompilda wouldn't go near it. That left croquet.

"I think croquet is our best bet," I said.

"I love croquet!"

"We'll need a fourth, though. Do you think your husband would play with us?"

Maribelle cringed apologetically. "I'm not even sure where he is," she said.

"That's all right." I looked around. I hardly knew anyone here. I'd have an impossible time finding a fourth player. You know, a nagging voice said, you could probably get Lady Relish to play. Roompilda wouldn't be able to resist supervising. I sighed. This was going to be a tedious game.

I was just about to tell Maribelle my plan when I heard my name.

"Evelyn," said Hugo Piminder, bowing as he approached. "How are you enjoying the fete?"

I couldn't tell whether I was blessed or cursed.

"Ah, it's lovely. Have you met my friend Maribelle? Lady Maribelle Frandsen, Lord Hugo Piminder."

"A pleasure to meet you," he said. Maribelle, meanwhile, was shooting me wide-eyed glances.

"How do you two know each other?" she asked.

"We met at the Courtenays'," I said. "Maribelle and I were about to play a game of croquet. Would you care to join?"

"I would be delighted."

Well, we had our final player. Now to convince Roompilda. "Now, we just need one more," I continued, hoping that if I talked loudly, no one else would offer suggestions. "Hmm . . ." I made a show of looking and walked directly after Roompilda.

"We could . . . ," Piminder tried to interrupt. "I believe I know someone . . ." He trailed off as I ignored him and followed in my wake.

As soon as Roompilda came within view, I started calling out.

"Oh, I know! Roompilda!" I shouted. "Come join us! We need a fourth for croquet!"

She turned around and stared at me incredulously. I marched my posse over toward her. "Here, you must meet Lady Maribelle Frandsen and Lord Hugo Piminder. Maribelle, Hugo, this is Roompilda . . ." My mind went blank. "I'm sorry, I can't remember your surname."

"Stidolph," she said. "Roompilda Stidolph."

"That's right. Roompilda trains young people for appearances at court. She gave Fan a few lessons."

Lord Piminder smiled politely, and Maribelle oohed appreciatively. Roompilda didn't seem impressed by them. You're supposed to be helping, Maribelle, I thought. Now she'd suddenly clammed up. How could I convince Roompilda to come with us? I remembered what Henry had—well, what I thought Henry would say. You're not that different. Give her business opportunities.

"A pleasure," she said tersely. "I'm afraid I—"

"Actually," I said brightly, interrupting before she could refuse, "Roompilda is a good person for you to meet, Hugo. What a coincidence! Hugo's son is about the right age to start thinking about marriage. I bet Roompilda would be able to help him make a more suitable match. And Maribelle has so many children. Are your boys going to have private tutoring, Maribelle?"

I gave Maribelle a pointed glare.

She gasped. "Oh, I hadn't even thought of that! They're going to be behind! How old should boys start lessons?" she asked, grasping Roompilda's arm. For a moment, I was impressed. I would never have suspected Maribelle had this much acting ability. Then, of course, I realized she was sincere.

"Please tell me six is not too old!" she continued. "Do you do private consulting?"

Well, we'd overcome our first obstacle. I immediately started leading us toward the croquet wickets. Like so many mortals, Roompilda couldn't react fast enough to an onslaught of Maribelle. In her bewilderment, she simply followed.

There was one croquet court left available. It was angled a bit away from the other courts and located not far from the exit to the hedge maze. The Allenbys had thoughtfully put out a few lawn chairs at each court.

"Looks like this one is ours," I said.

"Which rules shall we play?" Lord Piminder asked. "There's pell-mell, golf, and then the lesser known international version, nine wicket, which I would be happy to teach everyone."

"Well, they've only set up six wickets," I said, "so I was thinking good old traditional garden croquet. Let's have Maribelle and Roompilda be partners, and Hugo and I will be partners. Which color balls do you want?"

"Ah-ah, we must start with a coin flip." Lord Piminder pulled a coin out of his pocket. "Lady Frandsen, would you like to call it?"

"Ooooh . . . it's so much pressure! I don't know. . . Oh, fine. Heads!"

"Heads it is. Will you two play first or second?"

Maribelle looked at Roompilda, who seemed to be struggling between the need to be polite to a potential gold mine and her desire to stare daggers through Maribelle's skull.

Luckily, Maribelle just decided on her own. "We'll go first!"

"Very well. Evelyn, which colors shall we take?" Hugo said.

"Black and blue," I said and handed him the black ball.

"Ooh, can I have yellow? And you can have red to match your hair!" Maribelle said.

"We must start by getting all four balls into play," Lord Piminder said. "After that, we may decide which ball to play on our turn."

"This is so much fun!" Maribelle exclaimed as she set her purse on one of the chairs. I placed mine next to hers and watched Roompilda with some trepidation until she deposited the carpetbag in the next chair. I breathed a sigh of relief.

The game started. Maribelle squealed as she knocked her ball toward the first wicket. I motioned to Lord Piminder to go next, and he promptly hit Maribelle's ball.

"Now, when you hit another player's ball," he called out, "you are immediately allowed what's called a croquet shot to send that ball anywhere on the field." He lined up the shot and sent Maribelle's ball rolling across the court. "Then, you are allowed a continuation shot to move your own ball ever closer to the wicket."

Roompilda and I were not particularly enthusiastic students. She watched with an impassive glare; I suspect mine looked a good deal more hostile. I'd forgotten, apparently, how patronizing he could be. Maribelle, on the other hand, spontaneously applauded.

Lord Piminder then took his continuation shot, which should have given him excellent field position—except instead of rolling to a stop, his ball curved away from the wicket and trickled down what we all quickly realized was a hill.

"Hmm. We appear to be on a slope. That certainly adds a new wrinkle," he commented.

Roompilda was next, and to my surprise, she took a full swing and barely managed to hit the ball a few feet. Well, at least I knew she had one weakness: limp wrists. I took a quick glance toward Hugo to see if he was foolish enough to teach her how to swing a mallet. He seemed to be biting back advice.

My turn. I took a look at the course. We're on a hill, I thought. Maybe I wouldn't need Maribelle to cause a distraction after all. With my first swing, I sent my ball toward Roompilda's, tapping it gently. Then I lined up my croquet shot and sent her red ball flying down the hill.

"I might have hit it the other way," Lord Piminder said. "When she puts it back in, she can place it fairly close to the wicket."

I ignored him and quickly lined up a continuation shot. I was halfway through my swing when he interrupted me.

"No, no, no," he said. He stood behind me and placed his hands on my arms. "Remember, you're permitted to hit each other ball once before going through a wicket. If you tap mine right now, you can use the croquet shot to hit it through the wicket, and then use your continuation shot to send yours through the wicket. See?"

I just wanted my turn over before Roompilda got back, but he was breathing down my neck and tracing a line with his finger in the air, apparently showing me the angle I would need to hit his ball. Any second now he was going to grab my hands and help me make the shot. If he gets any closer, my body suddenly told me, I am going to bite him. Fine, I thought. I shook him off, hit his ball, sent it and then mine through the wicket, and finally ran over toward the purses.

"Oh good, you found it!" I heard Maribelle say. I abruptly sat down next to the purses, trying not to look suspicious and gnashing my teeth.

"Lord Piminder says you may place your ball so it will go right through that wicket," Maribelle said.

"I hate to hurt my own team," he began, "but I must be honest. According to section 1.6a of the official rules, an out-of-bounds ball can be placed within three feet of the spot where it left the field of play; no penalty given."

Maribelle gasped. "And we get to decide who plays on our turn, don't we? You should go! You'll get us a point!"

Roompilda carefully lined up her shot, and hit the ball a few inches forward through the wicket.

Unsurprisingly, Lord Piminder decided we should play his ball on our turn. I sat next to the purses, my fingers itching to rifle through Roompilda's carpetbag. I would need a distraction after all.

When Maribelle finished her turn, I caught her eye and motioned for her to sit next to me. She plopped in the chair with a wide grin.

"Sooo, Evelyn," she sang, "tell me about Hugo Piminder."

"Maribelle . . ."

"He is attractive for an old man."

"Maribelle!"

"Only, I thought you were on the side of Cl—"

"Maribelle, I promise I will tell you everything later if you stop," I hissed.

Maribelle closed her mouth and then pretended to lock it with a key.

"Besides, you're supposed to be helping me get into Roompilda's carpetbag!"

Recognition dawned on Maribelle's face. "Oh no, I completely forgot! What do I do? Should I stand guard while you look in the bag?"

"Lady Frandsen, Madam Stidolph?" Lord Piminder called. "My turn is complete."

"You can have a go, Roompilda," Maribelle called out. "I just went."

As Roompilda took the field, I whispered, "On Lord Piminder's next turn, I need you to talk to Roompilda. Ask her about her lessons, anything, as long as she's paying attention to you. Then, when it's your turn again, say your knee hurts or something and she should go again."

Maribelle nodded. "I won't disappoint you, Evelyn!"

With her floppy-wristed croquet swing, Roompilda could only inch her ball toward the next wicket. She gave her ball sort of a hard tap and returned to her seat. I nodded at Maribelle.

"Roompilda!" Maribelle said. She stood up, still holding the arms of the chair, and lifted so that the chair seemed to stand up with her. Then she waddled over and planted next to Roompilda.

I leaned over and undid the clasp on Roompilda's carpetbag. Maribelle was between me and Roompilda, but her back was to me. Just keep Roompilda's attention, Maribelle. I started to reach my hand into the carpetbag.

"Umm . . . ," Maribelle stammered.

"Yes?" Roompilda said. I thought I saw her eyes drift away from Maribelle and toward me. I snatched my hand back.

"Oh! Well, I just wanted to say . . . umm . . . now I can't . . . actually, I wanted to ask you . . ."

Of all the times in Maribelle's life to draw a blank! Every time Maribelle paused, Roompilda's gaze darted toward me. I'd placed my arm on the back of the chair holding the purses, my hand tantalizingly close to that carpetbag. Just give me a few seconds, Maribelle!

"I was just curious, umm . . . where did you get your carpetbag? The black and white stitching is really lovely!"

Well, that ensured a rather pointed glare from Roompilda in my direction. I cursed under my breath.

"Ladies," Lord Piminder said, bowing and gesturing toward the court.

"Oh, Roompilda, you should play again!" Maribelle said, in that slow and deliberate tone people use when they're obviously lying. "Umm. My toe hurts!"

Roompilda simply raised an eyebrow. As she walked onto the court, Maribelle turned and gave me a giant grin and winked. I smiled tersely back and began to reach back into the carpetbag, only to stop inches above the opening as Lord Piminder sat down beside me. I quickly patted all the purses until I reached my own, hoping I didn't look suspicious.

"Reaching for a sweet?" he asked, chuckling. "Don't worry, I won't judge."

Apparently, I had looked guilty, although only of being an older lady who kept sweets in her purse.

"You know," he began, "I'd forgotten how much I enjoyed croquet. It is such a game of strategy, don't you think? I've heard the really good players can link continuation shot after continuation shot so that their turns almost never end! I do wonder, in the nine-wicket version . . ."

While he droned on about croquet, I watched Roompilda. She was setting up a long shot to the wicket, and she had the unfortunate position of needing to hit it uphill. With her flimsy swing, she'd be lucky if the ball didn't roll right back to where it started.

Sure enough, the ball didn't stay put, but instead of rolling straight back, it took a little bit of a curve and landed a few inches away from my blue ball. You could knock it anywhere you like, I thought.

A loud burst of laughter came from the direction of the hedge maze. Another gaggle of young people had just made it through. I looked at the wide skirts of the young women. If a ball went into the crowd, those skirts would hide it. You'd have time to look through the carpetbag. You could find the queen's message, and figure out what she had planned for your daughter. I would not surrender Fanchon to Roompilda's whims. I would aim for the crowd.

As Roompilda left the court, I jumped out of my seat.

"I haven't played in forever, Hugo. Let me go."

I hustled into position before he could object. I knew if I just tapped her ball and sent it into the crowd on the croquet shot, I'd have the same problem as last time. I'd have to hit the continuing shot, and Hugo would interfere and try to teach me something, and I'd miss my chance at the carpetbag again. It had to happen now. I needed one mighty shot.

I swung the mallet hard and sent my ball screaming toward Roompilda's. The red ball took off toward the crowd of people, taking a bounce as the field leveled off and rolling its way into hiding. There were a few shrieks as ladies jumped out of its way. Oh, please land under someone's skirt, I prayed.

"Oops! Well, I suppose I'll need to wait for her before I can continue," I said as Roompilda trekked stiffly toward the crowd. "I just need to check something in my purse."

I hustled toward the chair and leaned over the purses, hoping it would look like I was rummaging through my own purse for sweets. My hand quickly found the envelope in the depths of Roompilda's carpetbag. I pulled the message out and read.

As requested, notes on the potential families
Rundle—Keen. Suave but arrogant. Demands seat on board of E.E. Will fit in at court.
Relish—Eager to please. Seems young. Will sell E.E. to his own firm. Will need to lie about that or E.R. will balk.
Farthingbras—No dowry demands. Father very influential. Doesn't (can't?) speak. Has already made poor impression on both F.E. and E.R. Unlikely.
I recommend Rundle or Relish. Preference and permission to proceed?
R.

Then, in a different handwriting at the bottom:
Rundle. Best to keep E.E. in the family. Proceed.

No dowry demands? Clearly, this was about marrying Fan. Damian wanted a seat on the board of Envers Enterprises, while Herb would sell it—to that weasel Norbert Easom, no doubt. E.R.—well, that had to be me, didn't it? Of course I would balk if someone tried to sell off my daughter's inheritance. F.E. was Fan, and R could only be Roompilda. She'd sent this letter to the queen, presumably, so that had to be the queen's response at the bottom. Proceed with what?

"Oh, Roompilda, I'm so sorry you had to walk so far!" Maribelle said.

I stuffed the letter and the envelope back in the carpetbag and stepped away from the purses. I hadn't put the letter back in the envelope, so she'd know I read it, but I was too angry to care.

"I can't believe you hit her ball so hard, Evelyn!" Maribelle finished.

"It was a complete accident!" I said, although it was obviously anything but.

Roompilda dropped her ball onto the playing field. When she turned toward me, one corner of her mouth was turned up in a haughty smirk, as though she knew what I was up to and didn't care. She thought she'd already won. I tried to smile sunnily, hoping I didn't look as troubled as I felt. I finished taking my turn, but my mind was no longer on the game.

She hadn't meant to prepare Fan at all! Perhaps that was a fortunate side effect, but all she really cared about was getting Fan to pick a husband. I should have wondered why she didn't send us calling, or why we never went to teas. Roompilda only engineered meetings where one of those three could woo Fan. The queen had made a list of families she wanted on Aiden's side, and Roompilda had come to ensure Fan married into one of them. The queen didn't care about Fan having a title in order to visit Ella. She was making a marriage alliance, and Fan was the pawn.

My turn completed, I returned to the chairs to fume. Just then, Roompilda pulled out her pocket watch.

"As delightful as this has been," she said, "I'm afraid I have to be somewhere else. It was nice to meet you both."

She sauntered past me, still smirking, and retrieved her carpetbag.

"Oh! Nice . . ." Maribelle trailed off, as Roompilda had already left, not bothering to wait for a response.

"Hmm. That was . . . abrupt," Lord Piminder said. "Well, perhaps we can still make this work. If Evelyn would like to take over Roompilda's ball, I would be happy to play black and blue. Although black and blue does have rather better field position. Why don't I take over red and yellow, and Lady Frandsen can come play black?"

"Sorry, I have to go as well," I said. I grabbed my purse and dashed off after Roompilda.

Where did she have to be? I briefly entertained the possibility that she just wanted to escape us, but my insides were churning, and I was certain something was wrong. I needed to find Fan, I thought. If I followed Roompilda, would she lead me right to her?

I chased Roompilda toward what seemed to me to be the entrance to the maze, keeping my eyes fixed on her hair. I didn't notice I'd walked through a tennis court until the ball whizzed past my head, but I ignored the jeers and stuck to my course. I likewise did not notice that Clarrie Babcock was running after me.

"Madam Radcliffe!" she called breathlessly.

I stopped and turned around. "Clarrie, I can't right now—"

"Why were you playing croquet with Lord Piminder?"

"What?" I studied her expression. She was trying to maintain her poise, but her eyes said she was terrified—terrified that I was double-crossing her, I realized. "He took a liking to me, and I've been using that to suggest things that will help you. That's why he lowered the amount. I promise I'm on your side, Clarrie."

She nodded. "My fairy godmother will help me, right?"

"I'm really confident she will. I just had to get Lord Piminder to set things up right. The fairies needed him to pick a date."

"It's just that Terence said that fairies hardly ever help anyone anymore, and we should forget about being together."

Uh-oh. The back of my mind was screaming that Terence's cold feet were a major problem. The front of my mind, however, was determined to find Fanchon immediately.

"Well, I think he's wrong. You do still want to marry him?"

Clarrie forced a smile and nodded. It was not a very good lie, but I didn't have time for this now.

"Clarrie, I have to go. But keep your chin up. I'll be in touch soon, all right?"

By now, of course, I'd lost Roompilda, so I ran toward the entrance to the maze, hoping that really was her destination. When I arrived, I scanned the crowd. Most of these people were in line for the maze, and Roompilda certainly wouldn't be among them—but Fanchon might, I thought. I looked through the line, then turned to the dance floor, and the luncheon tables, but to no avail. Where had Roompilda gone?

Then suddenly, I heard a gasp behind me. I turned to see people leaving their conversations to rise up on their toes and crane their necks, all trying to get a better look at something. I pushed through the crowd that was gathering near an old beech tree.

"Since the moment I met you, I have been captivated by your loveliness. I could sing your praises to the sun, the moon, and the stars!"

I froze at the edge of the crowd. Fanchon stood under the tree facing a kneeling Damian Rundle, who quite loudly proclaimed his devotion to her. She looked like she wanted to run away, but the crowd was quickly hemming her in.

"I can think of nothing I would want more than to spend eternity with you. Fanchon Envers, will you be my wife?"

The girls in the crowd oohed, and I heard a few cries of "That's so romantic!" I saw Fan glance up at the multitude, and I knew she was feeling the pressure of her audience. These were exactly the tactics I planned to use against Lord Piminder. This was why I wanted a throng waiting for Clarrie to emerge with her gold—how could Lord Piminder disappoint all those people? Every girl out there would hate Fanchon if she turned down such a "romantic" proposal. I needed to help, but how?

Before I could make a move, we heard another voice from the crowd. "Don't listen to him!" Heribert Relish stepped into the circle. "I may not have his way with words, but I think you are the prettiest, sweetest girl in the whole world. If you marry me," he said as he knelt next to Damian, "I promise I will take care of you as long as I'm alive."

"Did you hear that? He has not noticed your skin, soft as a doe's and white as snow; your lips, red as a rose's petals; your hair, black as—"

"Oh, come on! You stole that from a fairy story! He's just trying to impress you—he doesn't really care for you."

"And you do? At least I respect the great man that was her father!"

Herb leapt to his feet. "Well, I believe Fanchon should break free! Free from her father's tyranny!"

I raised an eyebrow. That was a false note, if you wanted to woo Fan. I would have thought Roompilda would have told him—I suddenly remembered the note. *Keep Envers Enterprises in the family,* the queen had written. The queen had chosen Damian, and Roompilda had sabotaged Herb.

Damian rose languidly to face Herb. "So you'll unload her inheritance, and then what? How's a groveling worm like you going to provide for a wife?"

"I work for Norbert Easom—"

"Name-dropper!"

"What about you, you pompous git? You're a glorified desk clerk! How are you going to pay for ball gowns on a government salary?" Herb shouted.

"I am a valuable advisor to the minister of the Treasury—"

"Prancing bore!"

"Fawning toady!"

"Say that again!" Herb postured, inching closer to Damian's face.

The two suitors seemed to have forgotten all about Fan. The more they fought, the more she faded into the background. I found myself hoping for a brawl. Then maybe I could help her slip out of here. Before Damian had a chance to respond, however, Justice Farthingbras emerged from the crowd and strode toward the two men. He put a hand on each of their chests and shoved them apart, then knelt down and held his hand out toward Fan.

"Hah! So the brute offers his hand?" Damian scoffed.

"Come on, Justice. Everyone knows you're a creeper!" Herb said.

The crowd gasped at the arrival of a third suitor. Any minute now, they were going to start clamoring for Fan to pick one. I had to step in, now. Unfortunately, I still wasn't sure what to say. I ruled out a logical explanation of how Fan didn't really know them and still needed time to think right away.

"Miss Envers, believe me when I say only I can offer you the life of sophistication your beauty deserves," Damian said, returning to his knees.

"I already have the connections! I can introduce you to a world of luxury and ease!" Herb dropped a knee as soon as he saw Damian move, not wanting to be the last left on his feet.

I can play the stepmother, I thought. I mean, obviously I was her actual mother, but I could forbid her from seeing any of them, just like a wicked stepmother would do. I was about to step into the ring when I felt a hand grip my arm.

"Don't," Roompilda said.

"Watch me."

She pulled on my arm even harder. "She must choose one of them."

"No, she's choosing none of them. You know perfectly well they want her money, not her. That's how you pitched her to them. You coached them on how to propose."

"Her Royal Highness has willed that Fanchon marry one of these three noblemen—"

"My daughter is not a political pawn!"

"Of course she is," Roompilda said. "The queen and the crown prince cannot pass up such an opportunity to make an alliance. Any of the three families is acceptable. Let Fanchon make her choice."

I looked at Fan, who'd finally managed to spot me in the crowd, and her eyes pled with me to find her a way out. So much for getting an invite to the palace, I thought. I was going to be in trouble for this.

I yanked my arm from Roompilda's grasp and started walking toward Fan. I still hadn't decided what I would say. Should I go wicked stepmother? I thought of that fairy tale book I'd bought. I could set some impossible tasks for them. But then what about when Fan really did want to get married? I needed something difficult, but not impossible, something we could control . . .

"Enough!" I shouted, silencing the squabbling boys. "In the absence of Fanchon's father, it falls to me to weigh these proposals and choose a suitable husband for my daughter. It saddens me to say that I cannot accept any of these suitors."

The crowd gasped. The three young men had twisted around to watch me. Herb's jaw had dropped, while Damian scowled at me. Justice was as expressionless as ever.

"Ever since the first day of summer, my daughter has been unable to smile or laugh. I know not whether this is some curse, but I cannot send her to her wedding day in such a sad state. Therefore, I will issue this challenge: the man who makes my daughter laugh is the one she shall marry!"

The crowd broke out into hushed murmurs—a good reaction, I thought. I'd have to see what people were saying later, but I thought that was a pretty spectacular speech, if I do say so myself. Especially for on the fly.

The boys stood up and slunk away, giving me dirty looks as they went. Not one of them, I noticed, had anything else to say to Fan. Roompilda had probably told them this would be an easy conquest.

I resisted the urge to find Roompilda in the crowd. I could well imagine her tight-lipped, cross expression, and it was altogether too soon for me to gloat. I held my arms out to Fan, who looked like she had avoided crying for as long as possible.

"Let's go home," I whispered.

CHAPTER TEN

"IS SHE ALL right?" Maribelle asked. She'd rushed over the morning after the party.

"She's . . . shaken up," I said. "She certainly wasn't expecting all that."

"I don't blame her! That was so inappropriate, proposing like that in public!"

"She only met them a few weeks ago."

"Is that what was in the message?" Maribelle asked. "The one from the pigeon?"

I nodded. "More or less. The queen sent Roompilda to make sure Fan married one of those three."

"But that's not fair! That's not romantic at all! Everyone's saying it was so romantic that they all proposed to her, but it wasn't! Romantic should have flowers, and candles, and it should feel special. Not a fight at a party."

"Yes, well, that's why I had to make up that whole bit about laughing. Everyone would have hated her if she'd said no, and I certainly wouldn't have let her say yes."

"So . . . she isn't cursed, then? Because I have noticed she's been down lately . . ."

"What? No! She has been down, but not because she's cursed. I suspect she's tired of being treated like a pawn."

Actually, Fan had looked at the whole event very differently than I had.

"How could they? How could they do that to me?" she'd cried, as soon as we were safely home. "I can't believe they would make fun of me like that!"

"Make fun of you?"

"Staging that fight with everyone watching, those fake proposals. Thinking that I would get excited, when everyone knew they didn't really like me. Oh God, it's like being fourteen all over again!"

"Wait, this happened when you were fourteen? But you had a lot of friends."

"I didn't have a dad. I didn't really have friends. Everyone was catty and mean, and so was I, because if I could find them someone else to pick on, it was more like I was in the popular circle."

"Sweetheart, I'm so sorry. I had no—"

"It's not your fault, Mom. It's not like I ever let you help, anyway. I'm just saying, I know those boys are trying to embarrass me."

"I . . . don't think they are, love."

"It's okay, Mom. You don't have to sugarcoat it."

"No, Fan, I . . . I found out that Roompilda has been talking to all three families. From the beginning. She was never here to train you, sweetheart. She was here to get you married to one of them." I left out the details of how I got the information.

"What? So—the queen didn't send her?"

"No, Her Majesty definitely sent her."

"But I thought this was all so I could visit Ella at court!"

"Yes. But with your husband, whose family is probably valuable to Aiden."

Fan was beginning to tremble, her body shaking with the effort of keeping all that fury inside.

"But the queen can't actually make you marry anyone. We have laws."

"Then what will she do if I don't pick one?" Fan said, hesitation creeping into her voice.

I shrugged.

"But she'll be really angry, won't she?"

"I suppose she might, but there's not something she can do to you. She can't put you in jail."

"She won't just let it go."

"Well, if we go visit Ella, I suppose she might be irritable toward us, but . . ."

"Could she make it so we can't see Ella?" Fan asked quietly.

"No," I said immediately. She couldn't stop Ella from seeing her own family. "I don't think she would do that."

"But she could," Fan said. "She's the queen. She can decide who gets to visit the palace. And Ella wouldn't disobey her. That was probably a hint, when she mentioned Ella in the letter to me! That's what she'll do, if I don't pick one of them!" The pitch of Fan's voice was rising, and she wavered on the verge of tears.

"Fan, don't panic. I'm sure if you married any nobleman of good station who could be a good ally to Aiden, the queen would see reason."

"Do you know what's really sad?" she said.

"What?"

"I think Ethan was going to propose to me."

"Wait, really?"

"Well, not soon, obviously, but I just think eventually he was going to work up the courage."

"But Fan, Ethan would be a great choice! The queen probably doesn't know about him, but if she did, she'd have to approve of him."

"But what if she didn't?"

"Fan, just please don't make a decision yet. This is your whole life—"

"My whole life without Ella," she whispered.

"Fan," I started, but before I could even try to reason with her, she ran crying from the room.

I sighed. I just couldn't imagine the queen would be so cruel as to force Fanchon and Ella apart. Then again, I wouldn't have expected she would try to manipulate Fan into marrying someone. Could Fan be right? Would the queen cut us off over this? No, I thought, I couldn't believe it—I couldn't allow myself to think it. We had to have a way out without losing Ella because I wouldn't let Fan marry one of those three fools. Not in a million years.

"All right. If you're sure she isn't cursed . . . ," Maribelle said.

"I'm sure."

"Two curses is a lot for one person." That seemed to be all Maribelle had to say about Fan. She was suddenly uncharacteristically quiet, sipping her tea and refusing to make eye contact.

"Is something wrong?" I said, which was the kindest way I could think of to tell her to spit it out.

Maribelle looked immediately guilty. "Oh, it's nothing! Except you did promise to tell me everything . . ."

"Oh. Right. Well, it's not that exciting," I began, trying to lower expectations, but Maribelle practically quivered, like a puppy wagging its tail.

"I'm thinking about—and I haven't made up my mind yet, I'm just thinking about it—I'm considering starting a business to help young people find their fairy godmothers."

"Really?" Fan said, poking her head into the room.

"Hi, Fanchon!" Maribelle said. "How are you feeling this morning?"

"Fine," she said quickly. "How are you going to do that?" she asked me.

"Well, I was thinking about how often people around here come up with these ridiculous fairy story tasks—like Clarrie Babcock having to spin straw into gold—but we never have any fairy godmothers anymore. And maybe that's because we don't teach young people the things that the fairies value."

"So you would train young people to be kind and honorable and hardworking like the heroes in the stories?" Fan said.

Maribelle gasped. "That's an amazing idea, Evelyn! It's genius! Oh, everyone will want you to help them!"

"Well, I don't know about that. But it seems to me that sometimes people have problems that could be better fixed by fairy godmothers than, say, lawsuits. Anyway, I'm just thinking about this. I haven't officially registered a business or anything. But I did agree to help the Babcocks."

"I wondered if you were up to something," Fan said.

"And all I'm doing," I said, building up to my biggest lie yet, "is making sure that Clarrie has done all she can to convince Lord Piminder that he should let her and Terence get married. I figure the fairies need a chance to find out that he's standing in the way of true love."

"Is that why you had dinner with him?"

"Oooooh! You had dinner?" Maribelle said.

"No, well, I needed—I needed him to do it right. He just wanted Clarrie to have it done by the end of the summer. I needed him to set a date so the fairies would know when to show up. Since he seemed to take a liking to me at the Courtenays, I thought . . ."

"You would seduce him!" Maribelle exclaimed.

"No. Absolutely not. No, no, no, no. I just wanted a chance to make a suggestion. And he did pick a date. Now I'm just concerned—from what Clarrie was telling me, it sounds like Terence might be getting cold feet."

"But if he doesn't want to marry her, then it isn't true love anymore, and then the fairies won't come!" Maribelle said.

"But the Babcocks owe Lord Piminder a lot of money," I said. "They were hoping a marriage would solve the problem, but if it doesn't happen, well, Lord Piminder will still definitely send the Babcocks to the poorhouse."

And I'll have lost my leverage. True love wasn't just important to the fairies—it mattered to the throngs of women I wanted standing outside the Babcocks' barn when Clarrie emerged. The same women, I was sure, who'd watched Fanchon's three-pronged proposal yesterday.

"Is that what Clarrie wanted to tell you yesterday?" Maribelle asked.

"Yes," I said, puzzled. "How did you . . ."

"Well, after you and Roompilda deserted me and Lord Piminder at the croquet field, Clarrie came and asked where you were. She said she'd seen you over there, and she needed to talk to you, and asked where you'd gone."

Oh no. "In front of Lord Piminder? Did she ask him or just you?"

"No, she asked us both."

"He'll know," Fanchon said.

"He'll suspect, at least."

"What? No! I'm sure he has no idea you're working for Clarrie Babcock! I was there, and I didn't guess. I had no idea until you told me!" Maribelle said.

Fan and I gave each other a look. Suddenly, we heard a pounding at the door, and all three of us flinched.

After a few seconds, Mina peeked around the corner. "Right, ma'am, I know this isn't exactly protocol, but there's a Miss Babcock here and she's really upset—"

"Bring her in! Come in, Clarrie!" I called.

Clarrie entered the drawing room in a state. Her eyes were puffy, like she'd cried herself to sleep, but at this point, she was much too tense to keep bawling. She'd clearly rushed here. Her dress looked a little crumpled, and a few curls stuck out at odd angles, as though she'd slept in her updo from yesterday and hadn't touched a brush yet.

"He moved the date up," she said. "I've got to produce the gold in five days!"

Five days? Oh, he knew. Damn. I wasn't close to having enough brass. I'd be up all night for the next few days just to get it done. And if he suspected anything, I couldn't cut corners—my fake gold had to be pretty convincing.

"But that's all right, Clarrie," Fan said. "I'm sure your fairy godmother can handle a bit of a rush job."

"Do you think she knows? I mean, my fairy godmother knows I need help, right?"

"Absolutely," I said. "The whole town knows. And they're on your side! I bet you'll have quite a lot of people there to support you when you present the gold."

"But—"

"What's wrong?" I asked.

"But I don't think Terence wants to marry me anymore!"

"Oh, Clarrie! I'm sure he'll change his mind when he sees that your fairy godmother helped you spin straw into gold!" Maribelle said.

I frowned. That was the problem with these stories—any man who changed his mind about you simply because you could spin gold and spit diamonds and rubies wasn't going to hold up in the long run. On the other hand, marriage at least meant the Piminders would essentially get the Babcock estate. It was one of my only bargaining chips, but I couldn't in good conscience advise Clarrie to marry Terence.

"Maybe, Lady Frandsen," Clarrie said. "But after the way he's acted, I'm not at all sure I want to marry him! See? It's not about true love anymore! And if the fairies don't help me, Lord Piminder will take away our home!"

"Clarrie, I'm sure the fairies—" I started without knowing how I would end that sentence. So marriage was off the table—the one thing I was pretty sure these fairies cared about. But I'd told the Babcocks I was going to get Clarrie's fairy godmother to fix this. I had to deliver, right? I couldn't say, 'Look, forget the fairies. They only care about marriage. You'll have to contest this in court, which will probably just get you into more debt.' I still needed to spin this into a fairy tale.

"But you'd still marry him if it meant you'd save your family, right?" Fanchon spoke up softly.

Clarrie was silent for a moment, frowning like she'd had to swallow something nasty. Then she nodded.

"Well, there!" Fan said. "It is still about true love, just for your parents, not Terence! If you're willing to make a sacrifice for your family, I'm sure your fairy godmother will still help you. She might even help you more! You might have enough gold to pay off the entire debt, and then you wouldn't have to marry Terence at all!"

Right, definitely not that last part. Not without a bigger oven. And some vats of lye. But I had to hand it to Fan—she knew exactly how to turn this into a fairy tale. Now I just needed to convince Lord Piminder it was in his best interest to forgive the Babcocks' debt for absolutely nothing in return. Why, exactly, had I gotten myself into all this?

At that moment, Mina skipped back into the room. "A message for you, madam. The messenger is waiting for a response."

I opened the folded card. My mouth twisted into a scowl as I read, and when I glanced up, I saw all four women staring at me.

"It's from Lord Piminder," I said. Maribelle gave an audible gasp. "He regrets that I had to leave our croquet game so suddenly and wonders if I would luncheon with him today."

"Augh-hah!" Maribelle wailed in a mini-swoon.

"So he definitely knows you were working with Clarrie," Fanchon said.

"Oh God, this is all my fault!" Clarrie cried. "That's why he pushed the date up so suddenly. I didn't even think about why you might be playing croquet with him! Oh, I'm such a fool!"

"I don't like this, Mom. What's he planning? Where does he want to meet you?"

"His estate."

"Well, you can't do that, madam," Mina said. "If you meet him at his house, he's in a position of power. You've got to go for a neutral location."

I was beginning to think Mina was wasted as a ladies' maid.

"Mina's right, Mom. Tell him you'll meet him in a public place. If he's angry, this could be dangerous."

"Eep!" Maribelle squealed.

"God, I'm so sorry," Clarrie wailed. "I'm so sorry. I'm an imbecile!"

"It's not going to be dangerous," I said. "Just uncomfortable."

Then what should I do? Mina was right—from a negotiating standpoint, I had less standing on his turf. But in a public place, we'd be overheard, and all anyone could glean from this was that I'd led Lord Piminder on. I could hear Henry: "Evie, maybe, just maybe, this is a good example of why we probably shouldn't practice deceit. It's just a thought."

"While I see Mina's point, I think I have to go to him. If we're in public, we'll be overheard, and I don't think it helps Clarrie for people to know I've been lying to Lord Piminder."

Except, part of me wanted to insist, were you really lying? To your dismay, you actually enjoyed his company. But you definitely hid your relationship with Clarrie from him, I countered. You're going to have to face up to it.

"At least put it off, ma'am!" Mina said. "Tell him you'll see him tomorrow. That's what I always do when a boy asks me out, so he doesn't think I like him too much."

I considered it. It's a way to take some control back, I thought. On the other hand, if he's got something else up his sleeve, I want as much time to prepare as possible. Four days wasn't a very long time.

"I think I'd better get it over with," I said. "Tell the messenger I accept."

A few hours later, I was walking up the path to the Piminder estate, and I couldn't help feeling I was walking into an ambush unarmed. Name any rule of negotiations—I was breaking it. I'd let him choose the time and place, I'd lost what few bargaining chips I had, and I was going in with no preparation or research. I could see my professors shaking their heads.

However, when his servant ushered me into the study, I had to suppress a grin. Oh, there was a table set up near the window, ready for a charming luncheon overlooking the garden, but it was painfully obvious what he was trying to do. If he thought I could be intimidated by some bookshelves, a mounted buck's head, and a masculine color theme, perhaps I had more going for me than I thought.

He rose from his desk and greeted me with a gracious bow. He pulled out a chair for me at the table and sat opposite, showing no signs of suspicion. Was it possible he hadn't connected the dots? Don't be wishful, Evelyn. You can't let down your defenses.

"I was very sorry you had to rush off so quickly after—what was her name?"

"Roompilda. Yes, she's had plans for my daughter the whole Season. When she took off I knew I had to see what she was up to. Turned out she'd arranged for three rich fools to propose to my daughter."

"My goodness. You know, an interesting thing happened after you left. Clarrie Babcock came looking for you."

"Yes, I know. She found me."

"Ah. Did she have anything interesting to tell you?"

"Oh, not particularly." I certainly wasn't going to admit that Clarrie'd had quite enough of his son.

"I wasn't aware you knew Miss Babcock."

"Somewhat. Not particularly well."

"Well enough to advise her on how to infringe on my rights as a creditor? As a father?"

I raised an eyebrow. "I'm advising her on how to get help from her fairy godmother. I don't know what you're talking about."

"I have the right to decide what is suitable for my son! How is it that you can decide your daughter's suitors are fools but I cannot?"

"Clarrie Babcock is a model young lady—"

"Oh yes, I'm quite aware! She's only been parading it in front of my face for weeks. Only someone putting on a show would be so blatant."

"What is she supposed to do if you won't give her the time of day? Have you actually met her? Have you seen her with your son? How is it you can claim our situations are the same? I've done my research!"

"It is still my decision, and you are still undermining my authority! Is that the reason you came to dinner? To manipulate me? When I brought you into my home in good faith?"

"I came in good faith."

He snorted. "Really." He'd leaned back in his chair so he could look down his thin hooknose at me, and his eyes conveyed an almost sinister level of condescension. I wanted to rip that crocodile grin off his face.

"You knew who I was," I said. "You made it clear from the moment I introduced myself that you knew what had happened to me. Did you think I wouldn't care? Did you think it wouldn't bother me that you were putting the Babcocks in the same position I was in? Last year, I was Clarrie Babcock! I was this close to living on the streets. I was this close to marrying a museum piece up on Squire

Hill just so I could feed my stepdaughter. Did you really think I wouldn't care that you were being cruel to a girl my daughter's age? You didn't invite me here. You invited an idea. You didn't think once about who I really was."

As soon as I said it, I felt like something in me had opened up, like I was free to be as blazingly furious as I wanted, with no more questioning of just how much was my fault. Finally, I'd named what was wrong with Husband #1. He cared only about my function: Did I look charming on his arm? Could I manage a household? Would I make a good impression on his clients? I might as well have been a doll.

And of course, this was exactly why I'd gotten myself into this mess.

I could tell that my words had bothered Lord Piminder. Maybe he had an inkling I was right, or perhaps he was offended that I'd suggest such a thing. Either way, he wouldn't look at me. He stood up and crossed to his desk.

"So you decided to sabotage me behind my back rather than take the mature option of simply telling me how you felt," he said.

"I did tell you!" I said, rising to follow him. "I told you this was cruel! But you fed me a cock and bull story about how if you helped one person, everyone would take advantage of you."

"Which is true," he said, sitting at his desk. "You cannot understand the finer points of—"

I slammed my hands on his desk and leaned in. "Why can't I understand? Because I'm a woman? You and I both know that restructuring or even forgiving the Babcocks' loan would be a loss, sure, but a drop in the bucket for your finances. And if you don't have anyone on your payroll who can spin the Babcocks' sob story into a plus for you, well—in fact, I'll make a deal with you. Hire me to do your PR. Forgive the interest accrued on the loan since your father died and structure a payment plan on the original loan that Patrick Babcock has a hope of paying off. I'll quit the Babcocks' employ right now, tell Clarrie to find a different husband, call off the straw-into-gold spinning, and instead I'll spin this so your reputation doesn't take a hit. You get to do the right thing, but you don't lose out in the long run, and I still get paid. What do you say?"

He'd already leaned back in an effort to get away from me; now, he kept his eyes fixed on some paperwork on his desk. I let him sit for a few seconds in uncomfortable silence, then stood up and crossed my arms.

"Very well, then. So much for the mature option. You told Clarrie she had five days. Am I correct in assuming you mean the twelfth?"

He nodded curtly.

"At what time on the twelfth?" I asked.

"Let's say dawn."

"Very well. In four days' time, Clarrie will enter her family's barn, where she will work all day and night, neither entering, leaving, nor admitting visitors, until dawn the next day, where she will emerge with the gold."

"I was rather hoping she'd do this publicly," he said.

"No, and I'm not going to let you put her in the stocks, either. I think you'll find that publicly humiliating Clarrie will go worse for you than her."

"But surely you understand that I cannot accept any part of her family's estate as the staging ground. There are simply too many avenues for cheating. In order to be fair, I will lock her in the southern tower on my estate."

Well, I certainly couldn't agree to that. I'd never be able to get the brass wires in to Clarrie. I had to produce neutral ground, and quickly.

"Of course not, for the same reasons you just listed. How about the abandoned round tower near the King's Wood? The city keeps it in good repair. Neutral territory."

"And both parties shall have the opportunity to inspect the site before Clarrie enters."

I had to grit my teeth and nod. What I most wanted was for the Piminders to stay as far away from the tower as possible so I could hide the brass in it, but I couldn't very well say that.

"Are we all agreed?" he asked.

"I believe we are," I said, extending my hand. We shook, and I turned to leave before he got it into his head to dismiss me.

"One more thing," he said, stopping me in the doorway. "In light of recent events, it seems to me that I must ask for the entire amount of the loan in gold."

"After you already lowered it?" Oh no. This was one thing I truly couldn't work around. I didn't have that much wire or that much time. "Are you sure? Everyone in Strachey knows you reduced the amount Clarrie had to spin. If you go back on your promise now, you'll have branded yourself the villain, and I won't have had to lift a finger. Trust me, you don't want to."

"As it happens, Evelyn, I don't trust you. So I'm afraid I must insist."

I opened my mouth to press argument, but he stopped me.

"You may go now."

I wheeled out of the room and hurried out of the house. I didn't stop to take a breath until I was back in the street. I was flushed with anger; heat filled my head, burning from ear to ear.

I'd been so close! I was so close to having a deal I could work with—it was going to be challenging, sure, but at least I'd have had a chance. There was no way I could get tens of thousands of sovereigns' worth of fake gold wire in time, and without Terence's cooperation . . .

I ran through my half-baked plan in my head. Originally, I had thought that when Clarrie emerged with the brass, the crowd would erupt with excitement. I wasn't expecting Lord Piminder to believe it was really gold, but if Terence took that moment to propose to Clarrie, the crowd would be so enthused, Piminder would lose every client in Strachey if he backed down. Now, Terence would stay silent, Lord Piminder would say the gold was insufficient, and everyone would be disappointed and a little embarrassed for Clarrie.

Not to mention, I realized, Piminder would tell the whole town the gold was fake. My plan required that no one look at it too closely, but without a marriage proposal, there'd be nothing else to see. I couldn't let her walk out with an armful of brass wire—we'd both be ruined. I had to tell Clarrie to shut it down. But how was I going to convince her that her fairy godmother wasn't coming? Should I just let it go? Let her stumble out of the tower in tears, knowing that no fairies had come to save her?

I crossed through the center of town fairly oblivious to my surroundings, still seething at Lord Piminder. How had I let him dismiss me? I'd known it was coming, but he caught me having to have the last word—and then there was that rubbish about opening his house to me. He hadn't listened to me! He'd spent the whole night trying to impress me (and I'd fallen for it, a fact I glossed over as I ranted to myself), and he didn't listen to me at all. Did he even ask me about my daughters?

I was in such a mood, in fact, that I very nearly missed someone calling my name.

"Madam Radcliffe?"

I spun around, looking for the voice.

"Mr. Sherman?" I exclaimed as I recognized my solicitor sitting on the patio of a teahouse.

He looked just as anxious and timid as the last time I saw him. Actually, if it were possible, he looked even more world-weary than usual.

"It's good to see you, Madam Radcliffe. I suppose congratulations are in order," he said. "A royal wedding! That's something. I'm very, very glad things worked out for you, Madam Radcliffe. Very glad."

"Thank you. What brings you to Strachey?"

His timid smile turned glum. "Lord Dorplin has me on retainer."

"To take care of his will?"

"No, he's hoping to cement some business arrangements while he's here, so he brought me to draw up the contracts. Brought my wife too. Insisted that we get to experience all the parties."

"Well, the Season can be a bit—"

"I've got nothing to do! Nothing to witness, no contracts to draw up until he makes an agreement. I'm eating limitless lemon ices and watching my wife spend money," he wailed.

As I was trying hard not to laugh, an idea struck me. Leverage, Evelyn. You need leverage.

"Do you do loan contracts, Mr. Sherman?"

"I can do. Are you looking to borrow money?"

"No, I'm more curious about defaulting on loans, debt collection, invalid contracts. That sort of thing. I suppose that's more investigation and court time than you really do."

"I look into that occasionally. You need a barrister to bring the lawsuit, of course, but I might gather the evidence. Why?"

"It's a bit of a complicated story, but a friend of mine is in some trouble over a loan his father took, which he didn't know about until recently. The creditor is demanding full payment plus interest, which puts the amount quite out of reach."

"Well, for starters, in the case of an inherited debt, the creditor is required to give the debtor a copy of the contract within so many days of the original debtor's death. If your friend's creditor didn't do that, he could easily argue for a suspension of interest until the notification was given. Other than that, I'd have to inspect the contract for any other advantages. There's always the possibility that the creditor might do something to invalidate the contract, but that's rare, of course. You said this was for a friend?"

"Yes. Mr. Sherman, would you like some work to do while you're waiting around?"

His eyes lit up, and then he immediately tried to cover that he was excited to do work. "Why, I . . . well, if you need something . . ."

"I'll send you the details. Care of Lord Dorplin?"

He nodded.

"Thank you, Mr. Sherman. I'll be in touch soon."

I couldn't help walking away with a grin on my face. Don't count your chickens, Evelyn, I warned myself. You can't be sure Mr. Sherman will find anything strong enough to persuade Lord Piminder to cooperate.

But oh, I prayed, I hope he does. Because with enough leverage, I would wipe the floor with Hugo Piminder's smug grin.

CHAPTER ELEVEN

I SPENT THE next two nights making batch after batch of brass wire until I had a heaping wheelbarrow full of what I hoped looked like gleaming straw. I was utterly exhausted.

On the third day, I went to the tower. Lord Piminder and I had agreed that I could get the tower ready for Clarrie. Then, the next morning, we would inspect it together, bring in the straw, and leave Clarrie to her fate. I had one chance to hide the wire in the tower before Clarrie took occupancy, and it would have to pass Lord Piminder's inspection.

So I trudged through the neighborhood that morning, fresh off my alchemical experimentations, pushing a wheelbarrow packed with a sack of wire that I'd carefully topped with blankets, pillows, and a broom. In my satchel, I'd packed hemp twine, a hammer, nails, shears, pliers, glue, parchment, ink, a pen, and at the last second, I'd thrown in chalk, just in case. I did know I'd gone overboard, but I still had no idea how I would pull this off.

Fortunately, I didn't have to lug everything through the center of town. Our home wasn't far from the King's Wood, which was a selling point for Henry when he bought it. It was a quieter neighborhood, a little bit out of the way, and the perfect environment to transport a wheelbarrow of brass wire unnoticed. Unfortunately, the tower was on a small hill. I bent low, put my back into it, and pushed.

The tower itself was quite simply round and tall and had stood there far longer than any of the nearby homes. Most assumed it had been a watchtower, although I wasn't sure it was tall enough to spot anything but the leaves on the trees. It belonged, I supposed, to the city, or the nation, or the queen, perhaps. I had no idea who kept it standing.

I approached the door of the tower—or rather, the door at ground level. Directly opposite and facing the woods was a door about six feet off the ground, the purpose of which historians continued to debate. The city, for its part, had simply built staircases on either side of the door.

Lord Piminder had asked the mayor for permission to use the tower and had received the key, which he passed on to me. Since it rarely occurred to me to ask for permission, I'd planned on picking the lock and apologizing afterward, but clearly, wealthy men had a different way of doing things.

As soon as I pushed the door open, I was hit with a cloud of dust. When the sneezing abated, I surveyed the ground floor. Someone had filled the space with crates, piled haphazardly throughout the room. They'd all had a board or two pried up and then bent back into some kind of shape so they could be stacked, although the person doing the stacking had not been meticulous, by any means. I peeked inside a few crates. Empty.

The crates were an obvious answer to my problem. Simply pack the wire in the crates. However, they were so obvious, Lord Piminder would be immediately suspicious. I could well imagine him ordering someone to open the crates; the question was, would he insist on opening every one? The wire would fit in a few crates, and I could easily hide them among the empty ones. How thorough would he be?

I could also pack all the crates with a layer of—well, what? Fabric scraps? Shredded newspapers? That would take a lot of newspapers, I thought. Besides, would Lord Piminder simply demand that the crates be unpacked? And how would I get Clarrie to open them? It didn't really seem like fairy magic to hide your reward in used packing crates.

What I'd really wanted was to hide the wire under the pile of straw. Then Clarrie would uncover it as she attempted to send straw through her spinning wheel. That's the sort of thing fairies would do—you find their magic after you've tried and tried and it all seems hopeless. You've got to suffer a bit before your fairy godmother shows up.

I sighed and went to work. The crates all had to be stacked along the tower wall to make room for the straw and the spinning wheel. I swept up the dust and dirt that had accumulated, and by that I mean I pushed it out the door. Then I went upstairs and pushed the second-floor dirt into the fireplace. It was a little cramped downstairs with all the crates, and I certainly didn't want to remove them all. Clarrie could sleep on the second floor and work on the first floor, so I didn't need to clean the third.

I did go up and look at it, however. I don't know what I expected to find—a secret cupboard? A hollow spot in the floor? Unfortunately for me, from top to bottom this tower was quite ordinary. I ran through my options. I couldn't hide the wire in the straw. The crates were much too big a risk.

There was also the option of sneaking the wire in during the night. I'd surely have to use the floating door, but Clarrie still might catch me. She might decide to stay awake all night trying to spin, and if I opened the door, she'd spot me immediately. And if Lord Piminder set someone to watch the tower . . .

I returned to the ground floor and examined everything one last time. Was there anything else Clarrie would need? The summer heat wave had just hit, so she wouldn't be cold. There would be no need to use the fireplace. Wait. The fireplace. Could I hide the wire in the flue?

I got on my knees, stuck my head into the first-floor fireplace, and twisted around to see the opening. That has to be big enough, I thought. I stuck my hand up the flue—unblocked. I could shove the sack of wire up the chimney. I just needed a way to hold it in place, and a way to make it drop.

I crawled back out of the fireplace and looked around the room. I had an awful lot of wood available. If I stuck a board in the flue underneath the sack of wire and propped it up with a couple of planks, I'd simply have to remove the props and the gold would fall into the fireplace.

I pulled one of the crates from the stack. The one thing I hadn't brought was a saw, sadly, so I focused on the board that had already been pried up, hoping it had been weakened enough that I could break it in half. Blessedly, these crates had been shoddily constructed, so it only took most of my strength to crack the board at its weak spot.

When it finally snapped, the piece flipped out of my hands, hit me in the knee, and clattered on the floor while I flinched and shut my eyes, trying to avoid flying wood splinters. I picked up the piece and held it up to the flue. A decent fit. Now I needed the props, so I pried off two of the diagonal planks that reinforced the sides of the crate.

I removed the sack of wire from the wheelbarrow. It was, of course, much, much lighter than actual gold, which would end this whole thing rather quickly if Lord Piminder got his hands on it. But he won't, I told myself. That's why you hired Mr. Sherman. You'll press your legal points on Piminder while the ladies of Strachey ooh and ah over Clarrie. Leverage.

I shoved the sack up the chimney. Then, holding the small board underneath the sack, I reached for one of the support beams and stood it on its end. It was long enough to keep the board hovering just below the narrow opening. I added the second prop and stepped back.

It held. I breathed a sigh of relief. I mean, there were two wooden planks standing straight up in the middle of the fireplace, but at least the wires were out of sight.

To trigger the falling sack, I only needed to remove the props. I pulled out my twine and tied one end around the middle of one of my spare planks. Then I placed that board behind the two props. One good tug and we'd have a fairy surprise. I just needed to run the line outside.

I gently unwound my twine, keeping it close to the tower wall, until I reached the wooden stairs leading up to the floating door.

I unwound quite a lot of twine from the spool and cut. Then I threaded the end up between the planks that formed the little landing right in front of the door.

Now I had to get the door open. I placed one shoe on the line to hold it in place and then hobbled outside and up the outer stairs and unlocked the door. I pulled the twine through the door, tucking it in the corner, and tied it to a nail I hammered into the side of the platform.

Back inside the tower, I surveyed my handiwork. The twine, I thought, would only be visible if you were looking for it. The boards in the fireplace, on the other hand, were obviously up to something. I took the rest of my demolished crate and piled it in the fireplace, arranging boards to look like I'd just dumped scraps in the hearth.

I bit my lip. It wasn't perfect, but how many people would look twice at a fireplace full of wood? Even if two beams were standing on end? More to the point, I supposed, was whether Lord Piminder would look twice at that fireplace. I couldn't afford to underestimate him, but I certainly didn't have any better ideas. If I didn't want him to look at the fireplace, where did I want him to look?

The crates. I'd pack them full of fabric scraps, newsprint, and brown paper, and tomorrow morning I'd let him waste his time taking them all apart.

The war council met later that evening. Mr. Sherman arrived after dinner to discuss his findings, while Maribelle, giddy with excitement, had invited herself over. And Fanchon, of course, lived here.

"You have a very successful argument that Lord Piminder did not provide notice of the loan to Lord Babcock in the requisite amount of time. I think a court could reasonably decide to deny Lord Piminder interest accumulated since the elder Babcock's death," Mr. Sherman said.

"That's good," I said.

"Unfortunately, I can't find any evidence that would completely invalidate the loan. If the senior Piminder somehow took advantage of the senior Babcock, it can't be proven. And there's nothing to suggest that Lord Piminder has actively interfered with Lord Babcock's ability to repay the loan. But as long as Clarrie's fairy godmother spins enough gold to cover the loan's principal, you should be able to convince Lord Piminder to accept it."

My heart sank. I wasn't going to offer Lord Piminder any gold at all. In fact, I suddenly realized, I had no way to spirit the gold away, so no one with a discerning eye would catch on. And now, if I had to hand it over to Lord Piminder, I needed to convince everyone that the gold had suddenly turned into brass wire in his hands. I grimaced. I wasn't ready for this. I was so far from ready, and Clarrie's future was marching on ahead. How could I have thought I could turn this into a business?

"Isn't that a good thing, Mom? Clarrie's fairy godmother will at least bring her that much gold, right?"

I looked around at the faces of my supporters. They all looked so hopeful. To them, the problem wasn't whether Clarrie's fairy godmother would come, it was whether she could possibly have enough gold to pay off the loan. And now she was bound to. I couldn't tell them the real reason I was worried.

"I'm just very worried that Lord Piminder won't accept it. What if he insists that it's fake?"

"But it's gold. If it's fake, he doesn't get it. He's not going to talk himself out of gold," Fan said.

"Unless he thinks he can get the Babcocks' land. The Babcocks owe Lord Piminder more than their estate is worth. Denying him the interest only means that he can take their estate and they'll be even."

We sat in glum silence, having apparently realized that fairies can't fix everything. You really should have known that, Evelyn. You should have told the Babcocks to seek legal counsel in the first place.

"Then we need someone to verify the gold," Fan said, unwilling to give up. "As soon as Clarrie exits the tower, we need a goldsmith to certify that it really is gold. Then Lord Piminder can't argue!"

Oh God, no, I thought. I'd have to bribe the goldsmith.

I shook my head. "Lord Piminder doesn't trust me, and I don't trust him. I'd suspect him of bribing a banker, and vice versa."

"Perhaps," Mr. Sherman said, "it is actually best if he does not accept the gold. If I were taking this to court, I would press the judge to order a payment plan so the Babcocks had time to pay back the loan."

In other words, Evelyn, it would have been best if you hadn't gotten involved.

"I think most judges would be willing to grant that," he finished.

"That's just it," I said. "Most judges. What if you don't have a sympathetic judge? And Lord Piminder has the resources to tie this up in court for ages, while the Babcocks are shelling out legal fees they can't afford."

"But the fairies are going to help!" Maribelle cried. "I just know Clarrie's fairy godmother is going to come! And it won't even be that little creepy man."

"Then we have to make Lord Piminder cooperate," Fan said.

"Don't you think he will? When he sees the fairy miracle?" Maribelle said.

"Well, I would," Fan said. "But I'd have been reasonable with the Babcocks in the first place. We've got to have a plan, just in case he doesn't have a change of heart."

"Oh, I think when she comes out carrying gold, his heart will melt, and he'll realize the error of his ways, and everyone will be happy, and—"

"Wait," I interrupted. "Are we the only ones who know Clarrie doesn't want to marry Terence?" They just stared at me, puzzled. "The original bargain was that if Clarrie could spin enough gold, Lord Piminder would let them get married. When I spoke to him, Piminder demanded the full loan amount, but I didn't say anything about the marriage. We all know this is about the Babcocks' loan, but doesn't everyone else think this is about true love?"

Fan's mouth dropped open while she thought, her eyes scanning the ceiling for answers. "Well," she began, "she told you, me, and Maribelle a few days ago that she didn't want to marry Terence. I haven't told anyone." She looked at Maribelle.

Maribelle shook her head. "Everyone's been asking me about you. Sorry, dear. I did change the subject to Clarrie, but I think I only talked about fairies. I'm pretty sure."

I could believe that, so I spoke up before Maribelle could spiral into indecision. "Then when Clarrie comes out of the tower with gold, everyone there will expect Lord Piminder to give his blessing to their wedding. And if he doesn't—"

"Ooh, people will be really angry!" Maribelle exclaimed.

"I think he'll cooperate if he realizes he's the villain." What I didn't add was that Clarrie's fairy gold would come with a caveat: it becomes worthless in the hands of the impure, or some such nonsense. Lord Piminder would neither like it nor believe it, but I prayed he would be swayed by the disapproval of his peers—or at least, their wives. "We need as many people there as possible. Maribelle—you've got the most connections. You've got all of tomorrow to get people to the tower at dawn the next day."

Maribelle nodded so seriously I thought she might salute.

"I can drop a mention to my wife," Mr. Sherman said. "She's not well connected, but she does like to talk. I will, of course, be there tomorrow and the next day."

"Can you bring your wife tomorrow morning?" I asked. "I don't want Lord Piminder to know we've hired a solicitor until the last minute."

"Oh, certainly. No need to give him time to hire ten. I will appear as an innocent bystander."

"Well," I started, suddenly feeling the need to give a speech. We needed a good team rally, I thought.

"Are people really asking about me?" Fan suddenly said.

Maribelle nodded with a sympathetic pout. "They just want to know who you're going to pick. And if I think one of the lads can really make you laugh. Also, they're wondering if you're cursed not to laugh."

"Then tell people I'll be at the tower. And that you've heard the boys each have plans to make me laugh."

Maribelle gasped. "Oh, that's good! People will want to see that! It's not lying, is it? They do have plans?"

Fan shrugged. "They do if Roompilda has anything to say about it."

I gave Fan a weak smile. "Thank you, sweetheart," I said. "Thanks to all of you. Now go home and get some sleep. We've got a busy few days ahead."

I lay in bed for a good while that night before I fell asleep. If I hadn't gotten involved, the Babcocks would have been ruined. Yet my interference wasn't shaping up to be much help—except in humiliating me. I pushed the anxieties out of my head and lulled myself to sleep with one last problem: How could I convince everyone that fairy gold was only pure in the hands of Clarrie Babcock?

CHAPTER TWELVE

I STOOD THE next morning at the door to the tower, face-to-face with Lord Piminder. It was going to be swelteringly hot today; although it was early morning, the air was still, promising a stationary heat that would cling to your hair and face and hands. At least Clarrie wouldn't even think about using that fireplace.

Terence stood at Lord Piminder's side, arms folded with a smug grin. Behind them were five of Lord Piminder's valets and a wagon full of straw. My ragtag contingent was spread out a few yards back from the tower. Maribelle and Fanchon watched with tense anticipation; a few busybodies were casually watching the proceedings, probably to see if it would be worth coming back tomorrow. I saw Mr. Sherman and his wife mixed in among them. Finally, Clarrie Babcock stood in front of the onlookers, one hand gripping her spinning wheel and the rosiness drained from her cheeks. Her father had his hand on her shoulder, although it was less a supportive gesture and more an actual need to steady himself—he swallowed hard, as though he was biting back bile. Her mother looked very, very cross.

"Are we ready?" Lord Piminder said, and it was obvious that smugness ran in the family.

"Lead the way," I replied, unlocking the door and handing the key back to Lord Piminder.

He entered the tower, and I took a step to follow, but Terence pushed in front of me and muscled his way in. I rolled my eyes and walked in.

I could tell Lord Piminder's attention was immediately drawn to the crates, as it should have been—I'd stacked them all against the wall on the left-hand side. You practically ran into them as you came through the door. I pretended to ignore them.

"The straw can go over there," I pointed, "and she can set up the spinning wheel in the center."

"What are these?" Piminder asked.

"Crates," I said. "The city's, I assume. I stacked them against the wall."

"Hmm," he said and moved toward the second-floor stairs.

This time, I motioned for Terence to precede me, so I wouldn't take another shoulder to the chin. He strode past me, and I followed leisurely.

"Is she planning on sleeping?" Lord Piminder scoffed as he saw the blankets. "I should think she'd use all her time to spin."

"Have you ever manned a spinning wheel for twenty-four hours straight?" I asked.

"No."

"Neither have I. I thought she might need rest."

He bent down, picked up the pillow and shook it. Then he tossed it to the floor and picked up each of the blankets, shaking them and throwing them to the floor in a heap. Satisfied, apparently, that I hadn't hidden any gold in them, he returned downstairs.

"That was petty," I said and began to remake the little pallet.

"Call the men," I heard Lord Piminder tell Terence. "Tell them to search the crates."

This was it. I dropped the bedding and hurried down the stairs.

"Absolutely not," I said, moving to block the doorway so Terence and his servants couldn't enter. Lord Piminder grabbed my arm, as though he would drag me away from the door. I swatted his hand away, and suddenly, I didn't have to pretend to be angry. "Under no circumstances—"

"As I believe I have made clear, Evelyn, I don't trust you. All we are going to do is make sure you haven't hidden anything in the crates." He motioned to Terence to enter with the men.

I stuck my arm out, rather hoping to clothesline Terence. "Why on earth would I do something so obvious? The crates are in plain sight!"

"Nevertheless, in the name of fairness—"

"Fairness? And just how is it fair to Clarrie to let your men trample all over the place? They'll tear up the crates and make a huge mess, and then she'll be stuck with it all day. Besides, do you expect me to trust you? I might cheat, but you, you're beyond all suspicion? There's no telling what you and your men have planned!"

Actually, I was pretty sure they had nothing. I couldn't think of a single way for Lord Piminder to cheat at this stage. The thing about arguing with men like Lord Piminder or Husband #1, however, was that they didn't expect you to make sense.

"If you want to waste your time unpacking crates, fine," I continued. "But not in the tower. You and your son can carry them outside yourselves. Then I don't care what you do with them."

Lord Piminder met my eyes with his supercilious glare, as if he were trying to determine whether I was bluffing. As much as I wanted to stare him down, I swallowed down the rising gall and looked away. Let him think I was lying.

"Very well. Terence, if you would. We shall deliver these crates to the men outside."

His servants backed off, and I removed my arm from the doorway to allow Terence entry. As both Piminder and his son exited the tower bearing crates, I pulled Henry's old pocket watch from my pocket.

"I'm not allowing this to eat up any of Clarrie's time, either! I shall time exactly how long this farce takes you, and it will be added to her deadline tomorrow!" I shouted as I stepped out onto the grass.

As the parade of crates began, I moved toward our audience.

"What's going on?" Lilla Babcock demanded.

"Lord Piminder wishes to examine the packing crates left in the tower," I said, loud enough so the crowd could hear. "Apparently, he believes we have cheated, although how I'm not sure. None of us has that much gold, which is precisely how this all started. Besides, I have full faith that Clarrie's fairy godmother will come to her aid, and I plan on simply letting her do her job."

Maribelle gave a little gasp and started to applaud, but then stopped when she realized no one was joining her. I was about to turn and supervise the crates when Lilla came up to me.

"This had better work," she said, her red face as close to mine as she could reach. "If you're putting my daughter through all this, all I can say is it had better work."

I repressed a shudder. "Don't worry, Lady Babcock. Clarrie will be just fine. I'm sure this will work."

I hurried away from Lady Babcock and watched the spectacle. Lord Piminder's men were trying to pry up enough boards that they could remove the muslin and newsprint I'd stuffed in the crates.

"My Lord," I heard one of them say, "we could really use a crowbar. Should one of us run back and grab one?"

"We don't have time for that," Lord Piminder snapped. "Just keep working."

Before long, sweat stained the shirts of everyone but Lord Piminder, who hadn't deigned to open crates himself. The ground was littered with strips of paper and cloth but of course no gold.

"It has been nearly an hour," I shouted, checking my watch with a theatrical flourish. "Are you finished with your wild-goose chase?"

"Almost," Piminder said through clenched teeth. "We are being thorough!"

A few minutes later, he left the demolished crates and marched over to me.

"Well?"

"I believe we are ready to begin."

I looked at the watch again, just to be obnoxious. "Then let's load in the straw."

This time I did allow his valets to help. They carried the straw bales into the tower, then cut the cords holding the bales together, leaving Clarrie a pile of straw nearly as high as her waist. When they were finished, Clarrie and I carried her spinning wheel into the tower.

"You can do this," I whispered. "It'll be a long day. You can take breaks. Sleep if you need to. Your fairy godmother will come."

"What are you telling her?" Lord Piminder asked.

"I am merely assuring Miss Babcock that her fairy godmother will come help her. Thank you, Lord Babcock," I said as Patrick handed me a little stool for Clarrie.

Clarrie came to the doorway and kissed her father on the cheek, and he stepped back from the door. Then Lilla came forward and held out a hamper for her daughter.

"What is in that?" Lord Piminder demanded, reaching out a hand to lift the lid.

Lilla snatched it back. "Food, for my daughter. Or were you expecting her to starve all day?"

"Really, Lord Piminder," I said, coming up behind Clarrie. "I'll put that inside." I took the hamper and flipped up the lid to show him a glimpse of the bread, cheese, and cold cuts within. The Babcocks had also filled several waterskins for Clarrie, which I took from Patrick as Clarrie hugged her mother.

"Are we quite ready?" Piminder asked.

The Babcocks stepped away from the door and I exited the tower.

"I believe we are," I said, nodding at Clarrie.

"Then we will see Miss Babcock and her gold tomorrow at dawn," Lord Piminder said, raising his voice so the crowd could hear.

I gestured toward the wreckage of crates. "One hour and seven minutes after dawn."

He gave me a thin false smile and replaced the padlock on the door.

"Who keeps the key?" I asked. "In case of emergency?"

"We are not far from the Indigo Goose. The publican knows me. I am sure he would be willing to hold the key for us. In the name of fairness."

I nodded. If Clarrie were really in trouble, of course, there wouldn't be time to run to the Goose and back. I'd examined the padlock, however, and it was a common model. I was certain I had a key that would fit it. I just didn't want Lord Piminder holding on to the real one.

I held out my hand, and as we shook, Terence stepped up behind his father, sweat dripping down his face.

"Until tomorrow," I said. "Don't worry, young man. I am positive Clarrie's fairy godmother will help you marry your sweetheart."

Terence turned a shade greener, although maybe that was just heat stroke. As we walked away from the tower, I heard him ask, "The back door—it is locked, isn't it? Does it use the same key?"

"It does," Lord Piminder answered. "But you remind me I have not checked it. Go see if it is locked."

My breath caught, and I turned around, hoping I was keeping my expression free of panic. What if he sees the twine coming out from under the door? What if he kicks it, or trips on it? What if he sets the whole thing off?

I held my breath as he examined the padlock on the back door and gave the door a good tug. I slowly exhaled as he returned.

"It's locked," Terence said. He had neither noticed the twine nor heard everything crash down. "Do you want me to take that to Lonzo?"

Lord Piminder gave him the key, and Terence ran off down the hill. Piminder nodded to me and turned away, gesturing to his valets to accompany him home.

I gave him a few steps before I shouted, "Are you going to clean that mess up?"

He merely waved his hand dismissively and kept walking.

I shrugged. "It's your littering fine," I called back.

He stopped abruptly and gave a terse command to his valets. I was quite certain he swore. I turned away with a grin on my face and joined Fan and Maribelle in the dispersing crowd.

"Oh, bravo, Evelyn! This is so exciting!" Maribelle gushed.

"That was really awesome, Mom. You totally humiliated him with the crates. I looked around. People were giving him some really dirty looks. Did you plan that?"

"The crates were in the tower. I filled them with cloth and newspapers so he'd make a spectacle trying to inspect them."

"Well, I think you won that round," Fan said.

"I hope so," I said. "Lilla Babcock will throttle me if this doesn't work."

"Oh, I don't see why! Clarrie's going to have the chance to meet her fairy godmother!" Maribelle said.

"I still wouldn't want to be her," Fan said. "It would be so boring to sit in that tower all day. I hope she at least brought a book to read. And what if you did all of this, and your fairy godmother turned out to be that little man? Honestly, this fairy story is the worst to be in, and I had frogs fall on my head."

Now that the Piminders had left and their men were occupied, Mr. Sherman approached the huddle.

"Hello, Mr. Sherman," I said.

"Well done so far," he replied. "Are you going home now?"

I shrugged. "I know it's unlikely, but if Lord Piminder does plan on sabotaging Clarrie somehow, it would be while she's in the tower. I don't feel good about leaving it unwatched. Besides, if Clarrie gets ill or needs help, someone has to be here to get her out of the tower."

I still wasn't sure how Lord Piminder could cheat. I'd tried to examine the spectacle from his point of view, and it was simply a matter of whether he believed Clarrie had a fairy godmother. If he didn't, victory was his. If he did, what could he do? But although I suspected Piminder was overconfident, I didn't think he'd leave things entirely up to fate. He could have someone steal the gold before she left the tower. He could, I supposed, try to discredit Clarrie—make it seem like she'd had a male visitor in the night. I didn't think he was quite that sinister, but he certainly didn't mind ruining the Babcocks financially. At any rate, I wanted the tower under observation.

"I'll take turns with you," Mr. Sherman said. "My wife is on to her next engagement. I'm happy to watch the tower."

"Thank you. I'll come back in a few hours and give you a break. Maribelle, it's on you now. Get us a crowd for tomorrow."

"I won't let you down, Evelyn," she said fervently, grasping my hand.

"Right. Um. Thank you. Well, good work, team. Let's break. Disperse."

That had gone rather well, I thought as Fan and I walked home. My distraction had worked. They'd paid so much attention to the crates, they never noticed my fireplace setup or the thin twine hugging the wall. Lord Piminder had made a fool of himself tearing up those crates. Nevertheless, nerves still clawed at my stomach because none of it mattered. I hadn't hidden real gold in the fireplace, and no marriage proposal was coming to bail Clarrie out of handing over a sack of brass.

At sundown, Mr. Sherman and I stood in the field a few yards from the tower. He'd come wearing a rather oversized tunic underneath a long overcoat, as well as a stocking cap pulled down over his ears, which combined with his large round spectacles made him look a bit like one of those gnomes people put in their gardens. I raised a skeptical eyebrow.

"My wife," he said. "She's always worried I'll catch a chill, even when it's warm out."

"You really don't have to stay, Mr. Sherman," I said.

"You can't stay awake all night," he said. "One of us can sleep while the other watches."

I frowned, hoping he wouldn't see it in the dimming light. At some point, I needed to pull the twine and send the brass crashing down—and deliver some message about it becoming worthless in the wrong hands—and I couldn't let Mr. Sherman see me. I hadn't expected him to be this dedicated, but he was like a very skinny, squeaky bulldog. As long as he really did go to sleep . . .

Fanchon helped me carry two garden chairs and a stack of blankets from home.

"Aren't you going to want a lantern?" she asked.

I shook my head. "Then we'll be totally blind outside the lantern's circle. Our eyes will at least adjust to the starlight."

I took the first watch, sitting in my chair with a blanket over my knees, watching the stillness. I'd debated when I should trigger the falling brass. I wanted Clarrie's excitement to be fresh, but I also couldn't be caught by early gawkers, so I'd decided to wait until a few hours before dawn. Mr. Sherman would have a turn watching, and then after we switched for the second time, I would work my fairy magic.

My few hours passed uneventfully. I woke Mr. Sherman and curled up uncomfortably in the chair, the armrest digging into my back. I dozed off picturing Fan walking down the aisle on her father's arm, his leering face taunting me.

I awoke to Mr. Sherman shaking my shoulder.

"Evelyn! Evelyn!" he whispered.

"Already?" I mumbled as I tried to work the kinks out of my neck.

"Shh! Look!" He pointed toward the tower.

A light bobbed across the field and climbed the hill toward the tower.

"Someone's there!" I whispered.

"We need to know who it is," Mr. Sherman replied.

The light crossed in front of the tower and headed toward the stairs that led to the floating door.

"We can hide in the woods," I said and crept off toward the trees.

Neither Mr. Sherman nor I was stealthy enough to creep through a forest in the middle of the night without stepping on at least a few sticks. Luckily, our visitor was oblivious to his surroundings.

I watched from behind a tree as the visitor set his lantern down at the top of the stairs and began to fiddle with the lock on the door. We were close enough now that I could see the visitor a bit more clearly. He was indeed male, tall, and slender, and although I could only see his back, that was enough for me—I'd already been clipped by those shoulders once today.

"That's Terence Piminder," I whispered.

"That's where I would have laid my money," Mr. Sherman said. "I thought he was too interested in the back door earlier."

Terence had succeeded in removing the padlock and now carefully pushed the door open a crack.

"We have to stop him!" I said and probably would have burst out of the forest had Mr. Sherman not grabbed my arm.

"He's going to interfere!" I hissed.

"Exactly! He's going to intentionally sabotage an attempt at loan repayment!"

I stared at him, wide-eyed. I noticed his eager expression, eyes distortedly magnified behind his spectacles. My jaw dropped.

"Courts have voided whole loan contracts for something like that," I said.

Mr. Sherman nodded.

I looked back at Terence. He'd peeked his head through the door and was now slipping into the tower.

"I'm not going to let him hurt Clarrie," I said to Mr. Sherman.

"Of course not. But we do need proof."

I nodded. "I can't be seen. This is up to you. Follow him, or whatever you need to do. I'll take the chairs and blankets home so it's not obvious we were camping here all night. I'll be back here before dawn."

Before Mr. Sherman could reply, we heard a loud crash—a crack, like the splintering of wood—from inside the tower. I could almost feel the blood drain from my face. The sack of brass had fallen. Terence had tripped the line somehow, and the sack had fallen into the fireplace, ready to be discovered by Clarrie's erstwhile sweetheart. I was stunned—how was I supposed to recover from this? I didn't have extra brass. Besides, Terence would know what I'd done. I had to chase him off now! Or should I pretend to be a fairy and reason with him? In a few seconds, my mind raced with panicked thoughts. Then, I heard another crash.

The sack can't fall twice, I thought.

Mr. Sherman snuck up to the tower, hesitating only for a moment before he tiptoed up the stairs and peeked in the room. There was another loud crack. What was going on? I fidgeted impatiently.

I decided to get just a little bit closer. I stepped out of the woods and stood with my back against the wall at the back of the stairs, with Mr. Sherman on the landing right above me.

After the fourth crash, I heard a faint voice from the second floor.

"Who's there?" Clarrie called. "G-godmother?"

At the same moment, Mr. Sherman stepped into the doorway. "Give that to me," I heard him whisper. Give him what? What did Terence have?

I wasn't sure if Terence responded, because all I could hear was Clarrie. "What was that? Did you say something, Godmother?"

"Hand it over," Mr. Sherman tried again.

"Oh, sorry, Godfather! Hand what over?" Clarrie asked. Then she gasped. "This is the part where you ask me for jewelry! But I don't have a necklace or a bracelet. We don't have money for fancy jewelry!"

"You're in over your head," Mr. Sherman continued to whisper to Terence. "This is going to end badly for you if you don't cooperate."

"Well, yes, I know that!" Clarrie cried. "I know I can't spin straw into gold! But I don't have any jewelry! What could I give you? Umm, Mother packed too much food for me. Would you like a corned beef sandwich? They're very good."

"You've made a mistake," Mr. Sherman said, "and you know what you've got to do. Now hand it over."

Clarrie wailed. "I can't! I won't do it! I won't promise my first-born child!"

Suddenly, there was a muffled thump, and I heard wooden planks rattling and something scraping on the stone floor.

"You'll regret this!" I picked out in the hubbub, followed by "Give it to me!" and "That's mine!" and "Ow!" One of the voices had to be Terence's, but I couldn't tell them apart. Had Mr. Sherman and Terence gotten into a scuffle?

"No!" Clarrie exclaimed. "Please don't be angry! Maybe—maybe I can guess your name! Um . . . oh, I can't remember what my book said! Is it Grumblepilson? No. What about . . . Lumpygilson? No, that can't be it."

Just then, I heard another thump, and Terence burst through the doorway. Only seconds behind, Mr. Sherman staggered out after him.

"Stay away from me, you creepy fairy!" Terence whispered as he raced down the stairs.

"Mr. Sherman, what's happ—" I hissed.

"I'm all right!" he said and sprinted off in pursuit.

"Wait!" Clarrie said. "Is it Mumblewitskin?"

Now that the two men were gone, the tower was completely silent.

"It is?" Clarrie said, surprised. "I got it!"

I heard the creak of Clarrie's feet on the stairs. She cried out in anguish.

"My spinning wheel! He must have destroyed it because he was angry with me!"

Her spinning wheel? That must have been what I heard splintering! Had Terence come to wreck her spinning wheel? Why? Surely he didn't believe she could really spin straw into gold. Unless . . . unless he was actually worried Clarrie might have a fairy godmother. I remembered his reaction when I'd mentioned him marrying his sweetheart. He was so concerned that he would have to marry Clarrie because of the fairies' help, he'd sabotaged her the only way he knew how. He must have thought the fairies needed a spinning wheel to turn the straw into gold—because in the storybook, I realized, that little elf actually does the spinning.

I almost wanted to laugh. Clarrie, of course, wasn't finding it funny. Well, I thought, this is as perfect a time as any to make the gold appear.

I took my knife from my pocket and cut the line where I'd tied it to the nail. Then slowly I began to pull, gathering in the loose line. Finally, when the line was taut, I wrapped the end around my hand and gave it one strong yank.

Wooden planks clattered on the fireplace floor, followed by a giant whomp as the sack landed on top of them. I breathed a sigh of relief. Clarrie stopped sobbing, and I listened as she moved debris out of the way to get to the sack.

I heard her gasp. "Gold! It's gold straw! Thank you, fairy godmother! Oh, thank you!"

Now I hesitated. This was the moment to deliver a message, to tell her some rubbish about the gold only remaining pure in the hands of the worthy. But Terence Piminder was the perfect leverage—Lord Piminder would surely back down now to avoid a humiliating defeat in court. Besides, my fairy voice was weak, and since this wasn't in the storybook, I couldn't know that the crowd would believe it. It was best to keep silent—as long as Mr. Sherman really did return with proof. He would, I thought. He had to. I kept my mouth shut.

I cut the line once more so that it fell down between the planks of the stairs, and gently shut the door. I replaced the padlock and returned to our chairs. It took a moment for me to locate them in the darkness, but eventually I ran into one and almost tripped. I stacked them, piled the blankets on top, and staggered home.

CHAPTER THIRTEEN

AS WE LEFT the house just a few hours later, Fan's face was molded into a look of grim determination. I couldn't let her do this, which was a pointless thought, since I really couldn't stop her. Nevertheless, I took a deep breath and prepared for a fight, sanitized of course, by the fairies.

"Sweetheart, don't do this," I said.

"Don't do what?"

"Marry one of those three fools."

"I'm going to marry Damian. Whatever joke he comes up with, I'll laugh at it."

I started to groan.

"I'm not going to marry Justice, obviously," she interrupted. "And Herb isn't horrible, even though he did desert me after that man screamed at me, but I know he wants to sell Dad's company, and I want to keep it. That leaves Damian."

"No! It leaves literally anyone else in the kingdom!"

"Not according to the queen."

"She'll get over it. There are more than three families worth a marriage alliance. The Kingsleys, for example. She'll come around."

"But what if she doesn't?"

"Sweetheart, I promise if you marry Ethan, or whoever it is you want, I promise that I will offend Roompilda and the queen enough that they'll blame it on me. Roompilda probably already assumes you just do whatever I tell you."

"But they won't believe you made me do something I didn't want to do. They'll know you wouldn't be mean to me, Mom."

"Fan, this is your whole life. Your whole life, married to this arrogant man who treats you like you're stupid, and it only gets worse! He only gets less charming, trust me."

"Yeah, and you stayed with Dad because you didn't want to lose me, right? Well, I don't want to lose Ella."

"The queen won't really stop you from seeing Ella. Ella wants to see you!"

"But maybe she doesn't," Fan said, tears welling up. "Maybe she's glad to be rid of me because I was so awful to her, and now the queen's giving her an excuse to say, 'Oh, sorry, Fan, but you're not allowed to visit.'"

"Fan, that isn't true!"

"But you don't know that. And I'm not giving up on Ella."

"I understand, love. I just don't want you to give up who you are."

She didn't respond. Maybe she could only think of things the fairies wouldn't let her say.

We were the first people at the tower, and I immediately panicked that no one would show up. That's because you got here early, I tried to reason with myself. Nevertheless, I paced about with my hands on my hips, praying that Maribelle had managed to drum up a crowd.

Eventually the Babcocks arrived. Patrick waved at me tentatively. Lilla refused to acknowledge me. I tried to smile like everything was going according to plan. Then Maribelle hustled over to me.

"I talked to everyone I could think of," she said. "They all acted like they would come. They will, won't they?"

"I'm sure people will come," I said. I couldn't quite convince myself, but luckily Maribelle was more suggestible, as it wouldn't help to have Maribelle melt down into a bundle of nerves at my side.

My foot had almost tapped out the drum section of an entire symphony when the first noblewomen drifted onto the field. Then slowly but surely the crowd grew. There were young women, some snickering at the tower, others stealing glances at Fan. I saw mothers watching the tower with hands clasped earnestly. The men seemed split—some were disgruntled at being dragged out of bed while others waited with curious anticipation. This was actually going to work, I thought. I had the crowd, Clarrie had the gold, and we had the perfect leverage over the Piminders.

At least, we would as soon as Mr. Sherman got here. Where was he? I scanned the crowd. Was his wife here?

"I'll be back," I told Fan, and I stepped away to search for Mrs. Sherman.

Although I was quite pleased I had a crowd to weave through, it didn't make it particularly easy to locate either of the Shermans. I swept through the first few rows, making my way deeper into the gathering. I had just turned around to make another pass through when I caught a glimpse of Master Relish approaching Fan. He was saying something with a nervous grin, but I couldn't hear him. I pressed forward just in time to see him take a step back and bellow:

"But lo! What strange behavior doth my mistress evince,
When I but from her chamber walkéd thence."

He started marching in place, raising his knees high. After a few steps, he threw himself forward, pretending to trip. It was obviously planned—first, he fell as though time had suddenly slowed, and second, he turned toward Fan with a big grin on his face. When she proved a tougher audience than he'd hoped, he continued.

"She spoke in starts, betimes her brow bedewed,
Crosswise, atimes her back she shewed."

He slowly spun around, turning his back to Fan. I sighed. Herb was reciting Dwerryhouse, a monologue from one of his comedies. And from his overstated pantomimes to his wooden delivery, Herb was awful. It seemed to me he'd put a lot of faith in that slow-motion sprawl—his backup material wasn't as good, and Fan showed no signs of laughing.

Now, having illustrated what it meant to show one's back, Herb spun back around to face Fan.

"Thus she, born under such a merry star,
And though true reason 'twould seem to mar,
I'd say perhaps 'twas me she loved . . ."

At this point, he made an attempt at a double take and ended up looking straight at Fan with his already round eyes practically bulging and his mouth gaping in an exaggerated O. He inhaled deeply, and I cringed in anticipation of the punch line.

"But—um—but that—oh, sorry, that's not it."

The onlookers started to titter at his fumbling of the lines, but that actually seemed to embolden Herb. I suppose he thought his plan was working and that Fan was bound to crack soon, but that didn't help him remember his lines.

"I'd say perhaps 'twas me she loved," he repeated, "but—oh, dash it all! But something, something . . . I'm so sorry. It'll come to me any second."

Herb covered his eyes and racked his memory, and just as he did so, I saw Justice slip up behind him, hand in armpit. Herb opened his mouth to speak, Justice flapped his elbow, and Herb's monologue was interrupted by the loud frap of flatulence. Herb's eyes looked like saucers.

"That wasn't me! I swear that wasn't me!" He turned around and saw Justice slipping back into the crowd. "Damn it, Justice! I know it was you! You can't hide!"

Although the entire crowd was guffawing at this point, Fan hadn't budged. I wasn't inclined to crack a smile either. Butchering Dwerryhouse like that was just embarrassing.

"Madam Radcliffe?" said a voice behind me.

I turned around to face a breathless Mr. Sherman. He'd made a hasty effort to tidy up but had missed a few streaks of mud on his face and hands, and several strands of hair had broken free from his comb-over.

"Mr. Sherman! There you are! What happened?"

"So sorry, Madam Radcliffe. I've been trying to get a hold of that fellow at the Goose, but all the banging in the world won't rouse him, apparently."

"You don't think Terence ever gave him the key."

Mr. Sherman shook his head. "I was hoping to get a statement from him before the Piminders got to him."

"That's unfortunate. We'll just have to work with what you got last night."

Mr. Sherman cringed; his whole expression looked almost sick. "I followed Terence to the river," he said. "He must have thought he'd lost me, as I don't think he knew I was watching when he chucked his hammer into the muck."

He opened a pocket of his briefcase and pulled out the hammer, wrapped in a dishcloth. "Luckily, he's got a lousy arm. It landed in the mud instead of the water, so I retrieved it."

"Mr. Sherman, that's excellent!"

His face crumpled. "But there's no distinguishing marks! Nothing to say this belongs to the Piminders. It's still my word against his."

I pursed my lips. He was right, of course. A convenient set of initials would have been lovely. The word of the tavern owner would have been the nail in the coffin. Instead, it would all come down to how persuasive I could be, and I'd made some awfully foolish mistakes recently. Should I have given Clarrie a fairy message about the gold?

"We can still work with this," I told Mr. Sherman. "Keep that hidden. I'll signal you when—hold on just a moment." I'd been keeping an eye out for the Piminders, but instead, a glance told me Herb had finished his monologue and Damian was moving in.

There is a voice in my head that tells me not to meddle, but I can't remember ever listening to it. I hustled over toward Fan. I would not let Fan marry a replica of her father. I'd hinder Damian's advances as long as possible.

"Well, I imagine the Piminders will be here any minute now," I said. "Hello, Damian. How are you?"

He stammered a hello, my sudden appearance having apparently taken him by surprise. "I'm doing well, Madam Radcliffe," he recovered. He stood there awkwardly. That was all right with me. As long as he didn't start telling jokes.

Fan finally broke the silence. "I do hope Clarrie's fairy godmother came."

"I almost hope she didn't," Damian said. "Imagine all these people when Clarrie comes out empty-handed. So gullible, they're standing out in a field at dawn waiting to see if a fairy has brought gifts. Like children waiting for Old Man Winter." He chuckled.

That certainly wasn't the way to win Fan over. Not even the queen could make her think that was funny. Didn't he know about the frogs?

"Well, you're here," she said crossly.

"Yes, but I'm not here to see Clarrie, am I? What did—" he began, but I cut him off.

"Has your sister been enjoying herself, Damian?"

"Yes, I think so," he replied but kept his eyes on Fan. "How—"

"Good. I was thinking of her just the other day when I saw a group of younger girls," I lied. I figured talking about his sister was a sure way to put him off his game. "They were all gathered outside a tea shop. I hope she's been able to enjoy the lovely markets and shops here in Strachey."

Damian gave me a patronizing smile. Fan's expression was inscrutable. I couldn't tell if she was annoyed or grateful.

I took a breath to continue my inane monologue, a far cry from Dwerryhouse, although I wasn't quite sure what I'd babble about next, when I heard a hush flutter through the crowd. I turned, and sure enough, the Piminders had arrived.

"Oh, here we go," Damian said with a smug grin.

"Wish me luck," I muttered to Fan. She nodded and squeezed my hand.

I gave a pointed glance toward Damian. "Don't laugh," I mouthed as I walked away. She scrunched her mouth into a tight-lipped frown.

I intercepted the Piminders as they cut across the field.

"Madam Radcliffe. Are we ready?" Lord Piminder asked. He took a quick glance over the crowd and smiled, probably pleased that Clarrie would embarrass herself in front of so many people.

I opened my pocket watch and checked the time. "Right on time. We're ready. I assume you retrieved the key from the Goose?" I said, looking directly at Terence. He pulled the key out of a pocket and held it out but wouldn't meet my eyes for more than a few seconds.

"Why don't we let her parents open the door," I said.

Lord Piminder nodded his agreement. I gave the key to Lord Babcock and rejoined the Piminders.

Patrick Babcock knocked on the door. "Clarrie?" he said as he removed the padlock. "You can open the door now, love."

Immediately the door flung open and Clarrie stepped out of the tower, the sack in her arms and a joyous smile on her face. "Look," she cried. "Gold!" She opened the sack and removed a handful of the wire.

Pure pandemonium erupted. Lilla Babcock screamed and fainted. Patrick rushed to catch her, which gave the crowd a perfect view of Clarrie holding gleaming gold straw. It was an hour after dawn, after all, and the sunlight hitting the metal made it sparkle. There were gasps. There were shouts of amazement. There were cheers. And of course, there was one very angry gentleman.

"That can't be real gold!" Lord Piminder barked and moved as if he would confront Clarrie. I stepped in front of him.

"That's immaterial," I said, putting a hand up to stop his advance.

"Are you saying you won't let me inspect the gold?"

"Lord Piminder, you may not believe me, but I'm giving you an opportunity to save face. You're going to congratulate Clarrie on her efforts and cancel her parents' debt."

"Are you insane, woman?"

"Not in the least. You're going to do this because you want to avoid a court battle you will lose."

"That's preposterous. The Babcocks owe me money. Any court would order them to pay it. On what possible grounds could the contract possibly be voided?"

Mr. Sherman suddenly appeared at my elbow. "On grounds that you and your son have established a clear pattern of sabotaging the defendant's ability to reasonably pay back the loan, sir."

"Who is this?"

"Chadwick Sherman, sir, a solicitor in the employ of the Babcocks."

"And what, pray, is this alleged pattern?"

"Point the first: neither at the death of the initial debtor nor at any point afterward did you provide the inheritor of said debt with a copy of the contract he was inheriting. At minimum, a court would cancel all interest accrued since the death of the initial debtor. Point the second: when you verbally informed the debtor of the contract, you resisted any attempt to draw up a schedule of repayment, which is required by law for any debt exceeding a sum of seven hundred sovereigns. Point the third: last night, your son directly attempted to sabotage Clarrie's attempt to fulfill the contract you and she had made."

"What?" Lord Piminder had turned purple. "Think carefully, little man, before you falsely accuse my son."

Mr. Sherman acted as though he had heard neither threat nor insult. "Not falsely, my lord. I witnessed your son open the back door of the tower and smash Clarrie's spinning wheel to pieces. Using this." He displayed the hammer.

"That proves nothing," Lord Piminder said. "That hammer could belong to anyone. You have no way of proving you saw my son."

"Unless Terence recognizes the hammer, of course," I said, smiling sweetly at Terence. He squirmed.

"He does not," Lord Piminder said.

"And are you certain he will continue to assert that under the scrutiny of a court?" I said, not taking my eyes off Terence.

Lord Piminder finally looked at Terence as well, which only made the young man shrink further. "Of course," Piminder maintained with a tense smile. "I cannot believe my son would take such foolish, senseless action." Terence looked like he wanted to cry.

I pressed my point. "And when your tavern owner verifies that Terence never brought him the key?"

"Lonzo is—"

"A friend, I know. Are you sure you're paying him enough to lie to a magistrate?"

A spasm of rage flitted across his face, and he stepped suddenly toward me and leaned over me, his face mere inches from mine. I couldn't stop myself from flinching. I wasn't afraid of him, but it was a reflex, I suppose, conditioned by Husband #1.

"Are you threatening me? You, an untitled, middle-class house-wife? You have the gall to think you can intimidate me? You're an amateur, Evelyn. It is my son's word against your solicitor's, and I quite like my chances. Why on earth would I concede now?"

"Just listen for a moment," I said, stepping aside so that he could see Clarrie and the crowd.

People had gathered around the Babcocks to see the gold, and they listened to Clarrie's story with rapt attention. Those in the back of the crowd were marveling to one another. Some women were even crying.

"The little man did come," we heard Clarrie say. "But he wasn't my, well, godfather, I guess. I heard him, and he kept asking me to hand it over, but I didn't have any jewelry, and I told him I didn't want to give up my firstborn child, so he got really angry! I could hear him stomping his foot and jumping around. He even destroyed my spinning wheel! But then all of a sudden, I remembered his name! It was Mumblewitskin! Then he vanished, and my real fairy godmother dropped this whole sack of gold down the chimney! She saved me and my parents!" The crowd cheered.

I turned back to Lord Piminder. "See, you've never understood that you're the villain. All your wealth won't make you more pop-ular than a sweet young woman with a fairy godmother. You're an obscenely wealthy nobleman trying to turn a charming woman and her parents out on the streets, and if you take this to court, everyone is going to know. You've got one chance to redeem yourself, and that's to forgive the debt right now."

"What is this, some kind of elaborate blackmail?"

I sighed. "Sir, the Babcocks should have taken you to court weeks ago. If I'd simply hired a solicitor at the beginning, we could have avoided all of this. So it's ironic that the one person this fuss really benefits is you. If you force us into court, we'll win at least a reduction and a payment schedule, and what does that tell your other debtors? Your colleagues will jump out of the woodwork to take advantage of you. I'm offering you a chance."

I held my breath. That was my best argument. If this didn't convince him to concede, things were going to get messy. I could see in his eyes he had more fight in him, so I challenged his gaze. He was practically quivering with rage, and I waited for the firestorm of abuse and denial. He sneered at me, his mouth half-open with a defiant response on his lips, but to my surprise, he held his tongue.

"This is what you're going to do," I said. "Consider it some free PR. You're going to approach Clarrie. Not her parents. You're going to congratulate her and offer her Terence's hand, as you agreed upon."

Terence's eyes widened, and Piminder immediately opened his mouth to protest. I waved off their objections.

"Which she will refuse," I said. "Turns out, girls don't particularly like it when you tell them to give up. Then you'll agree to forgive the debt. Make a fancy speech, show that you've seen the error of your ways, and I bet you'll get applause."

With pursed lips, Lord Piminder walked stiffly over to Clarrie, Terence in tow. Silence fell over the crowd. I took the gold from Clarrie, tucked it inside the tower, and removed myself from the scene.

"Congratulations, Miss Babcock," Piminder began. "Your father was correct—you do have a knack for working with gold. As per our agreement, I . . . give my blessing to a marriage between you and my son."

Clarrie glanced at Terence, who couldn't quite stop himself from shaking his head a fraction of an inch. "With all due respect, my lord, Terence should marry someone he is truly in love with. I did this only to help my family."

"In that case, it is only right that I put your mind at ease. I . . . regret," he said, nearly spitting the word out of the side of his mouth, "making such harsh demands from such an obviously virtuous family. I hereby declare the loan given to your grandfather from my father forgiven."

Cheers burst forth from the crowd. There was applause. There were shouts of "Hip, hip, hooray!" I swear I even heard some stranger say, "We did it!" For a moment, Lord Piminder looked surprised, as if he hadn't expected that to work; bolstered by the attention, he then put on a gracious smile and used the spotlight to bow generously to Clarrie and shake her hand, all to thunderous applause.

I breathed a huge sigh of relief. I felt like I'd aged an extra five years this summer, although I wasn't sure how much of that was Roompilda and how much was Hugo Piminder. Sixty-forty in Roompilda's favor, definitely. Maybe even seventy-thirty? The high of defeating the Piminders had probably made me forget how nerve-racking it had been.

Lord Piminder and Terence left Clarrie to her admirers and walked away. Spotting me on the sidelines, Lord Piminder motioned for Terence to continue home and approached me.

"I suppose you're pleased with yourself," he said.

"I'm pleased for the Babcocks," I replied.

He snorted. "Yes, now you'll get paid. Still, I must confess your skill at public relations. For a woman, you are quite astute at crowd control. In fact, I'll make a deal with you," he said, with an air of sudden benevolence, as if whatever he was about to offer would be a gift I could never truly repay. "Come work for me. I'll pay you more than someone like Patrick Babcock ever could, you could expand your portfolio, and you can keep me from turning into a villain again. Discuss it with me over dinner?"

I was incredulously speechless for a few seconds, but I certainly didn't want him taking my silence for assent. "You know, Hugo, there was a brief moment—a very, very brief moment—where I actually, genuinely liked you. But I gave up a long time ago on men who refuse to see my true self."

As I turned away and left him standing there, I was, in fact, rather pleased with myself. And then I remembered Fan.

I strode into the crowd, scanning faces for Fan or Damian, until finally I saw someone familiar. A certain uptight redhead was directing two young women—I followed Roompilda's pointing finger with my eyes, and sure enough, there stood Fan and Damian in a circle of young people, about to be joined by two more. Damian and the hangers-on were talking and laughing. Occasionally one of them would pull a face, probably mocking someone not in the circle. Then they would all giggle. Was his goal to peer pressure Fan into laughing?

I picked up my pace, not letting my eyes leave Fanchon, but made it no more than a few feet when the Shermans manifested buoyantly in my path.

"Well done, Madam Radcliffe!" Mr. Sherman said.

I swallowed my frustration. I couldn't very well put off Mr. Sherman. He'd saved me, for the second time in my life.

"I couldn't possibly have done it without you."

He beamed like a small child.

"I can't thank you enough. Make sure you send me an invoice," I said.

He shook his head and waved his hands at me. "Oh no, I wouldn't dream of it!"

"Mr. Sherman. If I'm getting paid—"

"Please. We haven't had this much fun in years," he said, glancing up at his wife.

"I can't believe we actually witnessed a fairy tale!" she trilled. "This was better than all the balls combined!"

Mr. Sherman grinned and gave me a wink.

"Well, it's been a pleasure, Mr. Sherman," I said. "Take care."

"You too, madam. And if you ever need anything, you know where to find me."

I hustled on as they walked away. I could only partially see Fan's face, and she looked miserably uncomfortable. How could Fan laugh at this sort of mockery? It was exactly the sort of thing the fairies had forbidden, I thought, knowing full well the fairies weren't real. Don't do this to yourself! I wanted to shout.

Apparently, I need to pay more attention to my surroundings. I didn't see Maribelle coming. She flung herself at me, throwing her arms around my neck and nearly knocking me to the ground. As I regained my balance I realized she was sobbing.

"Evelyn, that was so beautiful!" she wailed. "The fairies really came, and Lord Piminder apologized, and Clarrie doesn't even have to marry Terence, which is good because I don't think he deserves her because she's so beautiful!"

"Maribelle . . ."

"I just can't believe there was really gold! And that creepy little man did appear, but he wasn't her fairy godmother—well, you know . . ."

She sobbed as she clung to me. I kept glancing at Fan. I needed help. I looked around. Who could help me?

"And I saw you arguing with Lord Piminder. I don't know how you convinced him to apologize, but you must have been amazing!"

"You helped with that, Maribelle."

"I did?" She stared at me wide-eyed, with dark streaks under her eyes where her makeup had smeared.

"He never would have listened to me if there hadn't been all these people here. And you found most of them."

This started the deluge of tears all over again.

"Maribelle . . ." I tried to peel her off me, but she wouldn't budge, and she couldn't hear me over the sound of her own sobs. I looked frantically around. If someone, anyone, could take Maribelle off my hands . . .

Then suddenly, my eyes spotted Ethan Kingsley, watching Damian hold court. He couldn't help me with Maribelle, but . . . I was all set to shout at him, when he turned toward me and met my eyes.

"Help," I mouthed, nodding my head at Fanchon. "Please!"

He nodded, clenched his fists, and worked his way into the ring. When Damian noticed him, he stopped his monologue and the laughter died down.

"Maribelle!" I hissed. "Shh! I need to be able to hear!"

"Hmm?" She stopped bawling and released her grip, and I moved her with me a few steps closer.

"You're a Kingsley, aren't you?" Damian said.

Ethan nodded.

"I thought I recognized those hand-me-downs." The group snickered. "What do you do, Kingsley?"

"I'm interested in shipping routes," Ethan said. "Right now, I'm helping Mum ship her—"

"You're working for your mother? Oh, well done. Tell me: Are you so inept you couldn't even get one of your brothers to hire you? Dear old Mum was the only employer who would take you?"

Ethan just stared daggers, giving no response to the laughter around him. Fan, on the other hand, wheeled on Damian.

"That's rude," she said. "Ethan is my friend."

Damian put his hand on her shoulder, and for a moment I thought she might bite it. "Him? You can do better than him. Kingsley, I heard that you took out a whole dessert table at the Courtenays." A round of jeering laughter spread through the group.

"Apparently," Damian continued, "he tripped, grabbed the tablecloth, and pulled it along with him as he landed flat on his face. Custard everywhere."

This got Damian's biggest roar of the morning. Even I had to admit it was slightly amusing. Fan wasn't laughing, but she looked frozen, staring not at Ethan or any of the jeering nobles, but past the circle into the crowd beyond. I disentangled myself from Maribelle and began moving around the circle, trying to follow Fan's gaze. Standing directly opposite Fan, positioned perfectly between the heads of two debutants, was Roompilda, reminding Fan merely by her presence that the queen expected to be obeyed.

What could I do? I briefly thought about running and tackling Roompilda, but what would that achieve? The damage had already been done. If Fan didn't want to risk losing Ella, all she had to do was pick one of Damian's jokes to laugh at. Her eyes flickered between Roompilda and Ethan.

"No," Damian said, "you don't want to tie yourself to someone like him. He's not worthy of your father's name. He'll simply drag you down with him—literally." Damian chuckled at himself and turned toward Fan, probably expecting that she would find this hilarious.

At the mention of her father, however, Fan's eyes narrowed and her fists clenched, and she broke free from Roompilda's gaze and turned on Damian.

"Did you think I would find that funny? You certainly know everyone's business. Did you know that just the other day someone screamed at me just because of my father? So no, you're right. He isn't worthy of my father's name. I wouldn't wish it on him!"

"I—I assure you, I had no idea," Damian stuttered, clearly not expecting Fan to get so angry. "I am terribly sorry for my poor choice of words. I was merely poking fun—"

"No, you weren't! That was mean! And it's mean to laugh along with you. And I know you know about the fairies and the frogs, because I'm sure she told you." Fan pointed at Roompilda. "You chose the one thing I for sure couldn't laugh at!"

"My darling Fanchon, I have been an ignorant fool, but nothing more, I assure you. I did not think—"

"You didn't think about me! You didn't think of me as different from any other girl!"

"Please, my dear—" he started, reaching out to grasp her shoulders.

"Don't patronize me!" she shouted.

He pulled his hands back. "You have every right to be angry with me," he said, adjusting his approach. "And you are correct, I do know that the fairies have granted you the luck you deserve. I also know that you are deserving of only the very best luck. Thus, I appeal to that kind, sweet nature of yours as I beg for forgiveness, hoping that surely you will take pity on me and grant me a second chance."

Fan's mouth opened and shut like a fish as she realized she was trapped. The fairies would want her to forgive him. Just as I thought she'd made up her mind to defy Roompilda and the queen, she was going to have to let this pompous fop back in, and eventually they'd all wear down her resolve. Not for the first nor the last time did I curse those frogs.

"Leave her alone," Ethan said suddenly, stepping into the center of the circle.

"Mind your own business, Kingsley."

"It's my business if you're bullying my friend."

"That's sweet, champ. Why don't you run home to Mum and—"

"Stop! Just stop!" Fan cried. "Leave him alone, you—" She froze, clamping her mouth shut. "Mmmgh!" she grunted in frustration.

"You—you—smug, boil-brained, fat-kidneyed ratbag!" Ethan shouted.

I winced. Not the snappiest insult I'd ever heard, although I could see the appeal of *ratbag*. The crowd, which had now grown beyond Damian's original circle of young nobles, was dead silent. Fan turned to stare at Ethan, her mouth gaping open.

"Did you—did you just insult him because you knew I couldn't?"

Ethan nodded. Fan snorted as a grin spread across her face, and then she erupted into uncontrollable laughter. The look of sheer panic on Ethan's face as Fan doubled over was matched only by the utter confusion on Damian's face.

"That's the nicest thing anyone's ever done for me!" Fan said, tears streaming down her cheeks. I tried not to take offense. I did only give birth to her.

Ethan smiled in relief as Fan wiped her eyes, her laughter subsiding to more of a chuckle. She looked at him, and her face lit up.

"You made me laugh!" she said. "That means you can marry me—um, if you want to, of course." She paused. "Do you want to?" she asked shyly.

For a split second, Ethan looked startled, but then he set his jaw and dropped to one knee so quickly he hit the ground with a thud.

"Um, Fanchon, would you—I don't have a ring." He smacked his forehead. "I'm so sorry I'm not prepared! But I really do—I really want—I really want to marry you. Will you marry me?"

Fan giggled. "Yes, of course! I proposed first!" She helped pull Ethan to his feet and threw her arms around his neck.

My enjoyment of the sweet spectacle was interrupted, however, by a high-pitched shriek a few feet away.

I turned toward the noise and saw Roompilda marching toward me, head lowered, moving people out of the way with a violent shove.

"You imbecile!" she shouted at me, her face flushing with anger. "Do you not understand who I am? I work for the queen! I work for the queen! You have interfered with royal commands!"

I was too speechless to argue. Her usual stick-straight posture and prim impassiveness had fallen to pieces. Her spectacles now sat crooked on her nose, and she was shouting so forcefully, beads of spittle had formed in the corners of her mouth.

"I had this!" she continued to scream. "I was so close, you ignorant, meddling peasant!"

I'd promised Fan I'd take the blame if she didn't marry Damian; apparently, that was exactly the message Roompilda was planning to convey to the queen. I was almost disappointed. I'd been looking forward to causing a scene. Well, perhaps I could be allowed one little parting shot.

"Do you have pen and paper?" I asked Maribelle, who'd followed along behind me.

She started rummaging through her handbag.

"I never lose!" Roompilda bellowed. "Do you understand me? I never lose!" Strands of hair shook loose from her updo and fell in her face.

"Ooh!" Maribelle exclaimed. She pulled a peppermint sweet from her bag, unwrapped it, and popped it in her mouth. Then she handed me the brown paper wrapping. "Here you go! Now, I don't usually carry ink with me . . ."

"I'll tell the queen everything!" Roompilda hissed. "She'll hear my full report!"

"I have my son's charcoal pencil," Maribelle said, brandishing the crayon. "Will that work?"

"It'll do," I said.

"Listen to me!" Roompilda screamed. "The queen will never, ever—"

Her tirade was interrupted by a concerned nobleman, who put his hand firmly on Roompilda's shoulder. "Madam, I think it's time for you to leave," he said.

He tried to guide her away, but she jerked her arm free, swinging her carpetbag as she did so, and wheeled on him. "Take your hands off me! Do you know who I am?" she shouted. He could only stare at her, bewildered.

"This is Roompilda Stidolph," I said. "Royal etiquette coach. I wouldn't let her near your children."

Roompilda let out a strangled cry of rage.

"Come on, madam," the nobleman said, grasping Roompilda's shoulder once more. With a violent yank, she spun away, stomping her foot vehemently in frustration. Unfortunately, she didn't account for the curvature of the hill.

Her ankle buckled beneath her as she lost her footing, and she began to topple over, carried by the momentum of her swinging carpetbag. The bag flew out of her hand just before she tumbled to the ground, and since she was already mid-spin, she simply continued to roll until she hit the carpetbag, which had beaten her to the bottom of the hill.

"Oof," Maribelle whispered.

I finished scrawling my note and walked down the hill. Roompilda had managed to prop herself up on an elbow and was glaring at me through her bent and battered glasses. I reached for the carpetbag and opened it.

"Just a talking point," I said, holding up the scrap of paper. "For when you report to the queen." I dropped the note in the carpetbag.

It read:

Kingsley: E.R. approves.

CHAPTER FOURTEEN

I AWAITED THE wedding with tense excitement mixed with a bit of dread. I needn't have. Ella responded immediately to Fan's letter saying of course she and Aiden would come and of course she would be Fan's matron of honor, but I held my breath until the prince and princess actually arrived in Strachey. Both welcomed Ethan with unbridled enthusiasm.

Although I suspected Aiden didn't need to be impressed, I knew word would get back to the queen, and I was concerned—nay, certain—that I couldn't pull off a wedding that would justify my wholesale disobedience. Fortunately, Francesca Kingsley knew what she was doing.

I swear I never told her any of the sordid details of my rebellion. Apparently, she didn't need them. She volunteered her own ballroom, hired a decorator from the Capital, and called in a favor to bring in the archbishop to perform the ceremony. And most importantly, I thought, she'd made sure each of Ethan's siblings was present, with spouses—from the colonel, in full dress uniform, to the chief physician, in full academic regalia. Each shook the prince's hand. Each, so far as I could overhear, name-dropped all the nobles he or she had influence with. There was a chance, I thought, Her Majesty might forgive me.

At least, I fervently hoped so. Just before they left, Ella and Aiden told us their secret: Ella was having a baby. She made Fan and

I promise to visit. If the queen didn't want me there, I'd sneak into the palace. Nothing would keep me away from my grandchild.

This time, I was prepared for the post-wedding loneliness. Mina and I cleaned out Fanchon's room and prepared her and Ethan's new home while they were on their honeymoon. I went for walks with Maribelle. And, by myself, I finally went through some of Henry's things. He was the type to keep mementos—old journals from school, a picture Ella had drawn him, a note I'd written him. I couldn't bear to get rid of them, so I bought a large wooden chest that Mina and I lowered into the cellar, and I filled it with his memories.

Before I locked it up, there was one more item I needed to store away: a large sack of brass-coated wire, which I'd snuck away from the tower as the distracted crowds dissipated. After all, you never knew when a fairy godmother might need to spin straw into gold.

The next day, I ordered a sign, and within a short time I was standing on a kitchen chair hammering a metal bracket on the front of the house. I hung my sign from the bracket, stepped down from the chair, and took a critical look. I'd told the sign painter that the slipper absolutely had to look like glass. Instead, it looked a sort of milky bluish gray, not unlike my own attempt at glass slippers.

I smiled with pride anyway. Sure, the pressure had been intense, and I'd been inches away from getting caught—on multiple occasions—but I'd won. I'd outwitted Roompilda and Lord Piminder, and I was willing to take the risks to outwit others like them. Somebody had to look out for these girls.

I was open for business.

ACKNOWLEDGMENTS

First and foremost, I am grateful for the women who have raised and mentored me, who encouraged me whether I wanted to be a princess or an athlete, and who recognized my anxieties and helped me find my strengths. To Mom, Pat, Nita, Cecilia, and many others, thank you for teaching me how beautiful humor is in the face of adversity.

I am doubly indebted to my mom, who did the lion's share of the editing on this book and, despite our differences on comma placement, bears a lot of the responsibility for this being better than it began.

I'm grateful to my dad, for unabashedly sharing this with everyone he knows, and for being my first writing partner, on a play containing my very favorite punchline, when the princess informs the vizier, "I'd rather wear red and pink together than marry you!"

I'm thankful to my brother, who played every bizarre game I imagined, created some unique ones of his own, and has challenged and encouraged my imagination our whole lives. May you always find the stolen White House plans.

My thanks to the entire Inkshares team for helping a new author find her voice, and for doing so with patience and cheer.

Finally, this book was crowdfunded, which means it would not exist without the friends, family members, friends of friends, and complete strangers who preordered enough copies to turn it into reality. I am so grateful for your support and enthusiasm. Thank you for sharing this with your friends and for investing in my dreams.

GRAND PATRONS

INKSHARES

INKSHARES is a reader-driven publisher and producer based in Oakland, California. Our books are selected not by a group of editors, but by readers worldwide.

While we've published books by established writers like *Big Fish* author Daniel Wallace and *Star Wars: Rogue One* scribe Gary Whitta, our aim remains surfacing and developing the new author voices of tomorrow.

Previously unknown Inkshares authors have received starred reviews and been featured in the *New York Times*. Their books are on the front tables of Barnes & Noble and hundreds of independents nationwide, and many have been licensed by publishers in other major markets. They are also being adapted by Oscar-winning screenwriters at the biggest studios and networks.

Interested in making your own story a reality? Visit Inkshares. com to start your own project or find other great books.

CPSIA information can be obtained
at www.ICGtesting.com
Printed in the USA
FSHW010908061118
53559FS